KINGS OF MAFIA

GOD OF VENGEANCE

USA TODAY BESTSELLING AUTHOR
MICHELLE HEARD

Cover Designer: Okay Creations

Editor: Sheena Taylor

TABLE OF CONTENTS

Dedication

Damiano is for all my readers who love their book boyfriends dark, ruthless, and broody.

Songlist

Keep On Fighting – Tribal Blood

Trust is a Cruel Friend – Tessa Jackson, Darius Timmer, Glenn
Herweijer & Ben Sumner

Everybody Wants To Rule The World – Lorde

Castle – Halsey

Keep My Head Up – Anna Mae

With the Devil I'm Going Down – Steelfeather

Control – Zoe Wees, 2WEI & ABBOTT

Let Me Hurt – Emily Rowed

Anything Can Happen – Tors

Here – Tom Grennan

I Will Rise – Steelfeather & ASHBY

Who We Are – Tristan Prettyman

Anyone – Tommee Profitt & Fluerie

Synopsis

I was born into the Cosa Nostra, so I've always known an arranged marriage loomed in my future.

When the *Capo dei Capi* of the Cosa Nostra comes to Sicily to give his approval for his cousin, Stefano, to take me as his bride, I know my fate is all but sealed. Marrying Stefano is the last thing I want, but being a woman, I don't have a say in the matter.

Damiano Falco is merciless and rules the Cosa Nostra with an iron fist. Everyone fears him and won't dare go against him.
I'm still trying to accept that I'll have no choice but to marry Stefano when Damiano utters the last word anyone expects to hear.
"No."
He doesn't give his approval, nor does he offer any explanation.

But if I think his refusal will set me free, I have another thing coming. Instead, my bags are packed, and within hours, I find myself sitting on a private jet with the head of the Costa Nostra.

The ruthless man doesn't tell me anything, and I have no idea what my future holds.

To say I'm terrified is the understatement of the century.

God of Vengeance

Mafia / Organized Crime / Suspense Romance
STANDALONE in the KINGS OF MAFIA
Book 5

Authors Note:
This book contains subject matter that may be sensitive for some readers.
There is triggering content related to:
Graphic and extreme violence
Abuse
Kidnapping
Death of a loved one
Trauma & PTSD

18+ only.
Please read responsibly.

"All is fair in love and war."

— **John Lyly**

Chapter 1

Gabriella

Damiano Falco; 38. Gabriella di Bella; 23.

"This is a great honor for the family," my mother says as her eyes slowly sweep over every inch of me. "Don't disappoint us."

She's referring to my impending marriage to Stefano Ferraro. That's if the Cosa Nostra approves of the union.

Or rather, Damiano Falco. The *Capo dei Capi* of the Cosa Nostra. He's the only one who still has to give his approval, which he'll do tonight at the dinner party that's being held in his honor.

The stories I've heard about Damiano are enough to make my blood run cold in my veins, and I'm not looking forward to meeting him.

But first, I need to get through an entire afternoon of smiling and pretending I want nothing more than to become Stefano Ferraro's wife.

God help me.

A chill creeps down my spine because the last thing I want is to marry Stefano. The man is in his late forties, and I've only seen him a handful of times. Every interaction with him didn't bode well for my future.

Not once has he offered me a smile or a kind word, but instead, I've been treated like I'm nothing more than a pawn in the great game called the mafia. His touch is always brutal, and his words demeaning.

My mother's eyes stop on my hair, and she lets out a displeased sigh. "I wish you didn't cut and color your hair. It looks awful."

The corner of my mouth almost lifts, but I manage to keep my face schooled with an obedient expression.

My hair used to be black and reached to my butt, but I colored it light brown with blonde streaks and cut it in a stylish bob. I did it because Stefano started calling me his black beauty, always pulling my hair to force me to look up at him. It was my way of giving him the middle finger.

My parents prefer that I wear modest clothes, no makeup, and keep my eyes lowered when we have company, and Stefano seems to be cut from the same cloth as them.

But that's not me. It never has been.

I love playing with makeup and different hairstyles.

Her gaze drops to the tight silk dress I'm wearing, which stops mid-thigh, and the black five-inch heels on my feet.

I'm aware the outfit is risky and a little too revealing, but today, I can't stop my stubborn streak from showing.

Shaking her head, Mother mutters, "Did you have to spill coffee on the dress I chose for you to wear?" She lets out a disgruntled huff. "I suppose it will have to do. We can't keep the men waiting."

Without checking to make sure I follow her out of the room, she continues to say, "Remember, Stefano is Mr. Falco's cousin. You're marrying into the greatest family, so you'll wait hand and foot on Stefano. Do whatever the man wants to ensure you get him to the altar."

When I keep quiet, my mother stops in the middle of the hallway to glare at me. "Do you understand, Gabriella?"

I do, but I sure as hell don't agree.

When I stare at my mother for seconds too long, her arm swings through the air, her palm connecting with the side of my head.

There's a burst of destructive emotions in my chest as my hands fist at my sides. The sting from the slap fades quickly while I swallow hard on the urge to tell my mother to go to hell.

With every slap, demeaning sentence, and controlling order, I become more defiant. I can't stop it, and I know it's only a matter of time before my stubbornness will land me in deep trouble.

They want a prim and proper little princess, but I'll give them a defiant queen.

And one day, it might kill me.

Through clenched teeth, she hisses, "You will not ruin this deal for your father and brother."

I swallow hard on my pride and temper as I bite out, "Yes, Mother."

Rosa di Bella has never been a mother to me. Since I can remember, she's kept a controlling grip on my life, telling me what to eat, how much to weigh, what to wear, and how to behave.

I'm nothing more than a bargaining chip, while my older brother is the crowned prince who will take over from my father. Santo can do whatever he wants and gets away with murder. Literally.

I was an accident. My parents were content with only having Santo, but then I came along, burdening their perfect lives with my unwanted presence.

16

They can't wait to pawn me off on Stefano Ferraro. They'll get a son-in-law who's related to the most powerful man in our world. And they'll be rid of me.

My mother gives me another glare before she takes the stairs down. As I follow reluctantly behind her, I hear my brother shout, "He's here!"

When the foyer comes into view, it's in time to see Santo open the front door.

A man comes up the steps, his head bowed while he unbuttons his suit jacket. He shrugs off the jacket, and without glancing back, he hands it to a man who seems to be his guard.

As he lifts his head, I suck in a desperate breath of air, my gaze stuck on the *Capo dei Capi* of the Cosa Nostra. With his features carved into a ruthless expression that promises agonizing pain and death, he looks like the God he is.

The dominance and power exploding from him keep my attention imprisoned.

I can't tear my gaze away from him. Even if I wanted to.

He's tall, dark, and utterly handsome. The man gives me the impression of a thunderstorm moving over the world, engulfing everything in darkness.

17

Damiano Falco.

As I think his name, his dark eyes lock with mine, and I swear they're black as death. An intense shiver shudders over my body, and I can't stop myself from taking a step backward.

Suddenly, Mother grabs my wrist, and I'm yanked forward. My shoes slip on the floor the servants polished until they could see their reflections on the shiny surface.

Before I can try to catch my balance, I fall to my knees while my mother's fingers tighten around my wrist, making a sharp pain shoot up my arm. My free hand slaps against the tiled floor to stop me from face-planting in front of everyone.

"Get up," Stefano growls beneath his breath.

Intense embarrassment burns through me, and before I can scramble back onto my feet, Damiano walks right by me, his steps filled with confidence and threats of death.

Mother yanks at my wrist, sending another sharp pain up my arm. "You're embarrassing us," she hisses between clenched teeth.

I struggle to my feet, in time to see all the men rush after Damiano. Even though this is his first time here, he heads straight for the living room.

Stefano shoots me a dark glare that promises nothing good for me before he disappears from my sight.

I'm yanked again, and I barely have time to fix my dress as my mother hurries to catch up to the men.

"Stop yanking me," I snap at Mother while managing to rip my wrist free from her hold.

She shoots me an angry glare, that's usually followed by a slap, but we enter the living room, making her restrain herself because of present company.

I notice Damiano's pouring himself a tumbler of my father's best bourbon while all the men look at him with anticipation on their faces.

My eyes dart over the gun tucked into his pants' waistband before locking on his broad shoulders. He turns around, and as he takes a sip of the drink, his eyes slowly creep over everyone in the room.

"You must be tired, cousin," Stefano says. "Why not take an hour to rest before we sit down for the meeting?"

Damiano doesn't even acknowledge what his cousin says, and when his eyes lock on me for a second time, the shiver rushing over my body is more intense than before.

His lips part, and I swear I can feel everyone hold their breaths as they wait to hear what the *Capo dei Capi* has to say.

"Come," he orders. His low and deadly tone is filled with ice, making a wintry chill spread through my veins.

When I don't move, Mother shoves me in Damiano's direction.

With every step I take closer to him, my legs feel like they'll turn to jelly and give way beneath me.

I suck in an audible breath when I stop mere inches from him and force my spine to straighten so I don't cower in front of the dangerous man.

Lifting my head, my eyes meet his, and every muscle in my body tightens as dread pours through me.

Caro Dio.

He's easily a head taller than me, and I'm wearing high heels. Barefoot, I'd probably only reach the middle of his chest.

I have no doubt he can kill me with a single punch.

Damiano downs the last of the amber liquid in the tumbler, and as he holds it out to his side, Santo has to hurry to catch the glass when Damiano lets go of it.

He couldn't even be bothered with putting the damn tumbler down on the table.

The *Capo dei Capi's* ruthless gaze moves from my head to my toes before flicking back to my face.

Even though my body starts to tremble with fear, I somehow manage to keep my chin raised.

Damiano locks eyes with me, and when it feels like he's digging his way into the deepest parts of my soul, I can't stop myself from taking a step backward.

My hands fist tightly at my sides, and swallowing hard, I force myself not to move further away from him.

His eyes narrow on me, and he slowly tilts his head.

Dio.

My mouth grows bone dry under his intense scrutiny.

Suddenly, a hand slaps against the back of my head, and I'm forced to look down.

"I apologize, Mr. Falco," Father mutters angrily. "She's usually more obedient. I don't know what's gotten into her today."

With my father's fingers wrapped around the back of my neck, I'm yanked backward and shoved toward Mother.

She grabs hold of my arm and drags me out of the living room.

I hear Damiano let out a sigh, making it sound like he's bored with the entire spectacle, then he orders, "Show me to a room where I can have privacy."

Mother doesn't stop walking until I'm shoved into my bedroom. The door slams shut, and as I turn to face her, she starts to slap me wildly, her palms burning over every inch of my face and torso.

In a moment of absolute madness, I bring my arms up between us and shove my mother away from me while shouting, "Enough!"

My outburst shocks her so much she stares at me with wide eyes. "Have you lost your mind?" she gasps.

My bedroom door opens, and as Stefano steps into my private space, he mutters, "I'll deal with my fiancée."

Mother shoots me an enraged glare before giving Stefano a trembling smile. "Thank you."

When she leaves the room, dread spins in my stomach as I try to brace for what's to come.

Chapter 2

Gabriella

When Stefano glances at me while he removes his jacket, a weird sensation creeps over my skin.

"You embarrassed me, Gabriella," he mutters as he drapes his jacket over the back of the chair by my dressing table.

His tone brims with anger, and it has me glancing at the door.

Suddenly, he lets out an incredulous-sounding chuckle. "You're not even going to apologize?"

Pride has me lifting my chin, and I force myself to lock eyes with the man I'm going to marry. If I don't stand my ground today, he'll make my life a living hell.

"I didn't do anything wrong," I say, my voice sounding much stronger than I feel.

When Stefano starts to undo his belt, a wave of terror-filled pins and needles coats my skin.

Dio.

"You can't take my virginity until we're married," I say as if the words will stop him.

Stefano's mouth lifts in a smirk. "You already belong to me."

"No." I shake my head. "Mr. Falco hasn't given his permission."

"I don't plan on fucking you right now. First, I'm going to give you the beating of your life so you don't dare embarrass me again," he growls. "I'll have your virginity for dessert after dinner."

The leather wooshes through the loops of his pants, and not thinking twice, I run for the door. I manage to yank it open just as the belt lashes over my shoulder and neck. The sting is intense, making me fall into the hallway.

I scramble to my feet, but I can't get away before Stefano grabs hold of my hair.

I should've shaved it all off.

My head's yanked back, and as his breath hits my ear, he says, "You better be the best fuck of my life tonight for all the trouble you're causing."

Strands are ripped from my skull as I'm pulled back, then thunder cracks through the air as Damiano snaps, "Enough!"

Stefano shoves me into the bedroom, then I hear him say, "I apologize for disturbing you, cousin. I'm dealing with the problem."

"The *problem* can wait," Damiano mutters. "Everyone back in the living room. Now!"

My entire body is trembling, but somehow, I manage to adjust my dress around my thighs and pat my hair into a neat style. My scalp stings from where I lost a chunk of hair.

After composing myself as best I can, I walk right by Stefano and follow Damiano to the living room. I struggle to keep my eyes from darting over the black fabric of Damiano's dress shirt that stretches tightly over his muscled back.

Entering the living room, I find safety behind an armchair, and in less than a minute, my family and Stefano stare at Damiano with bated breaths.

"I've made my decision," the *Capo dei Capi* mutters.

My breath stalls in my throat, and my heart sinks.

"Do you give your blessing, cousin?" Stefano asks.

Damiano's eyes lock with mine, and once again, they narrow as he stares at me.

I lift my chin and clench my jaw as I hold the gaze of the man who's killed people for the mere pleasure of feeling their blood seep through his fingers – the man who is about to condemn me to a life of hell.

His lips part, and a second later, a single word breaks the tense silence.

"No."

"What?" Mother gasps.

"Cousin?" Stefano says, the word filled with confusion.

"Mr. Falco?" I hear my father ask.

He said no.

Air bursts from my lungs, and the relief is so intense I have to place my hand over my heart to keep it from beating out of my chest.

I won't be forced to marry Stefano.

He won't get to take my virginity.

My eyes drift shut from the overwhelming happiness coursing through my body, making me feel faint.

When I hear movement, my eyes snap open, and I watch as Damiano pours himself a drink.

I almost thank him for not giving his blessing, but something tells me to keep quiet.

Damiano glances at his guard. "Get the men to pack Gabriella's belongings. We're leaving."

"On it," the guard answers before he stalks away to carry out the order.

What?

Mother gasps, and my father's mouth opens and closes like a fish out of water.

Stefano is the first to recover, and shaking his head, he dares to ask, "What are you doing?"

Damiano downs the bourbon before shoving the glass into Stefano's hand. Without a single word of explanation, he walks out of the living room.

Everyone stands frozen for a moment before life returns with one hell of a bang.

Mother rushes to me, a smile spreading over her face. "I can't believe the *Capo dei Capi* has taken an interest in you."

What?

It's the only question that keeps playing on an endless loop in my frazzled mind.

"Holy shit," Santo breathes, shaking his head in disbelief.

Looking confused, my father asks, "Mr. Falco is taking Gabriella?"

"Damiano!" Stefano shouts, going after his cousin. "What's the meaning of this?"

Mother once again grabs my wrist, and I'm dragged out of the living room. As we rush through the foyer and up the stairs, I hear Damiano's voice rumble like fire and brimstone as he says, "I'm taking the woman. It's not open for discussion. Find someone else to marry."

Holy crap.

Damiano is a million times worse than Stefano. There's no telling what he'll do to me.

Before I can hear more of the conversation between Damiano and Stefano, I'm pulled into my bedroom, and seconds later, five men come into my private space and roughly start throwing my belongings into bags.

I can't think a single coherent thought as Mother thrusts an outfit into my hands before shoving me into the bathroom.

"Get changed. Hurry," she orders before yanking the door shut.

I hear my bedroom being torn apart while I stare at the doorknob.

This isn't happening.

"Hurry, Gabriella, or I'll come in and dress you myself," Mother threatens.

In a stunned daze, I start to undress and quickly put on the light pink pantsuit. The pants are three-quarter in length and look good with the black five-inch heels.

Mother forgot to grab a blouse, but I shrug on the jacket and fasten the two buttons. A sliver of black lace from my bra is visible.

Taking a moment for myself, I wash my hands and pull a brush through my hair before I open the cupboards to dig out toiletry bags. I quickly pack my perfume, toiletries, and bath and skincare products.

I can't believe I'm leaving with Damiano Falco. I have no idea what it means for my future, and it terrifies the hell out of me.

But I hurry because I don't dare keep the man waiting.

If I take too long, he might just kill me for wasting his time.

Dio.

My fear multiplies by the second as I realize I'll be at the mercy of the *Capo dei Capi* of the Cosa Nostra. I'm leaving my life in Sicily behind to start a new one in New York. Everything will be foreign and dangerous.

The bathroom door slams open, and when Mother sees I'm busy packing, she comes to help.

When I walk into my bedroom it looks like a tornado swept through it, the drawers and closets standing open.

The guard that's been at Mr. Falco's side since they arrived holds a bag open and orders, "Throw your toiletries in here."

I do as I'm told.

"Is there anything we missed that you'd like to bring?"

I quickly check all the drawers, the closet, and the bathroom, shocked at how quickly my life's been packed up.

When I shake my head Mother holds out a black pouch to me. "This contains your personal documents. Don't lose it."

"I'll take it," the guard says, swiping the pouch from Mother's hand.

When she grabs hold of my wrist again, the guard says, "Miss di Bella will come with me."

Holy shit. In a matter of minutes my family no longer have any authority over me.

I pull free from my mother's hold, and not even sparing her a glance, I follow the guard out of the bedroom where I've spent most of my time.

Crap, this is really happening.

My dire circumstances really start to sink in as I take the staircase down to the foyer and walk with the guard toward the front door.

"Let us know when you land in New York," Mother calls out.

I'm too worried about my own survival to pay her any attention.

As I step out of the house, it's to see Santo and my father standing near an SUV with blacked-out windows.

Father hurries closer to me. "Find out what he wants with you and let me know," he orders.

The guard takes hold of my arm, his touch not biting like I'm used to, then my eyes widen as he pushes Father out of my way.

The guard opens the back door to the SUV and nods toward the backseat for me to climb inside.

"Mr. Falco," Father says, hoping to get the *Capo dei Capi's* attention as I slide into the backseat. "Why are you taking Gabriella?"

Damiano is busy typing something on his phone and doesn't even bother acknowledging my father's question.

The guard shuts the door, and I can only suck in desperate breaths when I find myself alone with Damiano.

Luckily, his attention remains on the device in his hands.

I dare to slowly turn my head to glance at the imposing man beside me. The expensive fabric of his pants clings to his muscled thighs, and for a moment, I notice the way-too-big bulge behind his zipper before I quickly turn my head away.

Caro Dio.

I suck in another desperate breath as my eyes land on my family.

I don't feel any heartache when the guard climbs behind the steering wheel and starts the engine. When the SUV begins to move, my eyes dart over the house.

I haven't known any love and never felt safe between those walls.

My eyes lower to my hands, and seeing the red marks on my arms and around my wrist, I brush my fingers lightly over them.

What will become of me?

Chapter 3

Damiano

Halfway to the airfield where the private jet is waiting, I tuck my phone back into my pocket.

Stefano's pissed off that I didn't give my blessing and instead took the woman he wanted to marry, but he'll just have to get over it.

The di Bella household is a fucking mess, and I refused to stay there a second longer. I'm used to violence. It's second nature to me, but having to see Gabriella degraded and mistreated tested my patience. If I'd stayed for dinner, instead of leaving, there would've been a blood bath.

I glance at Gabriella and notice she's changed her outfit. She looks glamorous in the pink suit, and even though I have zero interest in her, I notice her cleavage that's on full display.

She might be on the shorter side, but she has curves in all the right places. She's beautiful, but that's not why she's sitting beside me.

When she held eye contact with me, I was actually a little stunned. It showed she has more guts than most of the men in our world.

No matter how she was yanked, shoved, and hit, she kept lifting her chin and straightening her spine.

I think she's fucking strong and would be a perfect match for Dario, one of the other heads of the Cosa Nostra.

Dario's like a little brother to me. Annoying as fuck, but still, I love him and want the best for him. He needs a strong wife who will take care of him.

Even though I don't give a shit about the woman beside me, I'm sure she'll appreciate being married to a man who won't mistreat her.

She'll be thankful that I've chosen a good man for her, and in return, she'll make Dario happy.

I'm surprised when she asks, "Are we going to New York?"

Usually, people don't dare speak to me without my permission.

My eyes flick to her face, and I notice the red welt across her neck from where Stefano hit her with his belt. The sight of the bruises fuels my anger.

Not bothering to talk, I nod.

"Why are you taking me with you?"

Annoyed by the questions, I mutter, "Silence."

Relaxing in the seat, I rest my elbow on the doorframe and rub my fingers over the scruff on my jaw as I stare out the window.

I hate traveling.

I hate leaving my house. Period.

I hate people.

I hate noise.

I hate the daylight.

I hate everything.

If it wasn't for the love I feel for the people closest to me, I'd think I was incapable of loving anyone or anything.

I only care about six people.

My mother.

Carlo, who's my most trusted man and hardly leaves my side.

Angelo, Franco, Renzo, and Dario – the other four heads of the Cosa Nostra.

Nothing else matters to me. Not even Angelo, Franco, and Renzo's women. Vittoria, Samantha, and Skylar only fall under my protection because they matter to my friends.

I've never made an effort to get to know any of the women, and I never will.

My thoughts return to work, and when I think about the fucker that's trying to sell drugs in my city, rage burns through my chest. I want Miguel dead as soon as possible so I can focus on the new construction projects that have been put on hold for too long.

Carlo brings the SUV to a stop near the private jet, and not waiting for him to open my door, I shove it open and climb out.

My eyes scan over the area for any threats as the rest of my men spill from the other SUVs to offer me protection as I walk to the plane.

I head up the steps and straight to my seat. A second later the flight attendant places a tumbler of whiskey down beside me.

"Anything else, sir?" she asks, her tone filled with respect and fear.

I shake my head, then my eyes lock on Gabriella as she takes a seat as far away from me as possible. She looks pale as fuck, and even though I can feel the worry and fear coming off her in waves, she keeps her head raised high.

As I enjoy the whiskey, her eyes meet mine, and instead of quickly lowering her gaze, she holds my stare once a-fucking-gain.

Besides my mother, Gabriella is the first woman to look me dead in the eye for longer than a few seconds. Usually, the female species cower before me, unwilling to meet my gaze.

But not this one.

Weirdly, it makes me feel curious to see how hard I can push before she'll kneel at my feet.

When I tear my gaze away from hers, I notice some of my men appreciating the view of Gabriella's cleavage a little too much.

Turning my head to my left, where Carlo is seated, I murmur, "Have Gabriella put on a blouse. I don't want her distracting the men."

"Okay."

When Carlo gets up and walks to Gabriella, her eyes widen slightly. Without saying anything, he takes hold of her arm and pulls her up from the seat.

He checks through three bags before finding the one he's looking for, then takes her to the bedroom. Once she's inside, he orders, "Put on a blouse beneath your jacket."

When he shuts the door, I order, "No one looks at the woman."

I hear a chorus of "Yes, boss."

"When she comes out, I want her sitting beside me," I inform Carlo.

I know very little about the woman and will need some information to give Dario. It's the only reason I want to talk to her.

Gabriella takes a couple of minutes too long before she comes out of the bedroom. Before she can return to her seat, Carlo gestures for her to sit next to me.

Her features tense, but without any argument on her part, she comes to take the seat.

A whiff of her perfume hits me. It's fresh, and surprisingly, I find myself taking a deeper breath instead of being annoyed by the feminine scent invading my personal space.

She crosses her legs, her movements elegant as fuck.

Gabriella di Bella has the grace of a queen.

Even though her hair is on the shorter side, the light brown and blond coloring suits her. Her slender neck draws my gaze, her skin looking silky soft.

Our eyes meet for a moment, and I notice the green flecks hidden in her light brown irises.

She has beautiful eyes. They're expressive.

The flight attendant comes to collect my tumbler, then says, "We're ready for take-off, sir."

I nod, and as she does her final checks, I put on my safety belt.

The private jet starts to taxi down the runway, and after gaining enough speed, it lifts into the air.

Gabriella suddenly grabs hold of my forearm, and if it weren't for the shirt I'm wearing, her nails would draw blood.

I turn my head toward her and see she has her eyes squeezed shut, her face so fucking pale, I worry whether she's about to get sick next to me.

I look at where her slender fingers are gripping my arm, and when my anger doesn't spiral out of control because she's touching me without permission, my eyebrow lifts.

Don't look too deep.

The seatbelt sign goes off, and it has me muttering, "My arm."

I hear Gabriella gasp as her fingers jump away from me. "I apologize," she murmurs, her voice coated with fear.

She glances in my direction, and a moment passes before her eyes meet mine. "It's my first time flying."

When she doesn't lower her gaze, I take in the green flecks in her soft brown eyes, then, to test her, I let my expression grow dark.

I let every ounce of power I possess radiate from me.

She starts to tremble and swallows hard, but still, her eyes remain locked on mine. There's no staring her down.

"Are you brave or stupid?" I ask, the anger constantly skirting around the edges of my mind, making my tone sound harsh.

It takes a few seconds before her glossy lips part, and her honest reply trembles with the fear I'm accustomed to hearing as she says, "I'm stubborn by nature."

Her answer actually amuses me, and once again, I'm caught by surprise as the corner of my mouth lifts. It's fleeting before I forcefully school my face with an impassive expression.

I glance at my men to see if any of them noticed the brief smile, but half are napping while some watch TV.

Focusing my attention back on my original plan to get information for Dario, I ask, "How old are you?"

"Twenty-three."

Eight years younger than Dario.

Sixteen years younger than me.

I ignore the unwanted thought and ask the next question, "Virgin?"

I feel an intense burst of energy from her, and turning my eyes back to her, I notice a blush creeping up her face.

Her reply falls softly between us. "Yes."

I know everything about everyone that matters. Before I laid eyes on Gabriella, I didn't care about her existence, and it's the reason I don't know much about her.

I tear my gaze away from her beautiful face. "Have you studied?"

"No."

"Work?"

"My parents don't approve of women working."

"From what I saw, I assume you're not close with your family?"

"I'm not."

Good. It will save Dario from having to worry about them.

"Friends or acquaintances?"

Sometimes, friends can be a bigger nuisance than family.

She shakes her head. "No."

"Your parents provided for you?"

I'm surprised when she doesn't answer immediately, and it has my eyes snapping back to her face.

She seems to be in two minds about something before she answers, "They provided for my basic needs."

"But?"

"You'll probably find out sooner or later," she mutters, sounding a little frustrated. "I get extra money from makeup and skincare tutorials on social media."

I find social media to be a waste of time, but I'm impressed that she's trying to earn her own income even though her parents don't want her to work.

Not commenting on what she said, I ask, "How's your health? Any problems?"

"No."

"Mental problems I should know about?"

"No."

"Contraception?"

Her cheeks flush again, and she sucks in a deep breath before letting it out with a huff. "There's been no need for contraception as I haven't been in a relationship."

"So, no previous boyfriends?"

"No boyfriends," she sighs, clearly annoyed by all the questions.

"But you were engaged to Stefano," I state.

"Not by choice, and you could hardly call it a relationship."

"My cousin isn't known for his patience," I say as I unbutton the cuffs of my shirt. While I roll the fabric to beneath my elbows, I ask, "Has he seen you naked or touched you in a sexual manner?"

"*Caro Dio*," she gasps, and for the first time, she glances down at her hands that are lying on her lap while her cheeks burn red with embarrassment. "No. He was waiting for your approval."

Good.

I'm surprised when a sense of relief trickles into my chest.

Not lifting her head, her voice trembles as she asks, "Will you answer my question from earlier?"

I shake my head and wave a hand toward the seat she previously occupied.

Carlo's up and quickly helps Gabriella to the other chair before coming to take his place beside me.

The flight attendant brings me another tumbler of whiskey, and I take a couple of sips before leaning back and closing my eyes.

Gabriella's answers fill my mind as I try to figure out who she really is. She seems strong and innocent, a combination I haven't encountered before.

Chapter 4

Gabriella

My heart is beating wildly in my chest, dread coating my skin, and my nerves frayed from the interrogation I somehow survived.

The past forty minutes of sitting next to Damiano were the most unnerving of my life.

My hand still tingles from gripping his arm. I was so scared when the plane took off I didn't realize I'd grabbed hold of him.

I can be glad I'm still alive after touching him without his permission.

The split second before I pulled my hand away, I felt his strength rippling beneath my fingertips.

Even where I'm sitting on the other side of the cabin, I can feel the violent energy coming from Damiano.

His refusal to answer my question makes me worry. It would be stupid to assume he took me for himself. He might have something worse planned for me.

Dio.

I suck in desperate breaths as a panic attack threatens to overwhelm me.

You'd think I'd be used to nerve-wracking situations after everything I've endured at the hands of my family, but sitting in a private jet with Damiano Falco and his men terrifies the living hell out of me.

Tension-filled minutes creep by slowly, a form of torture I've never experienced before.

I glance around the cabin, noticing most of the men are fast asleep. Including Damiano.

His guard, who's seated next to him, is the only other person awake. Besides the flight crew, of course.

I take a deep breath and let it out slowly, trying to ease my frail nerves. It's of no use because my uncertain future keeps making fear shudder through me.

Maybe he's taking me for someone else?

That's if I'm even going to get married. He might have taken me for a completely different reason.

But what?

Even though the Cosa Nostra isn't known for dealing in sex slavery, the terrifying thought still crosses my mind.

No, that's not the reason.

He made me put on a blouse, and I overheard him tell his men not to look at me. That means my virtue is worth something to him.

Virgins sell for a lot.

I swallow hard on the terrifying thought as my eyes lock on the *Capo dei Capi*. Even though he seems to be sleeping, he still looks dangerous as hell.

There's a frown between his eyebrows, and his mouth is set in a grim line.

I wonder whether he ever relaxes.

Is he capable of laughing?

The fleeting smirk I saw earlier pops into my mind. It was only for a second, but his face transformed from deadly to downright hot.

As I stare at Damiano, I take in his black hair, his features that could easily be carved from stone, and the dark bristles on his jaw.

My gaze lowers to his neck before drifting over his broad shoulders and down his muscled biceps.

When I see his forearms and the veins snaking beneath his skin, I feel a weird sensation in my stomach. It feels like something is twisting and turning in my abdomen, and as my eyes lock on his left hand, his ring finger bare, the sensation spreads to my chest.

When my eyes lift back to Damiano's face and I see the grim lines pulling around his mouth, I shake my head.

Then I lock eyes with his guard, who's watching me like a hawk.

He shakes his head slowly before murmuring, "Stop whatever you're thinking."

Crap.

I tear my eyes away from the guard's and wrap my arms around myself.

I hope the man doesn't think I was plotting to kill his boss.

At some point during the long flight, the flight attendant gives everyone food. Even though I'm not hungry, I eat some of the lamb shank and mashed potatoes because I have no idea when I'll get food again.

After we've all had our meals, I notice Damiano and his guard are caught in a serious conversation.

I hope the guard doesn't tell him I was staring at him while he was resting.

Lifting my hand, I wipe my fingers over my forehead, where a tension headache is forming.

I have no idea how long the flight is, and unable to sleep, I just sit and stare at nothing in particular. My thoughts are overwhelmed with everything that's happened and my uncertain future.

My family probably only cares about what they might gain from Damiano taking me. They're definitely not worried about my safety, and they sure as hell won't miss me.

No one cares about what happens to me.

The thought makes a forlorn feeling ghost through my chest.

Lifting my chin, I suck in a deep breath while I forcefully squash the gloomy feeling.

I have myself.

I've survived beatings, starvation, and years of neglect. I'll survive whatever lies in my future.

When the flight attendant announces that we're landing in ten minutes, my stomach turns into a queasy mess.

Crap, I shouldn't have eaten.

My hands grip the armrests tightly, my nails digging into the expensive leather as I try to brace myself.

"Come," Damiano's guard suddenly says as he unclips my seat belt.

Taking hold of my elbow, he helps me to my feet, and I'm once again steered to the seat beside Damiano.

As I quickly fasten the seat belt, Damiano places a paper bag on my lap.

"If you're going to get sick, use the bag," he mutters, his tone harsh.

"Thank you," I reply.

Sitting next to Damiano makes me feel a hell of a lot more tense, and I clasp my hands together on my lap.

I'm confused as to why he wants me to sit beside him.

It's probably to keep you close so you won't try to make a run for it once the plane has landed.

Suddenly, the plane dips, and my stomach rolls with fear. I squeeze my eyes shut, and not caring whether Damiano will be angry, I grab hold of his arm.

This time, there's no fabric, and I feel the heat of his skin.

The plane dips again, and I let out a squeak.

"Christ," Damiano growls beside me. "Your nails are sharp."

When he takes hold of my hand, my eyes fly open, and it's to see him moving my hand to his.

For a moment, I forget about the plane.

I'm stunned out of my everloving mind when his fingers wrap tightly around mine, but then the plane shudders as it touches down on the runway. If it weren't for the seat belt, I'd climb into Damiano's lap for safety. Instead, I turn my head and press my face against his bicep, another squeak escaping my lips.

The aircraft slams on its brakes, and my body jolts from the force. My other hand grabs hold of Damiano's bicep, and I press as close to him as the seat belt allows.

The plane slows down drastically, and the first thing I become aware of is the scent filling the air I breathe. It's warm and manly, with notes of spice and something rich.

I can smell the power before I feel it beneath my hands.

Before Damiano can say anything, I yank away while my face goes up in flames.

"I apo–"

"Stop apologizing for something you intend on doing again," he grumbles while unclipping his seat belt and climbing to his feet. "Come."

Again? Does that mean he plans to take me somewhere else?

I quickly free myself from my seat belt and get up. Once again, Damiano's guard takes hold of my arm and pulls me to the side so I'm out of his boss' way.

Half the guards leave the plane while Damiano straightens his sleeves before shrugging on his jacket.

Only when one of the guards signals that it's safe does Damiano head down the stairs.

I follow with his guard, and having the man's hand on me, I mutter, "If you're going to drag me around, I should at least know your name."

"Carlo," he murmurs. "I'm the head of security and Damiano's second in charge."

He must be just as dangerous as Damiano, if not more.

It's much colder in New York than Palermo, and I shiver as I walk away from the private jet.

Reaching an SUV, I climb into the backseat with Damiano. He pulls his phone from his pocket and keeps busy replying to messages and emails.

When Carlo starts the engine, I glance at the dashboard and notice it's nine pm. I forgot about the time difference between the two countries.

As we drive away from the airfield, I stare at the foreign landscape, or as much of it as I can see at night.

I wonder if I'll be allowed to explore New York.

Probably not.

It feels like I'm being transported from one prison to another, and God only knows what my new warden will be like.

Chapter 5

Gabriella

My eyes dart from one tall building to another, and I'm struck speechless at the hustle and bustle of cars and people so late at night.

After an hour's drive, the SUV enters an underground parking, and only when we climb out do I realize the other guards didn't follow us. I have no idea what's happened to my belongings.

"Come," Carlo mutters.

I follow Damiano and his guard into an elevator, the muscles in my body wound tight as I cautiously glance from one man to the other.

Being alone with them is super unnerving.

Instead of the elevator opening on a residential floor, the doors open on the roof.

When I see the helicopter, my stomach drops to my feet, and my mouth dries up.

Oh no.

This is why Damiano made the comment earlier.

The wind is icy up on the roof, and I try to rub some warmth into my arms.

The helicopter doesn't look as trustworthy as the private jet, and I start to tremble as I climb into it.

Damiano takes a seat beside me, sitting much closer to me because of the restricted space. Our sides touch, and I try to steal some of his body heat.

When the propellors start to chop through the air and noise fills the cabin, I press my lips tightly together so I don't make a panicked sound.

Damiano hands me a headset. "Put it on."

I do as I'm told, and it blocks the noise from the helicopter.

When the aircraft begins to lift into the air, there's no stopping a shriek from bursting over my lips, and this time, I grab hold of Damiano's thigh.

I duck my head and curl into myself while it feels like my stomach is free-falling to the ground below.

Once we're in the air, I hear Damiano's voice clearly through the headset as he orders, "Let go."

I pull my hand away and wrapping my arms around my middle, I dare to open my eyes. I'm met with a magnificent view of the city lights below and swallow hard, hoping to all that's holy I don't throw up.

The queasy feeling passes, and staring at the buildings as we fly over them, I wonder where we're going.

Soon, the view of the buildings falls away, and I notice the landscape changing.

My lips part as we fly over a lake, the water dark and smooth in the moonlight and the shores lined with tall trees.

Wow.

We approach a mansion, warm lights shining from the windows and the grounds lit with outdoor lights.

I'm overwhelmed by the beautiful sight, then notice the heavily armed guards scattered all over the property.

There will be no escaping my new prison.

My eyes dart to the mansion that looks as imposing as its owner. The three-story is easily five times the size of my parents' house.

When the helicopter starts to descend, I hold myself tighter to stop from grabbing Damiano.

We land on a helipad, and guards come to open the doors.

With a relieved sigh, I quickly take off the headset and place it on the seat before I climb out of the cabin.

It's freezing, and I shiver my butt off as I glance around. Nerves spin in my stomach, and unsure of what is expected of me, I look at Carlo.

He tips his head toward the entrance. "The guards will bring your belongings later."

I nod, and swallowing hard on the scratchy feeling in my throat, I follow Damiano and Carlo to the back entrance of the mansion.

I expected a cold penthouse somewhere in the city, not this beautiful property.

Approaching double French doors, Damiano walks in first before I follow. My eyes dart around, taking in the white walls, the art, and expensive décor.

Damiano doesn't spare me a glance as he breaks away from us, heading in the opposite direction.

I'm relieved when central heating chases the chill from my body as I follow Carlo up the grand staircase.

When we reach the third floor, I'm taken down a hallway where he opens a door and once again tips his head, saying, "You'll stay here for the time being."

I step into the room, and my lips part when I glance over all the luxury.

My family isn't poor, but I've never had so much space for myself.

A massive bed stands by a wall, the bedding white and welcoming. Floor-to-ceiling windows give me a stunning view of the trees and a lake. The view must be so much more beautiful during the day.

Unable to ignore Carlo, I lock eyes with him and ask, "What is expected of me?"

"Don't cause trouble, and you'll be fine. Get some sleep, and we'll talk in the morning," he mutters before leaving the room.

When the door shuts behind him, I let out a relieved breath while I lock it.

Finally alone, my unsure reality sinks in, and I worry about what will happen next.

Exhaustion creeps into my bones, and sucking in a deep breath, I look through the bedroom, a small sitting area, the empty walk-in closet, and a stunning bathroom.

The exhaustion keeps growing in my bones. Not knowing when my belongings will arrive, I decide to take a quick shower before trying to get some sleep.

Luckily, I find a bathrobe in the bathroom. I don't take my time and instead rush through my routine, using the products provided.

Leaving my dirty clothes and underwear in the bathroom, I shrug on the bathrobe. I place my handbag on the dressing table and dig out my cell phone.

Crap. I hope the guards packed my charger.

Checking the device, I realize I have no Wifi. I hope Damiano will let me have the password for his Wifi service.

I'll probably have to get a US SIM card.

Noticing my phone automatically adusted to the new time zone, I set my alarm for six am before I crawl beneath the soft covers.

I notice a remote control on the bedside table, and picking it up, I glance over all the functions. Seeing buttons for the curtains, I press one.

When the curtains start to slide closed, my eyebrows lift.

Wow. Fancy.

Placing the remote control back on the bedside table, I snuggle into one of the pillows and close my eyes.

It's already past midnight, and usually, I'm fast asleep. At home I had to be up at six in the morning and in bed by nine pm. There were so many rules and I'm sure Damiano has his own. I wish I knew what they were.

Am I allowed to leave the bedroom?

What about food? Do I have to ask permission like I had to do at home?

What does Damiano plan to do with me?

"Dio, I've been taken by the *Capo dei Capi,"* I whisper as the shock hits once again.

What will become of me?

My mind is preoccupied with the predicament I find myself in, but eventually, exhaustion wins, and I drift off into a restless sleep.

Chapter 6

Gabriella

Even though I went to bed late, I wake up before my alarm. I press the button to open the curtains, and climbing out of bed, I adjust the bathrobe I'm wearing while walking to the windows.

"*Dio*," I whisper when I see the breathtaking view of the sun rising over the lake.

Noticing a balcony, I find the door and unlock it. When I push it open, a cold breeze sweeps over me. I step onto the balcony, drinking in the exquisite sight of the tall trees on either side of the vast backyard.

It's the most beautiful view I've ever seen.

I take a seat on one of the wrought-iron chairs by a small round table and pull my legs up so I can cover my feet with the bathrobe.

Crap, it's much colder here than in Palermo.

I don't think my clothes are warm enough for the snowy winters New York experiences.

Staring at the scenic nature and the guards scattered over the property, I suck in a deep breath as I try to gather my thoughts.

Everything that's happened over the past twenty-four hours fills my mind, and I'm once again left worrying about my uncertain future.

Hopefully, Carlo will give me some answers today.

I hear someone knocking, but they don't wait for me to answer, and instead, they try to open the door.

I dart off the chair and rush to unlock the door. When I open it, I'm met with several guards who carry my belongings inside, dropping everything in front of the bed.

Not bothering to acknowledge me, they immediately leave again.

I shut the door behind them, relieved to have my belongings.

"I'll get dressed before unpacking," I whisper to myself.

Should I unpack?

I have no idea how long I'll stay here.

I'll ask Carlo when I see him.

With my parents not here to control what I wear, I search through the bags until I find a matching set of lace underwear and one of my warmer outfits.

The stylish pant legs flare around my legs, and I match them with a cashmere sweater that fits like a second skin.

After getting dressed, I slip my feet into a pair of cream heels before searching through the bags for my makeup supplies. A smile stretches over my face when I also manage to find my hair and skin care products.

I let out a sigh of relief when I see none of the products were damaged when the guards packed them.

Thank God for small mercies.

Heading to the bathroom, I brush my hair and teeth before going through my skincare routine.

Feeling much better, I take a seat at the dressing table and carefully apply my makeup.

Once I'm happy with the final result, I straighten the covers on my bed and search for my phone charger. Just as I plug the device in, there's another knock at the door.

I quickly open, and when I see Carlo, I feel relieved that I don't have to wait any longer.

Smiling politely, I say, "Morning."

He just nods at me then gestures down the hallway. "It's time for breakfast."

I step out of the bedroom and shut the door.

We start to walk, and I shoot him a cautious glance. "Can I ask questions?"

"Yes."

"How long will I stay here?"

"Until Damiano decides otherwise," he mutters.

Feeling brave, I ask, "Do you know what he plans to do with me?"

"You'll find out soon."

Not liking the answer, I frown at Carlo.

"Can I use the Wifi?"

"I'll get you the password."

Gazie a Dio.

"Am I allowed to leave my bedroom?"

"Yes." We stop at the top of the stairs, and Carlo locks eyes with me. "Stay away from Damiano's suite and office. You're not allowed to leave the property without permission."

I nod quickly. "Okay."

We head down the stairs, then Carlo mentions, "There is an elevator if you get tired of the stairs."

I nod, and sucking in a deep breath, I ask, "Am I allowed to help myself to food?"

"Yes. I'll show you where the kitchen is."

When we reach the first floor, Carlo says, "You'll meet Damiano's mother and mine. Mrs. Falco is blind. You're not to mention anything about her disability."

"Okay."

We walk into a state-of-the-art kitchen, and Carlo takes a few minutes to show me where everything is. I actually start to relax around the man.

A woman dressed in a black and white uniform comes into the kitchen with an empty tray in her hands.

"Martha," Carlo says. "This is Miss di Bella. She'll be visiting us for a while."

"It's nice to meet you, ma'am," she says politely.

"You too," I murmur. When we leave the kitchen, I glance up at Carlo. "Thank you for answering my questions."

"You're not a prisoner. Just don't cause any trouble, and you'll be fine."

His words ease more of the anxiety that's been tightening my stomach.

Maybe things won't be as bad as I thought.

When we enter an elegant dining room, my eyes jump from the two women who seem to be in their early or mid-fifties to Damiano. They're already seated at the table.

My gaze darts back to the woman sitting to Damiano's left, and I can't help but notice how beautiful she is.

Now I know where Damiano got his good looks from.

Damiano is sitting at the head of the table, busy cutting strips of bacon into smaller pieces.

Pushing the plate in front of his mother, he says, "Clockwise, the bacon is at three and the pancakes at nine."

She holds her hand palm up and when he places his hand in hers, she kisses his fingers, then asks, "How was the trip? Are Cettina and Stefano well?"

Carlo holds a chair out for me, and I take a seat across from Mrs. Accardi while Carlo sits down to Damiano's right.

As Damiano pulls his hand free from his mother's, his eyes flick to me. "We have a guest."

"Oh?" Mrs. Falco's eyebrow pops up while Mrs. Accardi gives me a curious look.

"I didn't give my permission for Stefano to marry Gabriella. Instead, I brought her to New York. She'll stay with us for a while."

My lips curve up in a smile as I glance between the two women. "It's nice to meet you."

"Welcome," Mrs. Accardi says.

It feels as if she's inspecting every inch of me.

Mrs. Falco only nods in my direction before turning her attention back to her son. "What did Stefano have to say about the matter?"

"Of course, he's not happy," Damiano mutters while cutting a piece off his pancakes. "I didn't see Cettina, but I'm sure she's well."

"Oh dear," Mrs. Falco sighs. "I'll have to call my sister-in-law and smooth things over."

"You'll do no such thing," Damiano orders.

Martha brings two plates of food and sets them down in front of Carlo and me.

Between bites, Mrs. Falco asks, "Why didn't you give your blessing?"

"I have other plans for Gabriella," he mutters, clearly annoyed by the conversation.

I focus my attention on the plate in front of me and begin to eat. Martha leans down beside me and softly asks, "Would you like juice, coffee, or tea?"

I give the housekeeper a warm smile. "Coffee, please." When she pours me a cup of steaming caffeine, I murmur, "Thank you."

"You look very young. How old are you, Gabriella?" Mrs. Accardi asks.

I keep my tone respectful as I answer, "I'm twenty-three."

Mrs. Falco turns her face in my direction, her eyes staring blankly ahead. "We'll get to know each other better after breakfast."

My eyes dart between Damiano and his mother before I reply, "I'd like that."

While I eat, Mrs. Falco asks Damiano, "Will you be home for a while?"

"I'll be between Manhattan and the mansion for the next few weeks," he answers before wiping the corners of his mouth with a napkin. Climbing to his feet, he says, "Have a good day, Mamma."

He leans over and presses a kiss to the top of her head before leaving the dining room.

Most of the tension in the room leaves with Damiano, and my shoulders relax a little.

A guard steps into the dining room, taking a seat next to Mrs. Accardi. His eyes flick between Carlo and me.

"This is Gabriella di Bella. She'll stay with us for a while," Carlo tells him. He gestures at the guard, then explains, "Gerardo oversees the mansion's security. He's Mrs. Falco and my mother's guard."

"Welcome," he says before his attention is drawn to Martha as she brings him his breakfast.

"Nice to meet you," I murmur.

"Gerardo, give Gabriella the Wifi password," Carlo orders as he climbs to his feet.

Mrs. Accardi also gets up from her seat and follows her son out of the dining room.

When I'm done eating, I'm not sure whether I should wait until everyone's finished or whether I can leave.

I glance at Gerardo and Mrs. Falco, and when she pushes her chair back, she says, "Gabriella, join me in my sitting room."

I dart to my feet, and unsure if I should assist her, my stomach fills with knots as I follow her.

I'm surprised when she walks down the hallway to a sitting room where the sun is streaming in through the windows.

She takes a seat, and with her head held high, she glances in my direction. "Please, sit."

I pick a chair opposite her and perch my butt on the edge, my hands folded on my lap.

"Don't be nervous," she says.

I almost nod but instead murmur, "Okay."

"Have you visited the States before?" she asks.

"No, this is my first time away from Sicily."

"Your English is good," she compliments me.

"My parents had me attend extra lessons," I inform her.

"Have you called them to let them know you've landed safely?"

I shake my head. "No. I have to get a SIM card."

"You can use the house phone."

I hesitate for a moment, but too scared to lie to Damiano's mother, I say, "I doubt they're worried about me, and they'll ask questions I can't answer, so I'd rather not call them."

Her left eyebrow lifts while a frown forms on her forehead. "You're not close with your parents?"

"Not at all."

"That's a shame," she murmurs.

Mrs. Accardi comes into the sitting room and sits down near Mrs. Falco. With both women facing me, I start to feel nervous again.

"What are we talking about?" she asks Mrs. Falco.

"We're getting to know Gabriella," Mrs. Falco answers. Turning her attention back to me, she asks, "Did you find everything to your liking in your suite?"

"Yes. Thank you. The room is beautiful."

"If you need anything, just let Martha know."

"Thank you," I murmur.

Mrs. Accardi gives me a curious look, then leans forward and whispers, "Do you know why Damiano brought you to the mansion? I asked Carlo, but he wouldn't tell me."

I shake my head. "Unfortunately, I don't."

Mrs. Falco's expression also becomes curious. "What happened at the meeting?"

"Not much," I answer. "Mr. Falco wasn't at my parents' house for more than an hour when he ordered his guards to pack my belongings. It all happened really fast. He didn't offer any explanation for why he didn't give his blessing."

"You said you're twenty-three?" Mrs. Falco asks.

"Yes, ma'am."

She scrunches her nose as if she's disgusted. "Stefano's almost fifty. That's twice your age!"

I swallow hard before agreeing, "Yes."

"Damiano did the right thing," his mother mutters as she leans back in her armchair. "What does Stefano want with such a young bride?"

"You know what," Mrs. Accardi grumbles.

Mrs. Falco shakes her head. "Stefano should marry someone his own age." She glances in my direction again. "Whatever Damiano has planned for you, it will be much better than marrying my nephew."

The words actually make me feel relieved and a little overwhelmed. I stare at the women as a weird sensation trickles into my chest.

"I really hope so," I whisper.

"Tell us, what do you like to do in your spare time?" Mrs. Accardi asks.

"I make skincare and makeup tutorials for social media."

"Oh, did you study to become a beautician?" Mrs. Falco asks.

I relax completely and actually start to enjoy the conversation.

"No. I learned everything from watching videos on YouTube."

Before they can ask me another question, Martha comes into the sitting room. "Can I unpack your belongings, Miss di Bella?"

"Oh, let me help," I say as I rise from the armchair. Looking at Mrs. Falco and Mrs. Accardi, I ask, "May I be excused?"

"Of course," Mrs. Falco replies. "Once you're settled, come join us again."

"Okay."

I follow Martha out of the sitting room, feeling much better after the pleasant morning.

By the time we reach my bedroom, the pleasant feeling starts to fade, and soon, the worry returns because I still have no idea what Damiano plans to do with me.

Chapter 7

Damiano

Standing out on the veranda with my eyes roaming over the backyard and guards, I don't glance behind me when I hear movement.

I recognize my mother's steps, and bracing myself for a million questions, I turn to face her.

She takes a seat on one of the lounge chairs, then says, "Greta says the girl is beautiful."

I move closer and sit down on one of the chairs. With my gaze resting on my mother, I mutter, "Aunt Greta is right."

"Did you take Gabriella for yourself?" she asks, getting right to the point.

"No." I glance at the open French doors before saying, "I'm going to arrange a marriage between Dario and Gabriella."

"Oh." Mamma's eyebrow flies up. "He's such a sweet boy. He'll be good to her."

72

"She better be good to him," I mutter.

"Always so protective," Mamma chuckles.

"Don't tell her. I need to talk with Dario before she's informed of the arranged marriage."

"Okay." She takes a deep breath before letting it out slowly, then asks, "Is Stefano very upset that you took his fiancée?"

"Probably."

My gaze drifts over my mother's face before they lock on the blank stare in her eyes.

She lost her sight the night I killed my father. It's been nineteen years, and I still remember every second of that night.

My mother's cries as he beat her.

The kick against her head that put her in a coma for three weeks.

Her blood soaking into the wooden floorboards.

I lost my mind and beat my father to death with my bare fists. He was unrecognizable by the time I was done.

It changed my entire life, and I became the head of the Cosa Nostra at nineteen.

At the time, Carlo's mother was our housekeeper, and having grown up with Carlo, he was the only man I trusted.

We moved our mothers into this mansion where a small army guards them twenty-four-seven.

Carlo's been by my side as I built my empire. The only other person I consider a close friend is Angelo, one of the heads of the Cosa Nostra.

I care about Franco, Renzo, and Dario, but I just clicked better with Angelo. He understands me.

"What are you thinking about?" Mamma asks.

"Everything," I whisper.

She stands up and holds her hand out to me. I take it and guide her to me before resting my head against her stomach. I close my eyes when she brushes her hand over my hair.

"You have too much resting on your shoulders," she murmurs. "I worry about you."

"I'm okay," I assure her. "Don't worry about me."

"To others, you are the *Capo dei Capi*, but to me, you'll always be my baby boy. I'll always worry about you."

The corner of my mouth lifts, and climbing to my feet, I lean down so I can wrap her in a tight hug against my chest. "*Ti voglio bene*, Mamma."

"I love you more, *mio figlio*."

Carlo steps out onto the veranda, asking, "Ready?"

I nod as I pull away from my mother, then say, "I'm leaving for Manhattan. I'll try to be home for the weekend."

"Okay." She pats my arm. "Be careful out there."

"Always."

Pressing a kiss to the top of her head, I walk with Carlo in the direction of the helipad.

Sitting in my private lounge that overlooks the entire club, I listen as Emilio and Vito give me updates regarding the construction projects and clubs.

"The unions haven't given any problems," Emilio says.

I nod. "That's good."

"Some fucker is planning to build a skyscraper near the hotel. It will obstruct the view of the Hudson River."

Letting out a sigh, I mutter, "Change their mind about building on the site and have them sell it to us."

My men are well-trained and will use any force necessary to get the job done.

It was one of the hardest things I had to learn – trusting my men to do their jobs and not just doing everything myself.

When they get up and Vito walks with a slight limp, it reminds me of when Angelo shot him in the foot for hurting Vittoria.

"Vito, how's the foot?" I ask.

"Gonna take a painkiller now, boss. Nothing to worry about."

I nod before picking up my phone. Bringing up the group chat with the other four heads of the Cosa Nostra, I start a video call.

When all their faces fill the screen, I say, "There's a meeting at my club tomorrow morning at nine. Don't be late."

"You could've sent a text," Franco mutters before yawning.

The man has triplets at home, so I let it slide.

"The babies keeping you up?" Angelo asks.

"Yeah. You know the drill," Franco chuckles.

Angelo and Vittoria are expecting their second child.

The family is growing, putting more pressure on my shoulders to keep everyone safe.

"See you all tomorrow," I say before ending the call.

"What's wrong?" Carlo asks.

"Nothing."

He pours me a tumbler of whiskey from my private selection. Handing me the drink, he lifts an eyebrow at me.

"They're all falling one by one and starting families," I mutter.

"Why is that a problem?"

"Just more people to protect."

"They have their own guards," Carlo says as he stands in front of the one-way glass overlooking the club's interior, and his gaze slowly sweeps over all the people.

"Not Dario. The fucker is stubborn and careless." I take a sip, letting the alcohol burn down my throat. "Remind me to talk to him about it."

"Will do."

While I enjoy the whiskey, my thoughts turn to Gabriella. When she walked into the dining room, it was hard not to stare. I'll never admit it out loud, but I love the way she dresses.

Christ. I need to get laid.

I can't remember when I was last with a woman.

Six months?

Frowning, I glance at Carlo. "When's the last time I got laid?"

"Fuck." He shakes his head. "The blonde?"

"What blonde?"

He lets out a chuckle. "Let's just say it's been a while."

Should I be worried that I haven't needed a woman's company in months?

Suddenly, the memory of Gabriella ducking against my side when the private jet landed pops into my mind, and I almost let out a growl.

The fuck, no.

Getting up, I stalk out of the lounge to get away from the unwelcome memory.

"Where are we going?" Carlo asks when he falls into step beside me.

"The penthouse."

I need solitude so I can recharge after being among people for the past two days.

When we climb into the SUV, Carlo asks, "Want me to order something for dinner?"

"Sure."

I glance out the window, and once again, Gabriella pops into my mind.

Last night in the helicopter, when she gripped my thigh, sent an unwanted burst of attraction through me.

A frown forms on my forehead, and as I wipe my fingers over my lips, I forcefully shove the woman out of my thoughts.

The moment Carlo brings the SUV to a stop in the underground parking, I shove the door open and climb out. My eyes roam over the area, and seeing all my guards at their posts, I walk to the elevator.

On the way up to the top floor, Carlo says, "I'll order steak."

"Okay."

The doors open, and I stalk into the penthouse. Loosening the tie from around my neck, I head to the bedroom while saying, "I'm going to shower. Let me know when the food is here."

"Will do."

Stepping into the bathroom, I switch on the faucets before getting undressed. Soon, the bathroom is filled with steam, and as I climb into the shower, the warm water pelts my body.

My thoughts return to Gabriella, and I let out a sigh. Once I've arranged the marriage between her and Dario, I'll have to start thinking about myself. I need an heir, and I'm not getting any younger.

But who?

Fuck, it doesn't really matter. As long as the woman is able to bear children, I'm good.

I let out a sigh as I start to wash my body.

The last thing I'm looking forward to is getting married. My time is limited, and having another person to care for will only add to my exhaustion.

It's not something to worry about right now.

I just have to focus on getting Miguel and his men out of New York. After the problem's taken care of and Dario is engaged to Gabriella, I'll revisit the idea of finding a wife for myself.

Chapter 8

Gabriella

It took me the whole day to get settled in the suite, and when I walk into the dining room for dinner, Mrs. Falco and Mrs. Accardi are already seated at the table.

"Where have you been hiding today?" Mrs. Accardi asks.

"I've been unpacking everything." I take a seat at the table and give Gerardo a tentative smile when he also joins us.

Martha brings out the food, and when she places a plate of spaghetti and meatballs in front of me, I whisper, "Thank you."

"I looked for you in your room and left the Wifi password on your bedside table," Gerardo informs me.

"Thank you."

Good, now I'll be able to check my social media pages.

Crap, I'll need an address for any promotional merchandise I get sent.

I glance at Gerardo, then push through and ask, "Which address can I use to receive packages?"

A frown forms on his forehead, and stabbing a meatball, he asks, "What kind of packages?"

"Sometimes I receive makeup and skincare products to promote on my social media pages."

He thinks for a moment, then says, "I'll arrange for a postbox where the stuff can be sent. Don't ever give out the mansion's address."

That won't happen, because I have no idea where the mansion is.

"Okay." I nod quickly, then add, "Thank you."

Mrs. Accardi cuts Mrs. Falco's meatballs into smaller pieces before focusing on her own plate.

I twirl some spaghetti onto my fork and take a bite. While I chew, I glance at my dinner companions, thinking things seem much calmer here than at my parents' house.

We never ate dinner as a family.

There were days I didn't eat at all.

My hand stills as my thoughts slip away to the times when my mother would lock me in my room for disobeying her.

Once, she forgot about me for four days. Luckily, I was able to get water from the bathroom.

"Is there something wrong with the food, *cara*?" Mrs. Accardi asks, pulling me out of my thoughts.

I quickly shake my head and force a smile to my face. "Not at all. It's delicious."

I continue eating, forcing the depressing thoughts to the back of my mind.

What doesn't kill me makes me stronger.

I constantly repeat the words to remind myself to remain strong no matter what life throws my way. I won't let anything break me.

"Can you cook, Gabriella?" Mrs. Falco asks.

"Yes. I was taught all the skills I'd need to make a good wife," I answer.

She stares in my direction. "What would those skills entail?"

"Cooking. Needle work. Cleaning. How to handle myself in social settings." I hesitate for a moment before I continue, hating the words as they spill over my lips, "How to be obedient to my husband."

A frown forms between Mrs. Falco's eyebrows, then she shakes her head before taking a bite of her food.

Did I say something wrong?

"What can you cook?" Mrs. Accardi asks.

"Mostly, Sicilian food."

"Do you have a favorite dish?" she asks before taking a bite of her spaghetti.

"*Coda alla vaccinara*," I murmur. "I love oxtail."

I once added too many vegetables and got hit over my knuckles with a wooden spoon until my skin turned blue.

My head jerks as I shove the memory away. Lifting my chin higher, I pick up my glass of water and take a sip.

What doesn't kill me makes me stronger.

"You should make it for us one day," Mrs. Falco says. "I can't remember when last I had *coda alla vaccinara*."

With a polite smile on my face, I reply, "I'd love to."

Once we're all finished with our meals, and Gerardo leaves with Mrs. Accardi and Mrs. Falco, I stay behind to gather all the plates and utensils.

"Oh, you don't have to do that," Martha says, rushing toward me.

"I kept you busy all day long. It's the least I can do."

She takes the dishes from me and shakes her head. "You're a guest, ma'am. Mr. Falco would be very upset if he heard about this."

Not wanting to get the housekeeper in trouble, I nod before leaving the dining room.

When I walk up the hallway toward Mrs. Falco's sitting room, I hear Gerardo ask, "Are you going to read one of those romance books again?"

"Yes, so you better make a run for it," Mrs. Accardi warns, her words followed by a chuckle.

Gerardo comes out of the sitting room and nods at me before he walks away.

Romance books?

"Let's see. Where were we?" I hear Mrs. Accardi say.

Mrs. Falco replies, "Beau was on his way to tell Daisy he loved her."

I stop right outside the door and listen as Mrs. Accardi reads, "I bring my truck to a screeching stop outside Daisy's house, and jumping out, I run up the path to the front door. I knock, impatient for her to open."

Mrs. Accardi pauses, then murmurs, "Oh, my heart."

"What?" Mrs. Falco asks. "Don't stop reading now!"

A smile curves my lips, and I lean my shoulder against the wall.

"When Daisy opens the front door, my hand flies up, and I grip her behind the neck. Yanking her toward me, my eyes lock with her startled gaze. 'I love you, Daisy Adams. I've always loved you. Stay in Paradise with me. This is where you belong.' I hold my breath while I wait for her to say something."

"Aww," Mrs. Falco coos. "Finally."

"Oh no," Mrs. Accardi mutters.

Mrs. Falco gasps, "On no what?"

"Daisy pulls away from me, shaking her head. 'No. You had years to tell me how you felt. Waiting until I'm leaving isn't fair.' My heart cracks down the middle when I see the anger in her beautiful gaze."

"No, Daisy," Mrs. Falco whispers, totally caught up in the story.

"Taking a step back, I shake my head. 'Don't do this to us, Daisy.'"

Mrs. Accardi pauses for a moment, and when she continues, emotion fills her voice.

"Her chin starts to tremble, then she says, 'You did this to us.' When she shuts the door, intense heartache bleeds through my soul."

I hear a soft sob, and peeking into the sitting room, I see Mrs. Accardi and Mrs. Falco sniffling because of the sad scene.

Mrs. Accardi spots me and smiles through her tears. "Come join us, Gabriella."

I quickly shake my head. "I don't want to intrude."

"Oh, hush. Come take a seat."

Stepping into the sitting room, I walk to one of the armchairs and take a seat.

"We love reading for an hour after dinner," Mrs. Accardi explains. "Afterward, we watch an episode of a TV show. You're welcome to join us at any time."

"Thank you."

"This book is too sad, and we're already three-quarters through it. Let's start a new one so Gabriella's not lost," Mrs. Falco says.

Mrs. Accardi stands up and walks to the bookshelf. While she's perusing the books, she asks, "What do you feel like reading?" She glances at me. "Do you have a favorite genre?"

I shake my head. "Growing up, I wasn't allowed to read romance books. I'm good with whatever you choose."

"*Caro Dio*. I would die without my books," Mrs. Accardi mutters. "What else weren't you allowed to do?"

Crap.

"Ahhh…" I hesitate, but not being one to lie, I answer honestly, "My parents were very controlling. Especially my mother. She decided everything for me." I let out an awkward-sounding chuckle. "When I started making

87

money from my social media pages, I bought my own clothes. It made her angry."

"Why?" Mrs. Accardi gasps. "I think your outfits are stylish."

"They preferred I wear modest clothes."

Mrs. Accardi grabs a book, and when she comes to take a seat, Mrs. Falco says, "It sounds like you didn't have a happy childhood. I'm beginning to understand why you didn't want to call your family to let them know you arrived safely."

"I don't come from a loving home," I admit.

My eyes drift over her beautiful face, and for a moment, I wonder whether she's always been blind.

Clearing my throat, I add, "I just want you to know I'm enjoying my stay here."

"That makes me happy," Mrs. Falco murmurs before lifting an eyebrow in Mrs. Accardi's direction. "Which book have you chosen? Read us the blurb."

Mrs. Accardi's mouth curves into a smile, then suddenly, she holds the book out to me. "I've been reading for years. It would be nice just to listen."

"Oh." Taking the book from her, nerves begin to spin in my stomach as my eyes dart over the words on the back cover.

I clear my throat, and lifting my chin, I begin to read, "Readers should brace themselves for an epic tale of love and found family. Caution: This erotic bestseller should be read with the AC on."

Erotic?

Feeling hesitant, I start with chapter one but soon get lost in the story.

When I reach chapter two, laughter bursts from me. "Uhm, so there are curse words in this book. Do I read them?"

Mrs. Accardi chuckles before answering, "You read every word, *cara*. Don't leave out anything, or it will take away from the story."

My tongue darts out to wet my lips, and as I continue reading, my eyes grow wide as saucers. "Staring at Josephine's curvacious … ahhh," I glance at Mrs. Falco and Mrs. Accardi, who are both waiting with bated breath, "curvacious ass, I can already tell she'll be a good … *Dio*."

My eyes jump over the page, and with every filthy word, they grow wider. "Oh wow," I whisper, then I read the part where the hero fantasizes about plunging into her wet core. "Holy crap."

Mrs. Falco lets out a burst of laughter, then says, "Put the poor girl out of her misery, Greta. Choose something tamer for her to begin with."

Mrs. Accardi chuckles as she retrieves another book from the shelf. "This one only has a three-chili pepper rating."

"What's a chili pepper rating?" I ask as I take the book from her.

"There are no more than four or five spicy scenes, and they aren't too hot."

Caro Dio.

I begin to read, and when I reach chapter three, and there is only a curse word here and there, I relax. The plot gets better and better, and I keep reading.

When I reach a scene where the main female character is betrayed by her best friend, I mutter, "What an awful friend."

"I think we should have some tea. You must be thirsty from all the reading," Mrs. Falco says.

"I'll prepare the tea," I offer as I set the book down on a side table.

When I get up from the armchair, Mrs. Accardi waves a hand in the air.

"We'll join you in the kitchen. I want to see if there are any of those chocolate cookies left that Martha baked."

I wait for Mrs. Falco and Mrs. Accardi to walk and follow them to the kitchen.

After I pour water into a kettle, I search through the cupboards until I find the teacups.

"Found them," Mrs. Accardi exclaims, and when I glance over my shoulder, I see her place a cookie in Mrs. Falco's hand then she comes to offer me one.

"Thank you," I murmur before taking a bite.

While I chew, I prepare chamomile tea.

I glance at Mrs. Falco and Mrs. Accardi, then think about the short time I've spent here.

So far, my stay has been enjoyable. It's a million times better than being at home with my family.

I hope I get to visit for a while before Damiano follows through on whatever plan he has for me.

Chapter 9

Damiano

When Carlo brings the SUV to a stop at one of my warehouses, I shove the door open and climb out. Straightening my jacket, my gaze sweeps over the area before I head toward the side door.

The moment my men see me, they straighten up.

Tommy rushes toward me. "We found the fucker trying to deal in Mott Haven. There were five other guys with him, but the fuckers put up a fight, and we had to kill them."

Nodding, I walk to where the drug dealer is sitting on the floor. My men have restrained him with zip ties and already gave him one hell of a beating.

Stopping a couple of feet from the prisoner, I say, "Dealing in the Bronx and Brooklyn is ambitious. What made you think it would be allowed?"

The man lifts his head, and when his eyes lock on me, they widen with fear.

Immediately, he starts to ramble, "We were just told to sell in those areas. They offered us good money for the work. Please, I have a family. It's tough out there. I just wanted to make a quick buck."

When I continue to stare at him, he starts to sob. "Please. I'm just a bottom feeder. A man by the name of Leroy gave me the job. That's all the info I have, boss."

Letting out a sigh, my eyes flick to Tommy. "Find Leroy."

"Yes, boss."

"So I can go?" the dealer asks, his tone filled with hope.

Not sparing him another glance, I turn around and walk to the side door.

"No! Wait! Wait!" he shouts right before a gunshot rings through the air.

Reaching the SUV, I open the passenger door and pause to say, "I want more men cleaning the streets. If we wipe out the bottom line, it will cut into Miguel's profits. Hit the fucker where it hurts most."

"On it," Carlo mutters.

Climbing into the SUV, anger and frustration simmer in my chest.

I want Miguel's drugs out of my fucking city.

I pull my phone out and go into the group chat with the other heads of the Cosa Nostra. I start a video call, and when only Angelo, Franco, and Renzo answer, I frown.

"Where's Dario?"

"He's probably at the ballet company," Renzo replies. "He's been busy with the upcoming show."

Right.

"There's a meeting at my club tomorrow at nine."

"It's a Saturday," Renzo mutters.

"Your point being?" I ask, raising an eyebrow at him.

He shakes his head. "I'll be there."

"You better have a lot of coffee," Franco says.

The corner of Angelo's mouth lifts. "See you tomorrow."

I end the call and glance out the window.

Carlo drives us to the penthouse, where the helicopter is waiting, and as we take the elevator to the roof, he says, "It will be nice to spend the weekend at home."

I just nod, my thoughts turning to my other problem.

It's been a week since I left Gabriella at the mansion.

I'll have to wait until after the ballet company's show before bringing up the subject of an arranged marriage to Dario.

We climb into the helicopter, and as it lifts into the air, I look down at my city.

I've worked my fucking ass off to make a name for myself. The blood I've shed forms a red carpet in the streets where everybody knows my name.

I want Miguel dead.

As we fly over Long Island, where Angelo lives, I think about how busy the other men's lives have become. Angelo and Franco are drowning in baby shit and diapers. Renzo is focused on his woman and the restaurant he opened for her. And Dario is working his ass off at the ballet company.

Once I've dealt with Miguel and arranged the marriage between Dario and Gabriella, I'll take some time off.

Maybe I'll take Mamma on a vacation. She seldom gets to leave the mansion.

The helicopter lands on the helipad, and climbing out, I glance at all the guards while I walk to the French doors.

When I step into my home, I suck in a deep breath of the familiar air and let it out slowly.

I head straight for my suite, and shutting the door behind me, I let the darkness wrap around me. My eyes drift closed, and I drink in the silence.

I've always been a bit of a recluse, and interacting with people exhausts me to my core.

Taking another deep breath, I switch on the lights and head to the bathroom. I open the faucets and while the water warms up, I strip out of my suit.

As I place my Glock on the counter, my eye catches my reflection in the mirror and staring at myself, I take in the fine lines around my eyes.

I see the emotionless expression and try to remember the last time I felt any kind of emotion.

A frown forms on my forehead when a memory flashes through my mind.

Gabriella keeping eye contact with me in the living room of her parents' house, caught me by surprise. When she took a step away from me but then caught herself and stood her ground, something shifted in my chest.

She was manhandled but kept her chin raised.

Stefano even hit her with his belt, and she didn't shed a single tear.

Gabriella is either fucking strong or broken beyond repair.

In my experience, I've learned broken people don't fight back. Which means she's the strongest woman I've ever encountered.

She'll be a good match for Dario with his soft heart.

Letting out a sigh, I step into the shower and let the warm water wash over my body.

I automatically go through my routine before switching off the faucets and drying myself. When I walk into the closet, I'm tempted to put on a pair of sweatpants so I can just go to sleep.

Check on Mamma first.

I grab a pair of chinos and a sweater. After getting dressed, I stop in the bathroom to get my Glock, and as I tuck it behind my back into the waistband of my pants, I leave my bedroom.

The mansion is quiet when I take the stairs down to the first floor, but nearing Mamma's sitting room, I hear Gabriella say, "The dresses are so pretty."

"Bridgerton is my favorite show," Aunt Greta murmurs.

Just as I'm about to enter the sitting room, Mamma says, "Describe the dresses to me, Gabriella."

"They have really high waistlines. They're elegant, and all the colors are pastel. Some have flowers printed on the fabric. They kind of remind me of the outfits they wore in Pride and Prejudice."

"I saw that movie," Mamma mentions. "Good, now I have an idea of what everything looks like."

"Aida hasn't always been blind," Aunt Greta says, and it has me stalking into the sitting room.

Gabriella startles, and Aunt Greta's eyes fly to me. I head straight for my mother, a smile already forming on her face.

She's always been able to feel whenever I'm close by.

"You're home," she murmurs, reaching out in my direction.

Taking hold of Mamma's outstretched hand, I help her to her feet, and without bothering to greet the other two women, I lead her out of the sitting room.

Mamma doesn't talk as we walk to the other side of the mansion where the sunroom is. I don't switch on the lights as I take her to one of the plush sofas.

The room is filled with indoor plants, and the glass ceiling allows moonlight to shine into the space.

Once we're seated, I lean back against the sofa and close my eyes.

Mamma leans against my side, then whispers, "Are you tired, *mio figlio*?"

Sucking in a breath, I let it out slowly. "Yes."

"You work too hard."

"If I stop, it will leave the family vulnerable," I mutter as I lift my arm and wrap it around her shoulders.

There's a minute's silence then she says, "I'm proud of you, Damiano."

"Thank you, Mamma."

She pats my thigh, then mentions, "Gabriella seems nice."

"Mmh."

"We've spent a lot of time with her the past week."

"Mmh."

"She made dinner tonight. *Coda alla vaccinara*," she mentions. "There are leftovers in the kitchen. You should have some. It's really good."

"Mmh."

I let out a sigh because I know where Mamma is going with this conversation.

"Don't sigh at me," she mutters. "Dario's still young, whereas you need to settle down or I'll never get to see my grandchildren."

I force my tone to sound calmer than I feel as I say, "Don't, Mamma. I got the woman for Dario. End of story."

"Such a pity," she sighs.

My eyebrow lifts, and my voice sounds almost playful as I ask, "Now you're sighing at me?"

"Tit for tat," she chuckles.

The corner of my mouth lifts, and I give her a sideways hug.

"When things quiet down, we should take a vacation. Where would you like to go?"

She thinks for a while, then answers, "The house in Manhattan. Just the two of us."

"That's not much of a vacation," I mention.

"It doesn't matter where you take me, Damiano. I just want to spend time with you without work interfering."

Ever since she was blinded, she lost interest in traveling to foreign countries. There's a stabbing sensation in my chest, and for the millionth time, I wish I could kill my father all over again.

"I'm going to head to bed," I say as I help Mamma to her feet.

"Try to sleep in tomorrow."

"I have a meeting at nine."

She shakes her head, not looking pleased.

I take Mamma back to her sitting room, where Aunt Greta is busy watching TV. Gabriella must've returned to her suite.

Once Mamma takes a seat in her favorite armchair, I press a kiss on the top of her head. I spare Aunt Greta a nod before leaving the room.

My phone starts to ring as I head upstairs, and seeing Dario's name, I answer, "What took you so long to call me back?"

"I was having sex."

Shaking my head, I mutter, "There's a meeting at my club at nine tomorrow morning."

"I'll be there."

The call ends, and I shove the device back into my pocket while shaking my head again.

The last thing I needed to hear was that Dario just had sex.

I hope it was a one-night stand and nothing serious, or I'm fucking stuck with Gabriella.

Chapter 10

Gabriella

With Damiano home, I've spent the entire day in my bedroom making a skincare tutorial.

Things were tense at breakfast, so I skipped lunch. When Martha came to check on me, I told her I was working and not to worry about me.

Knowing I can't miss dinner, I check my appearance in the mirror. I'm wearing a short, black cocktail dress with a low-halter top.

"You can survive dinner with Damiano," I whisper before I leave my room.

I walk down the hallway, and as I come around a bend, my eyes land on Damiano, who's coming from the other wing. I slow my pace so he'll head down the stairs before me.

His eyes only touch on me for a split second, and he doesn't say anything.

I haven't interacted much with him, but it's clear he's a man of few words.

I follow him down the stairs, my gaze drifting over his broad shoulders before locking on his gun.

Even at home, where we're surrounded by an army of his men, he's armed.

When I take the last step, my left heel gives way, and not thinking, I reach out to catch myself. My palm slams into the gun at Damiano's back, and instantly, the blood drains from my face.

Shit.

Damiano spins around, and as I suck in a breath to gasp, his fingers wrap brutally around my throat, and I'm twisted around before he slams me down onto the tiles.

Pain shudders through my hips and shoulder blades. The air explodes from my lungs, and the next second, the barrel of his gun is pressed against my forehead.

ShitShitShit.

Fear fills every inch of my body as I choke the words past his painful grip on my throat, "It was … an … accident."

Crouched over me, his features are carved from granite, his eyes twin pools of danger.

My heart thunders in my chest as I stare up at him, and I make a strangled sound as I try to suck in a breath.

"It … was … an accident," I gasp. "My heel … broke, and I …. tripped."

He moves an inch, and not easing his hold on my throat, he glances at my broken shoe. Seemingly satisfied with my explanation, he finally lets go of me and straightens to his full height.

Caro Dio.

I suck in desperate breaths of air as I quickly climb to my feet. Only when my eyes land on Damiano, who's already walking away from me while tucking his gun back into the waistband of his chinos, does anger begin to swirl in my chest.

The asshole. He just slammed me against the tiles and almost choked the hell out of me, and he can't be bothered to say a single word?

I rip the broken shoe off my foot and almost throw it at his back, but luckily, I catch myself in the nick of time.

Scowling at his retreating back, I slam my hand against the button on the wall to call the elevator. When the doors open, I step into the small space before glaring at the stupid shoe that almost got me killed.

My shoulders and hips still hurt, and I lift a trembling hand to my throat.

He didn't need to overreact like that.

Dio, like I'd try to kill him? I'm not stupid, and I certainly don't have a death wish.

Heading to my bedroom, I quickly change my shoes before rushing to the dining room.

I don't even look in Damiano's direction and offer Mrs. Accardi a forced smile as I take a seat next to Carlo.

Just get through dinner with your head held high.

From years of abuse, I've become a master at hiding my true feelings. I refuse to let people see my vulnerable side because I know they'll use it against me.

Reaching for my glass of water, I take a sip.

As I set the glass down, Mrs. Accardi's eyes lock on my neck. "Where did the bruises come from?"

"Bruises?" Mrs. Falco asks, her features tightening.

I feel the air tense around the table and know if I glance at Damiano, he'll probably give me a look of warning to keep my mouth shut.

My stubborn streak, that's taken a rest the past week, flares to life, making my anger grow.

I've never hidden my bruises, and I refuse to lie on someone else's behalf. It's landed me in trouble on many occasions.

The time Santo beat me for daring to swim on a hot day flashes through my mind. His friends came over and saw me in a bathing suit.

My brother dislocated my jaw that day, and when our priest visited during a house call, I didn't stay hidden as instructed.

Not that the priest did anything when he saw my bruised face. My little act of rebellion cost me two broken ribs and three days locked in my room without food.

Even though my smart mouth will probably earn me a beating, I can't keep the words from spilling over my lips. "I tripped and accidentally touched Mr. Falco's gun. He grabbed my neck and slammed me against the floor."

Mrs. Falco gasps, her face growing horribly pale. She makes a similar strangled sound as I did when her son almost choked the hell out of me.

Damiano shoots to his feet, and grabbing hold of his mother's shoulders, he crouches beside her chair.

His tone is surprisingly gentle as he says, "Breathe, Mamma."

Her breaths speed up, and it's clear she's having a panic attack.

Shit.

"I'm sorry," I say, feeling awful for not keeping my mouth shut. I didn't mean for Mrs. Falco to have a panic attack.

"Get out!" Damiano shouts. "Everyone!"

I'm up and out of the chair in a split second. When I rush into the hallway, I hear Damiano lovingly murmur, "It's okay, Mamma. I'm here. You're safe. He can't hurt you anymore."

Mrs. Accardi places her hand on my arm, giving me a worried look. "Are you okay?"

"Not now, Ma," Carlo mutters. "Gabriella, you should go to your room."

Nodding, I hurry away as the realization that I caused Damiano's mother to have a panic attack sinks like a rock to the pit of my stomach.

He's going to kill me.

When I shut my bedroom door behind me, I wrap my arms around my middle and shake my head.

Dio. What have I done?

Feeling like a caged animal that's about to be slaughtered, I start to pace up and down my room.

I shouldn't have said anything.

With every passing minute, it feels like the walls are closing in on me.

The growing tension becomes too much, and one after the other, the traumatic memories creep out of the shadows.

All the times my mother hit me.

The countless days I was locked in my room.

The endless hunger.

The day my father threw me over the balcony. He only tried to kill me that one time because, soon after, he brought Stefano home and announced our engagement.

My arms fall to my sides, and I stare at nothing as one memory after the other plays out in my mind.

By the time my bedroom door slams open, my breaths are rushing over my lips, and my body's a trembling mess.

What doesn't kill me makes me stronger.

I expect Damiano to pull out his gun and shoot me, but instead, he stalks toward me.

Even though I'm scared shitless, I don't move a muscle.

When his fingers, once again, wrap around my throat, and he shoves me back until I'm pressed up against a wall, a squeak escapes me. I grab hold of his wrist with my left hand while my right slams against his way too solid chest.

For an unnerving moment, Damiano's eyes burn into mine.

Somehow, I manage to notice that his grip on my throat isn't biting like before.

Anger pours from him in crushing waves, and I swallow hard when it becomes near impossible to hold his gaze.

His voice is a low rumble of thunder when he growls, "Don't ever say anything like that in my mother's presence again."

Once more, I'm too brave for my own good, as I say, "I won't lie for anyone, including you."

His jaw clenches so hard that a muscle jumps near his temple, and I expect to hear his teeth grind against each other.

He hasn't killed you yet. Don't push him.

For years, I've had to fight for myself, and it takes one hell of a swing at my pride when I whisper, "I regret upsetting your mother."

His grip loosens around my throat, and I'm surprised when his eyes lower to the bruises he left on me.

I feel his thumb brush over my skin, and it makes a surprised gasp escape my lips.

No man has touched me in a gentle way before.

My stomach starts to spin with nerves, not from fear but with a strange sense of anticipation. The scent of his cologne and manliness fills the air I breathe.

I remember how lovingly Damiano spoke to his mother, and he treats her like she's precious to him.

What would it be like to have the protection of such a powerful man?

No one would be able to hurt me.

His eyes flick to where I'm still holding his wrist, and I quickly let go. My arms fall to my sides, and glad for the wall behind me, I lean my weight against it.

Dio, the romance books and Bridgerton are getting to me. Damiano Falco is not a man you fantasize about.

He takes a step away from me, and I can't stop my gaze from sweeping over his muscled body.

When I read a steamy scene from one of the books, I felt a tightening sensation in my abdomen, and as I look at Damiano, the same sensation is back. Only, it's a hell of a lot stronger.

He tilts his head slightly, his eyes narrowing on me.

Crap.

For a moment, I lower my head, and banishing the attraction I'm feeling, I suck in a fortifying breath. When

I'm sure my face is expressionless, I lift my head and lock eyes with him again.

With his gaze still narrowed on me, he demands, "Tell me what you were thinking about before you lowered your head."

He didn't see it written all over my face?

When I don't answer fast enough, his expression starts to darken.

Unable to lie, my cheeks go up in flames as I admit, "I just noticed how attractive you are."

Surprise flickers over his face, but it's gone as quickly as it came.

Turning away from me, he glances around the room. His gaze stops on my dressing table, the surface covered with my makeup products.

Not saying anything, he starts to walk to the door, but then my phone vibrates and lights up with notifications from my social media accounts.

He pauses, and my heart jumps to my throat when he picks up the device where it's lying at the foot of my bed.

He unlocks the screen, then mutters, "No password?"

"No."

I gather my courage and step closer so I can see what he's doing with my phone.

Damiano checks my contact list and call history before entering my TikTok account.

I'm too anxious to get upset that he's invading my privacy.

As my latest video plays on the screen, he says, "You haven't called your family."

"No."

He looks at the video for a few seconds before handing the device to me.

When I take it from him, I clutch it to my chest.

He seems to hesitate, and when I give him a questioning look, he stalks away from me. The door shuts softly behind him, and I slump down on the edge of my bed.

With my lips parted, I stare at the closed door, wondering what just happened.

Damiano is known for showing no mercy. The horror stories I've heard braced me for death, but he didn't even hurt me.

I let out a breath of relief, then the past ten minutes replays in my mind.

I've never felt attracted to a man before, and I blame the romance books for my temporary lapse in sanity.

Dio, why couldn't I lie when he asked me what I was thinking?

My hand lifts to my neck, and I brush my fingers over the spot where his thumb lingered.

Getting up, I walk to the mirror, and when I see the red bruises, I shake my head.

Just because he didn't hurt you again doesn't mean he won't punish you in the future.

Chapter 11

Damiano

Feeling rattled, I walk to my mother's private suite, and knocking, I wait for her to answer before I enter.

When I shut the door behind me, I ask, "How are you feeling, Mamma?"

"I'm fine." She pats the space beside her where she's sitting on a sofa near the windows. "It's nothing to worry about, so don't take your anger out on Gabriella."

When I barged into Gabriella's room, it was with the full intention of killing the woman. However, before I could reach for my gun, I saw the same expression on her face I've seen countless times on Mamma's.

It's a blank look that masks years of trauma, and it's one of the few things in this world that makes me feel like absolute shit.

I witnessed firsthand how Gabriella was mistreated by her family and Stefano. I can only imagine what kind of abuse she's suffered throughout her life.

I shake my head as I take a seat, and resting my elbows on my thighs, I rub my palms over my face.

Mamma places her hand on my arm before moving it to my back.

Her voice trembles when she asks, "Did you hurt Gabriella?"

Hearing the question from Mamma makes me feel even worse.

"When I felt her hand on my gun, I just reacted. You know I don't care whether the person is male or female. If they're a threat, I'll kill them." I let out a sigh before I continue, "She practically weighs nothing, and I slammed her down harder than I meant to." I shake my head again. "The moment I saw a broken shoe was responsible for her losing her balance, I let go of her."

My mother scoots closer to me, her voice soft as she asks, "And the bruises?"

"At that moment, she was a threat, Mamma."

"You should apologize to her," she demands.

The fuck. I'm not going back to Gabriella's room.

I close my eyes as the memory of what happened after Mamma's panic attack plays out in my mind.

The instant I stepped into that suite, I was assaulted with Gabriella's fresh scent. Seeing her masking her trauma took an unexpected swing at my heart.

Feeling her tremble while she still held eye contact made me realize nothing would be able to break her. Even the threat of death didn't keep her from raising her chin and facing me head-on.

And then, the woman looked me up and down with interest shining in her eyes before she lowered her head to hide her attraction to me.

She belongs to Dario.

Christ, tonight has given me an emotional whiplash.

"Are you okay?" Mamma asks.

"Yes," I lie because my emotions are all over the place.

I've never hesitated to kill anyone before, but Gabriella managed to escape death twice in one night.

She didn't beg for her life.

She's probably not even five feet five inches, yet she stared me down with way too much bravery.

Leaning back against the sofa, I glance at Mamma. "You sure you're okay?"

"Of course. It was just a little slip-up."

I wrap my arm around her shoulders and tug her to my side. Pressing a kiss to her hair, I ask, "Do you want to go

116

out for dinner tomorrow night? Renzo's girlfriend opened a new restaurant, and I think it would be good to get away from the mansion for a couple of hours."

"Just the two of us?"

"Yes. Besides the guards, of course."

"I'd love to," she murmurs.

I hold my mother a little longer before I pull away and climb to my feet.

"Want me to walk you to the sitting room?"

Nodding, she gets up, and I hook her arm through mine.

"Thank you, *mio figlio*."

After I leave Mamma in the sitting room, I walk to the veranda and glance over the property.

There's a chill in the air, reminding me Christmas is around the corner.

Hopefully, Miguel will be dead soon so that I can enjoy the holidays with my mother.

My thoughts turn to the meeting I had with the other capos this morning. Dario didn't mention anything about getting laid last night, so I'm pretty sure it was a one-night stand.

Maybe putting off talking to him about Gabriella isn't such a wise idea.

Pulling my phone out of my pocket, I bring up his number and press dial.

Within seconds Dario answers, "I don't have any solid leads on Miguel."

"That's not why I'm calling," I mutter.

"Oh, did you miss me?"

I swear, sometimes he drives me up the wall.

Ignoring his question, I ask, "Was last night a one-night stand?"

"Huh?" he grunts in my ear. "Since when are you interested in my sex life?"

"I'm not," I snap. "Just answer the fucking question."

"No, it wasn't."

Fuck.

"You're dating?" I ask.

"Yeah. I found myself a little dancer. We're going on our first date tomorrow."

I let out a sigh. "Are you serious about the woman?"

"As serious as a heart attack. By the way, she lives in Brownsville. If you plan on attacking, give me a heads up so I can get her out of there."

Christ, what the fuck do I do with Gabriella.

"Why all the questions?" Dario asks, his tone growing suspicious.

"No reason," I mutter. "Just keeping an eye on you." I'm about to hang up, then add, "Get yourself some guards. You're way too careless."

"Aww ... I knew you ca–"

Before he can finish the sentence, I end the call and shove the device back into my pocket.

I hear movement behind me, and a moment later, Carlo comes to stand next to me.

With his gaze resting on the view of the lake, he asks, "You okay?"

I let out a heavy breath. "Yes."

"Your mother?"

"She's fine."

He nods, then turns his head to look at me. "What are you going to do with Gabriella?"

Fuck knows.

"I wanted to arrange a marriage between her and Dario."

"Wanted?" he asks. "You changed your mind?"

"Dario's dating some woman. It sounds serious."

"So what are you going to do?"

I feel eyes on me, and glancing over my shoulder, I see Gabriella standing near the doorway with a worried expression on her face.

119

Cautiously, she steps closer. "I'd like to hear the answer to that question." Her tongue darts out to wet her lips. "Seeing as it concerns me."

I turn to face her, and when my eyes lock with hers, Carlo says, "That's my cue to go." He takes the stairs down to the lawn and walks toward a group of guards.

Gabriella steps out onto the veranda and wraps her arms around herself.

When she tries to rub some warmth into her bare arms, I mutter, "Go inside where it's warm."

She lowers her arms and fist her hands at her sides. Her features tighten, and she lifts an eyebrow at me.

"What do you plan to do with me?" she demands.

I take a few steps closer, forcing her to tilt her head back so she can keep eye contact with me.

My tone is low when I answer, "At the rate you're testing me, I might just decide to kill you instead of sending you back to Sicily."

Panic flares in her eyes. "To my parents?"

She's not worried about me killing her.

Gabriella moves closer to me, and for the first time since I laid eyes on her, she gives me a pleading look.

"Don't send me back to my parents." It's not a question but a demand. "I have money. I can get a place of my own. I'll disappear."

Someone like her could never disappear. She'll always stand out.

"You want me to let you go," I murmur.

Her head bobs up and down, and I see a flicker of hope in her light brown eyes.

"You're a mafia princess," I remind her.

Her brows furrow, her expression something between sad and angry.

"I'm so tired of everyone treating me like a pawn in whatever game they're playing." The sadness fades until she looks like a powerful queen. "I'm not a possession."

Needing to test her strength, I close the short distance between us until our bodies almost touch.

"I own everything in this city." Leaning down, my eyes burn into hers. "Including you, *principessa*."

Gabriella doesn't back down. Instead, she surprises the fuck out of me when she presses her body to mine, rage tightening her features.

Her tone is just as low as mine when she doubles down and says, "I am not a possession."

No, she's not.

Instead of losing my temper, the corner of my mouth lifts, and my smile stuns Gabriella.

"You're quite the little spitfire," I murmur.

A frown forms on her forehead, and she looks at me with confusion. "You're not upset?"

I shake my head as her fresh scent drifts around me. I feel the slight tremble in her body, and before I can stop myself, I lift my hand to her neck.

My thumb brushes over the fading bruises.

I hate that I left marks on her skin and hope they'll be gone by tomorrow.

My eyes flick to hers, and I watch as her pupils dilate.

Letting go of the rigid control I always have, I allow myself to feel.

My heartbeat quickens slightly, and a need to touch more than just her neck pours into my veins.

Tension builds between us, and with every passing second, the trembling in her body grows.

Maybe this woman is strong enough to survive being by my side.

As soon as the thought pops into my mind, I let go of her and step backward.

"Go inside, Gabriella. I'm done with this conversation."

The stubborn woman remains standing in front of me and says, "You haven't answered my question."

"I haven't decided what to do with you."

"When will you decide?" she asks.

I'm starting to feel annoyed by all the questions, and tilting my head, I mutter, "Go inside."

She hesitates, then letting out a sigh, she turns away from me and walks into the house.

I should send her back to her parents.

I shake my head, not liking the idea one bit.

Not wanting to think about Gabriella for a second longer, I walk to where Carlo is talking to the guards.

Chapter 12

Gabriella

I was on my way to Mrs. Falco's sitting room so I could apologize when I overheard Damiano and Carlo's conversation.

While I shamelessly eavesdropped, it again dawned on me that Damiano could've killed me twice tonight, but he didn't.

It gave me the courage to confront him about my future.

Not that I got any answers.

Deciding to apologize to Mrs. Falco tomorrow morning, I head back to my bedroom. I feel too frustrated to talk to anyone right now. It's been a week since Damiano brought me to New York, and my life is still up in the air.

He said he wanted to arrange a marriage between Dario La Rosa and me. I don't know much about Dario, but I'm thankful he's no longer available.

The last thing I want is to marry a stranger.

No, there's one more thing that would be worse – returning to my parents.

Maybe I can convince Damiano to let me go. I won't be able to live a life of luxury, but I make enough from my social media accounts to provide for myself.

Walking into my room, I head to the closet and grab my pajamas. I always sleep in a matching satin cami and shorts set.

I let out a sigh when I enter the bathroom, and while the tub fills with water, I think about everything that's happened.

When I lost my temper, Damiano didn't get angry. Instead, he seemed amused.

When a smirk formed on his face, I was shocked by how hot it made him look.

I know he was testing me when he brushed his thumb over the bruises on my throat.

Did he feel the attraction?

Or is he playing with me?

I shut off the faucets, and stripping out of my clothes, I step into the balmy water.

What would it be like marrying Damiano?

Not that it would ever happen, but I can't stop my thoughts from going down that rabbit hole.

I would be safe.

I don't think he'll hurt me again, because it would upset his mother.

He's hardly home.

I get along well with Mrs. Falco and Mrs. Accardi.

Soaking in the tub, my thoughts turn down another path.

What if he sends me back to my parents?

What if he gives his approval for Stefano to marry me?

My eyes drift shut, and I shake my head.

Dio, anything but that.

I won't survive being married to Stefano.

A hopeless feeling trickles into my chest, and letting out another sigh, I start to wash myself.

When I'm done with my routine, I climb out and dry my body. I lather my skin with lotion before putting on my pajamas.

While I'm patting moisturizer over my cheeks and forehead, my thoughts are filled with worries.

I rub the remaining moisturizer into my hands, and walking out of the bathroom, my stomach grumbles.

Ignoring the hunger from missing lunch and dinner, I grab my satin robe and shrug it on.

As I fasten the belt, there's a knock at the door.

I freeze for a moment before saying, "Come in."

When the door opens and I see Mrs. Accardi, I let out a sigh of relief.

"I wanted to check on you before bed," she says as she enters the room. Her eyes lock on my neck. "How are you feeling?"

Lifting my hand, I rest my palm on my collarbone. "I'm okay."

Her eyebrows draw together, and she moves closer to me. "Really?" She lifts her arm and rubs her hand over my bicep to offer me some comfort. "From what I've learned and seen the past week, it's clear you haven't had an easy childhood. Tonight must've triggered you as well."

Staring into Mrs. Accardi's kind eyes, there's a twisting sensation in my chest, and a lump pushes to my throat.

I swallow the emotion down and force a smile to my face.

"You don't have to worry about me. I'm stronger than I look."

A compassionate expression softens her features. "I'm here if you need to talk or just need a hug."

A hug?

I can't remember ever being hugged.

Before I can stop myself, I whisper, "I'd really love a hug."

Mrs. Accardi doesn't hesitate to pull me into her arms. Emotions crash through me, and I hesitate before I return the embrace.

She starts to gently pat my back, and it causes tears to burn in my eyes.

"You're going to be okay, *cara*," she coos, her tone motherly.

Dio.

I squeeze my eyes shut, and it takes all my strength not to cry.

When I feel my resolve crumbling, I pull away from her and say, "Thank you."

"Try to get some sleep," she murmurs, a soft smile on her face.

"I will."

My muscles strain to keep the emotions from overwhelming me.

Mrs. Accardi walks to the door and opens it. Glancing at me, she offers me another caring smile. "Good night, *cara*."

"Night," I murmur, my voice strained.

The moment the door shuts behind her, and I'm finally alone, a breath bursts over my lips. I cover my face with my hands as a tear escapes.

From years of conditioning, I fight the emotion and refuse to let another tear fall.

It takes me a few minutes to calm down, and only then am I able to relish in how good the hug felt.

I wish I had Mrs. Accardi for a mother.

Letting out a tired sigh, I grab my phone and check my notifications. I try to stay busy so I don't spiral down a path of self-pity because of the stress I'm under.

Hours pass, and when my stomach grumbles for the tenth time, I set down the phone and wonder if I should risk going to the kitchen.

I check the time, and noticing it's past midnight, I feel it would be safe.

Everyone should be asleep.

I tighten the belt of my robe before I open my bedroom door carefully, so it won't make a sound. I sneak out and quickly make my way through the dark mansion.

When I reach the kitchen, a smile tugs at my mouth as I switch on the light.

Checking the pantry, I find a tub of Nutella. I fix myself a sandwich, and while I'm enjoying it, I prepare a cup of tea.

Damn, this could become my favorite midnight snack.

When I'm done eating, I quickly clean after myself before leaving the kitchen.

Feeling better after having something to eat, I walk through the foyer as I head toward the stairs.

The tiny hairs on the back of my neck raise, and feeling like I'm being watched, I glance around me.

Not seeing anyone, I quickly dart upstairs, and when I shut my bedroom door behind me, I let out a sigh of relief.

"That's enough stress for one day," I mutter as I switch off the lights.

I take off my robe and crawl into bed.

Hugging a pillow to my chest, I close my eyes and start to count to ten so I won't lie awake and overthink things.

Counting numbers doesn't work, though, and soon, I find myself replaying the day's events in my mind.

Chapter 13

Damiano

During the helicopter ride to Manhattan, my thoughts turn to the night before.

I caught Gabriella sneaking around the house after midnight, but when she just grabbed something to eat before heading back to her room, I returned to the sunroom.

I spent an hour thinking about the satin robe she wore and how the fabric flowed around her body when she moved. I got glimpses of her toned legs and way too fucking sexy shorts.

By the time I headed to bed, I felt agitated.

When the helicopter touches down on the helipad, I'm pulled out of my thoughts.

I help Mamma out of the aircraft and lead her to the elevator with Gerardo following us. I gave Carlo a rare afternoon off so he can spend time with his mother.

We're quiet on the ride down to the basement, and when the doors open, I see Vito and Emilio waiting by the SUV.

They signal for the other group of guards that we're leaving, and Gerardo opens the back door.

Once we're seated, with my mother between Gerardo and myself, Emilio starts the engine.

Vito glances over his shoulder from where he's sitting in the passenger seat. "How are you doing, Mrs. Falco?"

"I'm good. Excited to spend time with my son," she answers. "How's your foot? Did you try soaking it in Epsom salts?"

"Yes, thank you. It helped, and the foot's much better."

"That's good." She tilts her head, then asks, "How are your parents, Emilio?"

"They're well, Mrs. Falco. Thanks for asking."

With the pleasantries out of the way, Mamma relaxes against my side.

During the drive, silence fills the cab, and when we pull up to *Yukhaejang*, Skylar's restaurant, I shove the door open and climb out of the SUV. I glance over the area for any signs of threats before I help Mamma out onto the sidewalk.

Renzo's already waiting by the entrance, and as we near him, he says, "Wow, who's the beautiful woman on your arm?"

"Oh hush, Renzo," Mamma chuckles.

He leans down to kiss both her cheeks. "It's good seeing you again, Mrs. Falco."

I shake Renzo's hand before we walk into the restaurant.

"Damiano tells me you've finally found the one," she mentions while Renzo leads us to a private room.

"Yes. You'll meet Skylar today," he replies. His eyes touch on me, then he says, "You just missed Dario. He was here with a date."

"Oh?" Mamma's eyebrow lifts. "He's seeing someone?"

"Yep, we're all falling, one by one."

Christ, now that's all my mother's going to talk about during dinner.

We walk into a private room, and I pull out a chair before helping Mamma to sit.

Unbuttoning my jacket, I glance at Renzo. "Are you serving us?"

"You wish," he chuckles. "Brianna will be with you shortly."

I nod as I take a seat.

"Enjoy the meal," my friend says before he leaves us alone.

Knowing my mother would want to know, I say, "We're in a private room. The walls are decorated with bamboo, and there are lanterns. It feels quite intimate."

"Mhh…" A smile curves her lips while her hands carefully explore the set table to check where everything is.

"Thank you for bringing me," she says.

"You're welcome," I murmur, my eyes drifting over her face.

Even though she's fifty-seven, her looks are so youthful she could pass for my older sister.

My gaze locks on the scar on her temple, and anger sparks in my chest.

My parents got married when she was eighteen. It was against her will, and she suffered for nineteen years before I was able to end the abuse.

Since then, any kind of violence has been a trigger for her.

I try to keep her life as calm as possible, but Saturday was out of my control, and I hope it didn't take a toll on her.

"How are you, Mamma?" I ask.

A frown forms on her forehead. "You know I'm doing well. Why do you ask?"

"Just checking. It's my job to make sure you're happy."

"I am," she assures me. Her smile widens, then she says, "So ... Dario's seeing someone."

"I heard," I mutter, knowing exactly how the conversation will play out.

She raises an eyebrow. "You're the only single capo left."

"I'm well aware of the fact," I mutter.

"Are you going to consider marrying Gabriella?"

I let out a sigh, but before I can reply, the waitress comes in.

She gives us a rundown of the specials and after taking our drink orders, she leaves the room.

"So?" Mamma reminds me that I owe her an answer.

"I haven't thought about it," I lie because the thought has crossed my mind more than once this weekend.

"You should. You're not getting any younger and Gabriella is a lovely girl."

"Do you like spending time with her?" I ask.

"Yes. It feels like she fits in with us. I don't have to entertain her."

135

"That's good," I murmur, my eyes scanning over the room.

When the waitress brings our drinks, I place an order for Sushi, knowing Mamma loves the dish but doesn't get to enjoy it often.

Once it's just us again, she asks, "How's business?"

"It's going well." Glad for the change in subject, I expand on my answer by saying, "The hotel is almost completed, and I purchased a lot across from it. I might open another restaurant."

"And the other side of the business?" she asks.

"I have everything under control," I reply, not willing to give her more information.

Mamma nods and takes a sip of her glass of wine.

We're quiet for a moment, then she asks, "How are Angelo and Franco doing?"

"Good. They're knee-deep in diapers."

"You should invite them over. I'd love to spend time with Torri, Samantha, and the babies."

Not wanting to make any promises, I murmur, "I'll see what I can do."

A comfortable silence falls between us, and my thoughts return to Gabriella.

I'll have to come to a decision concerning her future.

Should I marry her?

She seems to be getting along with my mother and Aunt Greta.

She's beautiful. At least fucking her won't be a chore.

My muscles tense at the thought.

"What's wrong?" Mamma asks.

"Nothing," I mutter. I suck in a deep breath, then admit, "I'm trying to decide what to do with Gabriella."

Mamma reaches out to me, and when I take her hand, she gives me a squeeze. "You deserve some happiness as well."

"You think a marriage will make me happy?"

Mamma pauses to think before saying, "If you can learn to love your wife, and she loves you, a marriage can bring a lot of happiness."

Angelo and Franco seem to be over the fucking moon with their wives.

I suck in a deep breath and let it out slowly. "I'll think about arranging a marriage between Gabriella and me."

A smile spreads over Mamma's face. "Good."

The waitress brings our food, and once she leaves, I say, "The plate is rectangular with the sushi in a row."

"Got it," Mamma replies.

We enjoy our food while my thoughts keep returning to a possible arranged marriage with Gabriella.

She doesn't want to return to her parents, so I'm ninety percent sure she'll agree with the arrangement.

The attraction is there, and we can maybe build a friendship or, at the very least, a comfortable companionship.

That's if she doesn't fight me every chance she gets.

Then we might just kill each other.

I'll take a week or so to think about it before I make up my mind.

Chapter 14

Gabriella

When the closing credits of *Safe Haven* roll over the screen, I smile at Mrs. Accardi.

"I love the movie."

"I thought we'd watch it while Adia's out with Damiano. He doesn't allow anything with violence near her."

My curiosity gets the better of me. "May I ask why?"

"Damiano's father was a bastard," she says, but before she can continue, Carlo comes into the sitting room.

"Are you done with the movie, Ma?"

"Yes." Her gaze rests lovingly on her son. "Why?"

"I want to spend some time with you."

She darts up from the armchair. "I'll never say no to that." Waving at me, she says, "Enjoy the rest of your night, *cara*."

"You too."

Once I'm alone in the sitting room, I walk to the shelf and grab the erotic book Mrs. Accardi made me read aloud last week when she played the prank on me.

Sitting down on the armchair again, I curl my legs beneath me and open to chapter two.

My eyes dart over the words, and as I read page after page, my heartbeat speeds up. When I get to a scene where the hero grabs the female lead and kisses the hell out of her, I stop to reread it again and again.

I've never been kissed and wonder what my first time will be like.

If I'm forced into an arranged marriage, will my future husband even bother kissing me?

Maybe Damiano will decide to let me go.

And maybe he won't.

Shutting the book, I let out a sigh as I climb to my feet. I place the book back on the shelf, and feeling a little restless, I walk out of the sitting room.

I haven't explored much of the mansion. With Mrs. Falco and Mrs. Accardi spending time with their sons, I decide now's as good a time as any.

Walking through the foyer, I head to the right side, where I find another sitting room that's decorated with brown leather and books on construction and architecture.

It feels like a man's space, and I quickly leave to continue exploring.

At the end of the hallway, I walk into a dome-shaped room, and my lips part. There are plants everywhere, and moonlight shines through a glass ceiling.

I don't bother searching for a light switch because it's not too dark in the room.

Between potted plants are sofas and walking to the nearest one, I take a seat.

Leaning back, I stare up at the ceiling, a smile spreading over my face.

A peacefulness wraps around me, and I wonder why Mrs. Falco and Mrs. Accardi prefer to read in the sitting room when they could do it here.

Slipping my heels off, I curl my legs beneath me and enjoy the silence.

My body relaxes, but then I hear footsteps, and the peaceful moment shatters.

Just as I dart off the sofa, Damiano stalks into the room.

The moment his eyes lock on me, he stops dead in his tracks.

His voice sounds aggravated as he demands, "What are you doing in here?"

"I wasn't aware this room was off-limits," I say.

He walks closer to me, and when he's within reaching distance, he glances down at my bare feet.

I quickly slide my foot into my shoe, but when I try to put on the other one, I momentarily lose my balance.

My hand automatically darts out and my palm connects with Damiano's abs. The man is solid beneath my hand, and it makes my abdomen tighten so much I gasp.

Dio. Not again.

I shove my foot into the damn shoe and yank away from him. "Sorry. It was –"

"An accident." The words rumble from him. "You should consider wearing different shoes."

Yeah. High heels might get me killed around this man.

But then I realize, he hasn't lost his temper.

Yet.

"Uhm …" I tilt my head back to make eye contact. "Ah … have a good night."

Just as I take a step, his hand wraps around my bicep. Instantly, tingles spread over my skin, and my lips part.

"This room isn't off limits," he says. "You can stay."

Oh.

He lets go of me, and I watch as he unbuttons his jacket before taking a seat on the sofa. Tilting his head back, he stares at me.

I can't make out the expression on his face, and the atmosphere feels much tenser than usual with the room bathed in moonlight.

"Sit, Gabriella," he orders. He tips his head to the empty space beside him.

A weird mixture of apprehension and anticipation spins in my stomach as I sit down.

My spine is straight, and my body on high alert. I glance at the indoor plants before turning my head and meeting Damiano's intense gaze.

His eyes shine like dark pools of water, and I feel too unnerved to keep eye contact.

Needing to say something to break the silence, I ask, "Did you enjoy the dinner with your mother?"

He relaxes, and lifting his arm, he rests it on the back of the sofa.

His voice is deceptively soft when he answers, "Yes."

Silence falls heavy between us, and I struggle not to fidget.

"Relax, Gabriella," he mutters.

Yeah, that's not going to happen.

I scoot backward in the seat and force my muscles to loosen.

When I glance at Damiano, I see he's watching me, and I wonder if he can make out my facial expressions.

"You don't want to return to your parents."

The statement catches me off guard.

I wet my lips before I say, "No, I don't."

"Tell me about your childhood," he demands.

I shrug, and unable to hold his intense gaze, I glance at the doorway.

"There's not much to tell."

"I doubt that," he mutters. "Have they always abused you?"

His question has my eyes flying back to his.

I don't know why he's asking the questions, and not wanting to give him anything he can use against me, I keep quiet.

He stares at me for a moment, then nods. "It must've been bad if you're not willing to talk about it."

I fold my arms around me, then say, "It was nothing I couldn't survive."

He tilts his head, and it feels like he's trying to pry my darkest secrets from me.

"You don't fear dying."

A frown forms on my forehead.

"Last night, you were more worried about being sent back to your parents than the possibility that I might kill you."

That's because I'll suffer worse things than death at my parents' hands.

Remembering my concern about being forced to marry Stefano, I ask, "If you send me back to Sicily, will you give your permission for Stefano to marry me?"

"No." He shakes his head. "I never change my mind once I've made a decision."

Intense relief washes through me, and I whisper, "*Grazie a Dio*."

"You should be thanking me and not the heavens."

My gaze darts to Damiano's. "Thank you."

He lets out a sigh. "You don't want to return to Sicily, and I won't allow you to leave the mafia." His tone drops low, the timbre ghosting over my skin and leaving goosebumps in its wake. "What am I going to do with you?"

Instead of fearing for my future, the spicy book I was reading pops into my mind.

Now is not the time to think of erotic scenes.

The air grows even more tense, and it begins to feel like I'm in danger.

Of what, I don't know.

When Damiano moves his hand from the sofa and his fingers wrap around the back of my neck, my eyes widen.

My heartbeat instantly speeds up, and I fist my hands on my lap.

He tugs me closer to him, and I have to brace a hand between us so I don't fall against him.

He tilts his head, his dark gaze burning over my face. When he speaks, his voice sends another wave of goosebumps over my body.

"Do you like living in my mansion?"

I swallow hard but hold his gaze. "Yes."

"Do you enjoy my mother's company?"

"Very much."

He leans a little closer, and when I feel his breath warm my mouth, my heart beats even faster.

"Can you have children?"

Shit. I think I know where this is going.

I look at Damiano, not as the *Capo dei Capi*, but as a man I might marry. He's dangerously good-looking, so attraction won't be a problem.

At least not on my part.

I feel my cheeks heat as I answer, "My father had a doctor inspect me. He said there was nothing wrong with me, and I should be able to have children."

"Good," he murmurs, the word almost a growl

My abdomen clenches so freaking hard I slap a hand over it.

Damiano's eyes flick down before taking mine prisoner again.

He leans a little closer, then pauses. His features tighten until he looks downright predatory, and I suck in a desperate breath of air.

Before I can exhale, he closes the distance between us, and his mouth presses against mine.

I blink once before my eyes fall shut, an overwhelmingly intense emotion exploding in my chest.

I don't have any time to take in the feel of his lips on mine before he pulls back.

I open my eyes, and when I see the dark expression on his face, a tremble wracks my body.

His fingers tighten around my neck, then he moves fast. When his mouth slams into mine, I instinctively press my free hand against his chest. Whether it's to push him away or pull him closer, I don't know.

I'm too inexperienced to know what to do, and when his tongue sweeps into my mouth, all common sense vanishes from my mind.

Having a man like Damiano be my first kiss is the last thing I expected, and it's too overwhelming to process anything.

His tongue massages mine in a way that makes tingles engulf my entire body.

His lips nip at mine, leaving me completely breathless.

Just as quickly as he initiated the kiss, he pulls away from me.

My mind is a frazzled mess, my heart pounding against my ribs.

When I open my eyes, it's to see Damiano climbing to his feet. Adjusting his jacket, he asks, "Can you handle a gun?"

Huh?

I shake my head, absolutely confused out of my ever-loving mind.

"It's a problem that can be fixed."

Not understanding, my voice is hoarse when I ask, "Why is it a problem?"

"You'll find out soon enough," he mutters before stalking out of the room.

What?

Still in a daze from experiencing my first kiss, I blink at the doorway.

What just happened?

Damiano just kissed the hell out of you and walked away like it didn't mean anything to him. That's what happened.

I lift my hand slowly until my fingers brush over my tingling lips.

Was he testing the waters to see if he felt attracted to me?

The way he abruptly ended the kiss has worry pouring into my chest.

What if he didn't feel any attraction and decides to send me back to my parents?

No. Anything but that.

Chapter 15

Damiano

It's been a week since I kissed Gabriella in the sunroom, and even though I've made up my mind, I haven't been home since.

Work has kept me fucking busy, and then Dario's woman got kidnapped. It's been one shit show after the other.

I met Dario's girlfriend at a ballet show earlier tonight and could see how much he already loves her. He's fallen hard and fast, and if we don't get her back, I have no idea what it will do to Dario.

The drug dealers that grabbed Eden right from under our noses are either fucking stupid or brave. I don't know Eden at all, but you don't touch a capo's woman and life to tell the tale.

Angelo, Dario, and I are sitting in a helicopter while Carlo flies us toward a yacht where girls will be sold as sex slaves.

Dario got the lead on the black market, and I can tell my friend is about to lose his shit. The only thing keeping him in line is the authority I have over him.

When Carlo lands on the helipad of the supersized yacht, Angelo gets out first before Dario follows. I'm last to step onto the deck and notice a man approaching us.

"We weren't expecting a fourth party," the man says.

Carlo comes to stand beside me, his weapon already drawn as he fold his hands in front of him.

"We invited ourselves," Dario mutters, his tone laced with a fuck ton of impatience.

Kristian Anderson comes up a set of stairs accompanied by two armed guards, and I instantly feel agitated.

The flesh peddler doesn't bother looking at Angelo and Dario. His eyes lock with mine, then he asks, "What's the Cosa Nostra doing here? This isn't your territory."

The fuck it isn't. The bastard is selling girls just off the coast of New York and pushing his fucking luck.

One day I'll have to deal with the fucker.

I feel Dario's eyes on me as he asks, "You know him?"

"Kristian," I mutter. "Sex trafficker. Let me handle this," I order.

Feeling fucking exhausted, I step forward and say, "I'm here for a specific girl."

151

"We don't have anyone who belongs to the Cosa Nostra," Kristian replies.

Wanting this over and done with, I mutter, "Show us the girls, and we'll be on our way."

"Only you. The rest wait right here," he agrees.

When I start to walk, Carlo sticks to my side. I can feel the tension coming off him and know he won't hesitate to jump into action should shit go sideways.

By the stairs, a guard shakes his head at Carlo, and I give the fucker a dark glare. "Where I go, he goes."

"Let him come," Kristian snaps from the foot of the stairs.

I head down and follow Kristian to a room. He shoves the door open, and I glance over the five young girls who look drugged out of their fucking minds.

Disgust ripples over my skin, but not showing any emotion on my face, I turn around and walk back to the helipad.

Seeing the question on Dario's face when I reach him, I shake my head. "Let's go. We're wasting our time here."

We all pile back into the helicopter and when the aircraft lifts into the sky, I rub my fingers over the headache pounding against my temple.

My phone starts to ring, and thinking it's one of my men, I pull the device out. Not recognizing the number, I accept the call and press the device to my ear.

I'm fucking surprised when I hear Gabriella ask, "Damiano? Are you there?"

Just hearing her voice makes some of the tension ease in my shoulders, and it catches me by surprise.

When I kissed her to test the attraction between us, I almost got knocked onto my ass by the intensity. I haven't kissed a woman since my early twenties, and feeling Gabriella's lips tremble against mine stripped me bare.

I had to force myself to break the kiss and walk away so I wouldn't fuck her right there in the sunroom.

Christ. I still need to arrange shooting lessons for her. If she's going to be my wife, she has to know how to handle a gun.

Not wanting to talk to her in front of Angelo and Dario, I mutter, "I'm busy."

She sounds worried when she asks, "Are we going to talk about what happened between us?"

"No."

"Seriously?" When she talks again, her tone is tense. "Fine. Are you going to send me back to my parents?"

Christ. I can feel Angelo and Dario staring at me.

Needing to end the call, I grumble, "No."

"Then let's talk about the kiss," she demands.

Not wanting to give anything about our conversation away to the other men, I once again mutter, "No."

"Damiano," she says. "You can't leave me hanging like this. Talk to me."

I suppress a sigh. "No"

"This is hard for me. I can't keep living with my life up in the air."

Fuck. I didn't even consider her feelings.

Regret creeps into my chest, the emotion foreign and unwelcome.

"I know," I grind the word out.

"Please," she begs. "Just tell me what you plan to do with me."

Gabriella should never beg for anything. Instead, she should lift her chin and tell me to fuck off.

"Christ, I don't have time for this," I snap. "Don't call again."

I end the call and shove the device back into my pocket.

"Who was that?" Angelo asks.

"No one," I mutter. "Carlo, take us back to land."

"We don't have a choice," Carlo mumbles. "We need to fuel up if we're going to continue searching."

"I need to get to my system at my place," Dario says. "We're wasting time out here."

During the flight back to the mainland, I push my personal problems to the backburner so I can focus on finding Dario's woman.

Once all this shit is dealt with, I'll let Gabriella know I've decided to marry her. Only then will I feel comfortable letting the other four heads of the Cosa Nostra know about her existence.

At least my mother will be happy to hear I'm getting married.

And me?

Gabriella's a beautiful little spitfire. At the very least, she'll keep me on my toes.

The corner of my mouth lifts at the thought. It's fleeting, but it offers me a reprieve from all the tension bearing down on my shoulders.

Chapter 16

Gabriella

I'm going to lose my mind.

I keep alternating between worrying and feeling angry because Damiano won't tell me what he plans to do with me.

I've been at the mansion for three weeks, and even though I love spending time with Mrs. Falco and Mrs. Accardi, the uncertainty is eating me alive.

It doesn't help that Damiano hasn't been home for the past twelve days.

The man laid a life-altering kiss on me, only to disappear.

Earlier this week, it took all my courage to call him, but he was so abrupt over the phone I couldn't get an answer from him.

And I don't have the guts to call him again.

Suddenly, a hand settles on my shoulder, making me startle.

"Sorry, *cara*," Mrs. Accardi says. "You've been so quiet we wanted to check on you."

She helps Mrs. Falco take a seat on my balcony, where I've been sitting for hours contemplating my uncertain future.

I straighten in my chair, releasing the hold I have on the blanket that's wrapped around me.

Instantly, the early winter chill sweeps over my body, reminding me I need warmer clothes.

Mrs. Falco lifts an eyebrow, then says, "Out with it."

"With what?" I ask.

"What has you hiding in your bedroom?"

Mrs. Accardi's gaze inspects my face, her features tight with concern.

"It's nothing for you to worry about," I say to put them at ease.

Mrs. Falco reaches her hand in my direction, and I quickly lean forward to take it.

"*Cara*, tell us," she insists. "We might be able to help."

I suck in a deep breath before letting it out slowly, then I admit, "Damiano hasn't told me what he plans to do with me."

"Why does it worry you so much?" Mrs. Accardi asks. "Don't you like visiting with us?"

"Oh no," I exclaim. "I love spending time with you. I just wish I knew what was in store for me."

"That's understandable," Mrs. Falco murmurs. "I'll talk to him when he gets home."

Surprised by her words, I ask, "He's coming home?"

"Eventually." She gives my hand a squeeze before pulling away.

"You don't have to talk to him. I don't want him thinking I complained to you."

Because that will only land me in a world of trouble.

We hear the sound of a helicopter, and my head snaps in the direction of the lake.

"That must be Damiano now," Mrs. Falco says as she climbs to her feet. "Greta, help me to the veranda so I can greet him."

"Thank you for checking in on me," I murmur, my eyes darting between the women and the lake.

"Of course, *cara*. We expect to see you at dinner," Mrs. Falco says.

"Okay."

I watch as Mrs. Accardi leads her through my bedroom and out the door, then I turn to face the scenic view of the lake.

The sound of the helicopter grows louder, and when it comes into view, a freezing wind slams into me and I wrap my arms around myself.

The aircraft lands, and a moment later, Damiano and Carlo climb out. As they walk across the lawn, Damiano glances up and our eyes meet for a few seconds before he looks away.

The memory of the kiss bombards my mind, and a blush creeps up my neck while my eyes follow him until he disappears from my sight.

Picking up the blanket, I walk into my bedroom and shut the door behind me to keep the wind from coming in.

I fold the blanket and set it down on the foot of my bed. Glancing around the bedroom, I let out a sigh.

All I want to do is talk to Damiano, but I also don't want to attack him the second he walks into the mansion.

Now that he's home, my stomach begins to spin with nerves – from the kiss and wondering what he's decided to do with me.

I walk to my bedroom door, and opening it, I step out into the hallway.

Should I go downstairs?

I'm still trying to decide what to do when Damiano comes around the bend in the hallway. His eyes lock with mine, and my mouth instantly grows dry.

Without a word, he stalks past me and enters my bedroom. I follow him inside and a frown forms on my forehead when he heads for my closet.

He looks at my clothes, and my eyebrows fly up when something close to a growl rumbles from him.

He reaches into his pocket, and when he pulls his wallet out, I'm very confused by his actions.

Damiano takes a black card from the wallet and holds it out to me. "Get warm clothes for the winter and plan the wedding. There will only be fourteen guests. Excluding us."

"Wedding?" I gasp.

He stalks closer, and grabbing my hand, he shoves the credit card into my palm.

When he walks away from me, I ask, "What wedding? To who?"

"Ours," he mutters before disappearing into the hallway.

What?

An intense wave of pins and needles spreads over my body as I gasp.

Holy crap.

It takes a stunned few seconds before I rush after him.

Catching up to Damiano as he walks across the landing that leads to the right wing of the mansion, I say, "You can't just tell me we're getting married and stalk away."

Not even looking at me, he says, "I'm tired, Gabriella."

When he steps into his bedroom, I stop in the doorway. "Are we going to talk at some point?"

His eyes flick to mine as he loosens his tie. "Tomorrow."

My gaze drifts over his handsome face, and seeing the exhaustion etched deep into his features, I think to ask, "Are you okay?"

Looking surprised by my question, he stares at me for a moment, then replies, "I'm fine. It's just been a rough two weeks."

Nodding, I take a step backward. For a moment, I hesitate, then I ask, "Can I make you some chamomile tea? It will help you relax."

He shakes his head. "No, I'm just going to shower and sleep."

"Okay."

I turn around and start to walk away, but stop when he says, "Gabriella."

I glance over my shoulder.

"The credit card doesn't have a limit. Take a group of guards with you when you leave the mansion to get clothes. The winters are much harsher here than in Sicily, and you need to dress warmer."

My fingers brush over the credit card, and a smile curves my lips as I say, "Thank you."

He nods before shutting the door between us.

Instantly, the thought hits me like a ten-pound hammer.

I'm marrying Damiano Falco.

Caro Dio.

I rush back to my bedroom and stare at the name printed on the credit card.

Mr. DC Falco

Wow.

I struggle to process the new developments, and in a daze, I walk to my bed, where I sink down on the edge of the mattress.

I'm marrying Damiano.

Before he kissed me, he said he never changes his mind once he's made a decision, so nothing will stop this wedding from happening.

I'm going to be the wife of the *Capo dei Capi.*

Holy crap.

I sit in total shock until the room starts to grow dark. Only then does it sink in that I won't have to go back to Sicily. I never have to see my parents again.

Intense relief spreads through me, and my eyes drift shut.

Grazie.

Life has been really good here at the mansion, and with a little luck, it won't change much once I marry Damiano.

I'll get to spend more time with Mrs. Falco and Mrs. Accardi.

The mansion will become my home.

Opening my eyes, a smile begins to tug at the corner of my mouth until I remember the kiss Damiano gave me.

He wanted to know if I can have children, so he probably expects heirs.

My eyebrows lift when I realize what that entails.

Sex.

I always knew I'd have to share a bed with whoever I married, but knowing Damiano is the man who will take my virginity makes a wave of nervousness crash over me.

At least I'm not repulsed by the idea like I was with Stefano.

Sucking in a deep breath, I stand up and place the credit card next to my phone before leaving my room and heading downstairs for dinner.

Chapter 17

Damiano

I only manage to sleep for three hours before I'm wide-a-fucking-wake.

While I put on a pair of chinos and a sweater, my thoughts turn to the past week.

Luckily, we were able to find Eden, and after seeing Dario lose his mind, it's clear as fucking daylight the man loves her.

I have to admit Eden managed to impress me, which is a rare feat. She killed a fucker with a high heel.

I should be more careful around Gabriella and her five-inch heels.

A chuckle escapes me, and the sound actually startles me.

As I tuck my Glock in the back of the waistband of my pants, I leave my suite.

I head downstairs, and when I near my mother's sitting room, I hear Aunt Greta say, "I loved Queen Charlotte's season most."

"Me too," Mamma agrees.

When I enter the room, Gabriella's gaze darts to me. "Did you get any sleep?"

"Three hours," I mutter before I take hold of Mamma's hand and help her to her feet.

Glancing at Gabriella, I say, "Give me thirty minutes, and we'll have that conversation."

"Okay." She glances between Mamma and me. "No rush."

When I lead Mamma into the hallway, she asks, "What conversation?"

"You'll find out soon enough."

Instead of walking to the sunroom, I press the button for the elevator, and we head up to the second floor.

Entering Mamma's suite, I say, "I've decided what to do with Gabriella."

"Oh?"

The expression on her face tells me she's dying to hear my answer.

"I'm going to marry her."

166

A wide smile spreads over her face. "That's such good news!"

Clearing my throat, I say, "I need the engagement ring."

Emotion washes over Mamma's face, and I watch as she walks to her dressing table. She opens a jewelry box, and her fingertips brush over the rings before she picks up the right one.

The engagement ring has been passed down from my grandmother.

Mamma moves closer to me, then holds the ring out. "I think you've made the right decision. I hope with all my heart Gabriella will make you happy."

I take the ring from her and tuck it into my pocket before I pull my mother into a hug.

"Thank you, Mamma."

"Try to be a good husband," she murmurs against my chest.

"I will," I assure her. Pulling back, I look down at the only woman I've ever loved. "I won't disappoint you."

She lifts her hand and pats my cheek as if I'm a little boy. "I know, *mio figlio*."

Her fingertips brush over my face, then she asks, "Are you okay?"

"Yes. Just tired."

"When will you take some time off?"

"I'm just dealing with a problem. As soon as it's resolved, I'll take a vacation."

Mamma lowers her hand, then asks, "When will the wedding happen?"

"I have to talk to Gabriella, and it depends on work."

"Let me know as soon as you've set a date."

Taking my mother's arm, I hook it through mine and lead her out of the room.

As we make our way down to the first floor, I say, "I've given Gabriella a credit card so she can get warm clothes. I would appreciate it if you accompanied her on the shopping trip so you can teach her what to look out for when she's in public. As my fiancée, she'll become a target."

"Of course. I'll also be able to take care of the Christmas shopping."

Walking into the sitting room, I help Mamma to her chair before I look at Gabriella.

"Come," I order before heading to the sunroom.

I hear Gabriella's high heels on the tiles as she rushes to keep up with me, and I slow my pace.

Entering the room, I switch on the lights. It's not too bright, the room filling with a soft yellow glow.

"It's so pretty," Gabriella breathes as her eyes dance over the lights and potted plants.

I walk to a sofa that's partially hidden behind plants and remove the ring from my pocket before I take a seat.

Gabriella sits down beside me, her spine straight and her features tight with a nervous expression.

I stare at her, and once again, she doesn't break eye contact. Instead, she says, "You didn't get much sleep."

My eyes narrow slightly. "Are you worried about me?"

She scoots backward and relaxes. "Of course."

"Why?"

"You carry our whole world on your shoulders. If you fall, we all fall."

I let out a sigh, and glancing at my closed fist, I ask, "Is that the only reason?"

"No," she murmurs. "If I'm going to be your wife, it's my duty to worry about you."

"If?"

I hope she doesn't think she has a choice in the matter.

"When," she corrects herself.

I reach for her left hand, and bringing it to my thigh, I stare at her slender fingers before opening my fist.

"This ring belonged to my grandmother and mother. Once I put it on, you will never take it off."

I feel her hand start to tremble, and as I position the diamond by her ring finger, my eyes lock on her face.

"Look at me," I demand.

Her gaze darts to mine, and only then, do I push the ring onto her finger.

Tension builds in the air before I say, "With this ring, you become my fiancée. The wedding ceremony is only a formality." When she nods, I add, "You belong to me, Gabriella. No man is to touch you."

"Okay," she breathes.

I can see she wants to ask something, but she hesitates.

"What?" I mutter.

"Will you … ahh…"

A frown forms on my forehead. "Out with it."

She lifts her chin and holds my gaze. "Will you have affairs?"

I let out an unexpected burst of laughter that startles her.

"You think I have time to fuck around?"

Her eyes widen. "No. I didn't mean it that way." She lets out a slow breath. "Forget I asked the question."

"No, there won't be affairs, because I'm way too busy and you'll satisfy all my needs."

Her eyes widen again, and a blush creeps up her neck.

I glance down at my ring on her finger, and brushing my thumb over the diamond, I ask, "Do you have any questions?"

"When will the wedding take place?"

Lifting my gaze to hers, I lean back against the sofa. "Once I've taken care of a problem at work." Before she can ask when that will be, I add, "Hopefully, it will be soon."

She nods, and lowering her eyes to where I'm holding her hand, the nervous expression returns to her face.

"What are you worried about?" I ask.

She shakes her head but meets my gaze before she answers, "Marrying you is the last thing I expected."

She didn't even consider it?

"Why?"

"You're the *Capo dei Capi*. You could pick any woman."

"I can't pick just any woman," I mutter.

Her eyebrows draw together with confusion. "Why?"

"Because the woman I marry has to be fucking strong." My eyes burn into hers. "No matter what, she has to stand her ground. She can never back down."

171

Letting go of her hand, I lift mine to her neck and brush my thumb over the stretch of skin where the bruises used to be.

"The woman I marry must be able to survive by my side."

Her lips part, and she almost looks shocked as she realizes what I'm saying.

Her tone is filled with surprise. "You think I'm strong enough?"

I shake my head, and pulling her face closer to mine, I say, "I know you're strong enough." My voice is low as I add, "You will not bend the knee to anyone but me."

Gabriella's eyes dart over my face before she nods.

I don't make a habit of asking people how they feel about a matter, but still, I ask, "Are you okay with marrying me?"

She doesn't hesitate to nod. "I'm honored. I'll do my best to be a good wife." Her tongue darts out to wet her lips. "Can you tell me what you expect from me?"

What do I expect from her?

I have to think before I answer, "I expect absolute loyalty and respect."

"Okay." There's a moment's silence, then she asks, "What about the intimate side of things?" She lets out an awkward chuckle. "Are you even attracted to me?"

Instead of answering her, I lean closer until I feel her breath on my face.

A nervous expression instantly tightens her features.

Slowly, I tilt my head, and once her pupils dilate with anticipation, I press my mouth to hers.

Just like the first time I kissed her, a tremble wracks through her body, and she presses her hand to my chest.

Her reaction does something to me, and unable to keep the usual tight control on myself, I tilt my head as I thrust my tongue into her mouth.

It's instant. The need hits me like a lightning bolt, and I fucking devour her. I grab her hips and lift her onto my lap.

Gabriella lets out a squeak, and it tastes sweet and innocent.

I break the kiss and force her to straddle me. The position forces her dress to bunch high on her thighs, and the sight is sexy as fuck.

Lifting my hands, I frame her face to keep her in place as I growl, "Yes, I'm attracted to you."

She's already breathless, her cheeks pink and her eyes filled with desire.

I slam my mouth to hers and allow myself to get lost in the kiss.

I don't remember a kiss ever feeling this good.

My tongue strokes hers, and her inexperience allows me to do whatever I want. My lips possess hers completely, and when she lets out a soft moan, I almost lose my fucking mind.

Christ.

I'm rock hard, and when she presses down on me, I just react and shove her from my lap and to the side.

I dart up from the sofa and stalk a few feet away, my hands fisted at my sides.

"Did I do something wrong?" she asks, her voice laced with panic.

"No." I suck in a desperate breath before I look at her.

Fuck.

With her swollen lips and her dress bunched up, she's the most erotic sight I've ever seen.

"Go," I growl.

"What?" she gasps.

"Leave, Gabriella, or I'll fuck you senseless."

She darts to her feet and wisely rushes away from me.

I rub my palm over my face while taking deep breaths to regain control over the urge to take what I want.

I can't just fuck Gabriella, and I worry I won't be able to be gentle with her when the time comes to take her virginity.

I've only kissed her twice, and each time, I had to put distance between us so I don't give in to the need she creates in me.

No woman has ever affected me like this.

Chapter 18

Gabriella

I run straight to my room, and once I shut the door behind me, I suck in desperate breaths of air.

Holy crap, that was intense.

I press a hand to my stomach where it feels like a kaleidoscope of butterflies is out of control and fluttering like crazy.

I can still feel the powerful tingles from when I unintentionally rubbed myself against Damiano's bulge. My body just reacted to feeling him between my legs, and I pressed down on him.

Worry trickles into my heart.

No, Damiano said I did nothing wrong.

He wanted me to leave before he lost control.

Is that good or bad?

I lift my other hand to my face, my fingers brushing over my swollen lips.

He tasted like whiskey, wild and burning with passion as he claimed me.

Dio. He's too much man for me.

My thoughts return to the conversation we had before he kissed me, and my eyes lower to the ring on my finger.

It's a bit big but gorgeous, the design vintage, and the diamond large.

Damiano thinks I'm strong, and that's why he's chosen me to be his wife.

I lift my chin, and my gaze falls on the dark view beyond my balcony. I walk to the door, and opening it, I step out of the room. I place my hands on the railing and stare at the backyard that's lit up with garden lights.

This mansion is now my home.

I'm engaged to Damiano Falco.

No one will be able to touch me ever again.

Only Damiano.

A gust of icy wind slams into me, forcing me back into my bedroom.

Walking to my dressing table, I sit down, and as I touch up my makeup, my eyes lock with my reflection.

No more cowering around Damiano, no matter how much he scares you. He's going to be your husband. Show him how strong you are and that he made the right decision to keep you.

He has a lot resting on his shoulders, so be the perfect partner and make life easier for him.

When I'm satisfied with my appearance, I leave my bedroom and head downstairs. With my head held high and a smile playing around my mouth, I walk into the sitting room.

Mrs. Accardi's eyes dart to my face, then drops to my left hand. "She's wearing the ring!" she exclaims as she shoots to her feet.

"Congratulations, *cara*." I'm yanked into a hug and kissed on both cheeks before Mrs. Accardi takes my left hand. "It suits you."

When Mrs. Falco gets up from her armchair, I pull away from Mrs. Accardi and walk closer to my future mother-in-law.

"Damiano said the ring belonged to you," I say, respect tightening my voice.

"My mother gave it to me when I got engaged. It's of great sentimental value to me. She passed away before the wedding day."

"Thank you for passing it down to me. I feel so honored."

Her mouth curves with an emotional smile, and she reaches out to me.

I move closer and when our hands touch, she pulls me into a hug.

"Be good to my son," she whispers against my cheek.

"I'll do everything in my power to be a wife deserving of such a great man, Mrs. Falco."

She kisses my cheek, then says, "Call me Aida. After all, we're family now."

An overwhelming sense of gratefulness fills my chest, and I have to fight the urge not to cry.

"Can I call you Aunt Aida?" I ask before explaining, "Just using your first name feels a little disrespectful."

"Aunt Aida is perfectly fine, my sweet child."

"Oh, you're here. I'll go get Carlo," Mrs. Accardi says. "We need champagne to celebrate this wonderful occasion."

When I pull away from Aunt Aida, I glance over my shoulder and see Damiano watching us.

He comes closer, his eyes flicking between his mother and me. "Did I interrupt an emotional moment?"

I quickly shake my head.

"I'm happy to hear about the engagement," Aunt Aida says. "I wish you both a lifetime of love and happiness."

"Thank you," I murmur.

Damiano comes to press a kiss to his mother's temple, then says, "Thank you, Mamma."

She lets out a chuckle. "You won't kick me out of the mansion now that you're going to become Mrs. Falco?"

Caro Dio!

"No, never!" I exclaim, and grabbing her hand, I say, "Never think anything like that. This is your home."

"She's joking," Damiano mutters, then he surprises the hell out of me by playfully chastising Aunt Aida, "Don't give my fiancée a heart attack before we have an heir."

Aunt Aida smiles at Damiano. "Oh? When can I expect my first grandchild?"

"Babies don't fall out of thin air, Mamma," Damiano says, the playfulness gone from his tone.

All the talk of babies has my cheeks growing warm, but thankfully, Mrs. Accardi comes rushing back into the room.

Martha also comes in, carrying a tray of glasses and a bottle of champagne.

When Carlo joins us, he grabs the bottle, and while he opens it, he says, "Congratulations on the engagement."

"Thank you," I murmur, still feeling overwhelmed.

The cork pops, and he pours the bubbly liquid into the glasses. When we each have one, Damiano moves to stand between Aunt Aida and me.

He holds up the flute, then mutters, "I hate giving toasts."

"We know, but do it for me," Aunt Aida says.

Glancing down at me, his eyes lock with mine. "Here's to finding a woman who's stubborn enough to make eye contact with me and brave enough to not back down."

Not taking his eyes off me, he takes a sip of the champagne, and I do the same.

I'm not surprised when he places the glass back on the tray and says, "I have work to take care of."

"No rest for the wicked," Aunt Aida mutters playfully, but I notice the worry on her face.

After Damiano and Carlo leave the sitting room, Aunt Aida sits down again.

I don't want to drink more so late at night, and I place the champagne on the tray.

Seeing as Aunt Aida and Mrs. Accardi are still enjoying their drinks, I take a seat, then ask, "Can you tell me how Damiano likes things?"

"What kind of things?" Aunt Aida asks.

"Ah … his coffee? Food? His routine when he's home?"

"He drinks his coffee black and bitter. He's never liked anything sweet," she mentions, and I make a mental note of it.

"He eats anything, but his favorite is a home-cooked meal."

"Okay," I murmur to show I'm listening.

"He doesn't have a routine. Being unpredictable is a safety precaution. Whenever we leave the mansion, we do the same. We never go out at a specific time and always switch things up."

"Okay."

"Damiano said we can go shopping," she mentions much to my surprise.

"Yes, he told me to get warmer clothes."

"I'll arrange with the guards for an outing on Monday. When we go out, you do exactly as the guards say. Be cautious, and always be aware of your surroundings."

"Okay," I say, soaking the information up like a dry sponge.

"You'll have to be my eyes when we're out in public. Always be on high alert. If we're attacked, don't let go of me and stay with Gerardo. If we're separated from the guards, we must find a safe place to hide."

"Okay."

Dio, it's starting to sink in that I'll have to take the same precautions as Damiano. I'll be just as at risk as he is, if not more.

I'm a member of the Falco family now.

Chapter 19

Damiano

I managed to get another three hours sleep and feel a little more human. It's early the morning when I walk toward Gabriella's suite.

Knocking, I wait for her reply before I push her bedroom door open.

She's sitting by her dressing table, and it's the first time I see her without makeup.

"Oh," she gasps, quickly climbing to her feet.

"We need to start with your training," I say as I move closer to her, my eyes drinking in the sight of her natural beauty.

Makeup or no makeup, my fiancée is breathtaking.

"Training?" she asks.

My gaze sweeps over the pantsuit she's wearing.

"Shooting lessons. Do you have casual clothes?"

She nods. "I have leggings."

"Change into them." When she remains standing, I add, "Now."

"Oh … okay." She hurries into the closet.

While I wait for her to change her clothes, I walk to the window and stare at the view of the lake.

It doesn't take long before Gabriella comes back into the bedroom. When my eyes land on the tight-as-fuck leggings and her long-sleeve shirt that leaves nothing to the imagination, I grow hard in a split second.

Christ.

The sight of the gap between her thighs and her evident-as-fuck perky breasts almost has me throwing her on the bed.

"That's definitely not going to fucking work," I growl.

Her eyes fill with worry as she whispers, "It's all I have."

Grabbing her hand, I haul her out of her bedroom and head to my suite. I don't stop until we're standing in my walk-in closet.

Yanking a sweater from a hanger, I shove it over her head and bark, "Arms."

She quickly puts on the sweater, and when it hangs to the middle of the thighs, I feel a little better.

Grabbing hold of her hips, I lift her from her feet and set her down on the display case in the middle of the closet. I brace my hands on either side of her, and leaning forward, I capture her stunned eyes.

"Never wear leggings outside of the bedroom," I order.

She nods quickly.

"No cleavage in public."

A frown starts to form on her forehead. "Do you want me to dress more conservatively?"

"No. I love the way you dress. Just don't show what's mine to other men, or there will be hell to pay."

There's a flicker of relief on her face. "Okay."

I pull back, and when I see her in my sweater, one hell of a possessive feeling fills my chest.

"I like you in my clothes," I mutter.

"I like it too." She smiles at me as she slips off the display case. "It's snuggly and warm."

Gabriella's wearing sneakers, and without the height of her high heels, she only reaches the middle of my chest.

An overwhelming protective feeling joins the possessiveness in my chest.

And then I fucking realize she's only a few feet from my bed.

Besides Martha, who comes in to clean, no other woman has ever set foot in my suite.

Fuck.

My eyes flick from Gabriella to the bed, then back to her.

Before I decide to fuck my fiancée, I take her hand and almost drag her out of the room in my hurry to put a safe distance between us and the bed.

Only halfway down the stairs do I remember Gabriella's half my size, and I slow my pace.

Walking out the front door, I head to the outer building near the lining of trees where my armory and shooting range are based.

When I key in the code, and the door clicks open, I step inside and switch on the lights.

I hear Gabriella gasp. "Wow. That's a lot of weapons."

I glance over the guns and pick one for Gabriella.

"This is a SIG P365. It has a twelve-round capacity." I check the magazine, then hold the weapon out to her.

She takes it, her fingers wrapping carefully around the handle.

"How does it feel?" I ask.

"It's not as heavy as I expected," she admits.

"Good."

I walk to the back, where the shooting range is, and removing my Glock from behind my back, I say, "Watch what I do."

"Okay."

Gabriella's eyes are glued to me as I fire five rounds at the target, hitting the head and chest area.

When I look at her, I notice her cheeks are flushed.

Tilting my head, I ask, "You like watching me shoot a gun?"

"Ahh…" She maintains eye contact with me as she admits, "Yes."

"Come closer, *principessa*," I order.

When she's within reaching distance, I pull her to stand in front of me so she's facing the target.

Leaning down, I say, "Position your arms the same way I did."

She brings them up, pointing the barrel of the gun at the target.

"Pull the trigger."

She fires a shot, and it slams into the wall a good foot away from the target.

She glances up at me from over her shoulder. "Sorry."

I shake my head. "This is why we're here. So you can learn to shoot."

I tuck my Glock back into the waistband of my chinos, and wrapping my arms around Gabriella, I nudge her arms up.

I line up the shot, then order, "Pull the trigger."

She fires a round, and it hits the side of the target.

I adjust her arms. "Shoot."

This time, she hits the heart, and the corner of my mouth lifts. "Again."

Bang.

"Again."

Bang.

"Again."

Bang.

I lower my arms, and not even thinking, I pat her on the ass. "Good."

I fist my hands, so I don't reach for her because I want to feel every inch of her body.

My voice is hoarse as I order, "Keep shooting until the magazine is empty."

I load magazine after magazine into the gun and watch as Gabriella gets better with every shot she fires.

As she pulls the trigger again, my eyes land on the engagement ring, and I notice it's a little too big for her.

I'll have to get it resized.

189

I don't like the idea of removing the ring from her finger one bit.

"What's wrong?" Gabriella asks.

"The ring is too big," I mutter.

"I'm picking up weight. It should fit better soon."

My eyes drift over her body, and I like the sound of her being curvier. Not that there's anything wrong with her body, I just won't have to be so fucking careful not to hurt her.

A weird expression flashes over her face. "Unless you're against me picking up weight."

The fuck?

"Why would you think that?" I almost bark the question.

"My mother always controlled my weight. I thought maybe you'd want to do the same."

The. Actual. Fuck?

I suck in a deep breath, so I don't lose my temper and mutter, "I'm not against it. Just don't lose more weight. You're already as light as a fucking feather."

A smile spreads over her face. "Okay."

Crossing my arms over my chest, I ask, "What else did your mother do?"

Just like before, she shakes her head and replies, "Nothing I couldn't handle."

"Tell me," I demand.

She glances down at the weapon in her hands. "They just weren't happy when I was born," she answers, her tone sounding strained. "I wasn't planned."

She shrugs, then emotions tighten her features, and she tries to smile. "I got my first hug two weeks ago. From Mrs. Accardi. It was really nice."

First hug?

My blood turns to ice in my veins. "Your parents never showed you any form of affection?"

"No." She faces the target and lifts her arms to fire a shot.

"Put down the gun," I order.

Letting out a sigh, she places the weapon on a counter near the wall, then she mutters, "I really don't want to talk about my parents."

"Come here."

Her eyes lift to my face, and she moves closer to me.

Lifting my hand, I wrap my fingers around the back of her neck before pulling her against my chest. I lean down and lock my other arm around her, holding her tight to me.

I feel a tremor shudder through her body, and lifting her from the floor, I mutter, "Wrap your legs around me."

Gabriella does as I say, her arms circling my neck. I walk to a seating area, and as I sit down, I order, "Straddle me."

Once again, she does as I say, and when I'm comfortable, I hold her even tighter while pressing a kiss to the top of her head.

"You're just going to hug me?" she whispers, her tone tight with emotion.

"Yes." I begin to brush my hand up and down her back, then say, "Relax, *principessa*. Lean into me."

Pulling her arms away from my neck, she snuggles against my chest, and it has the corner of my mouth lifting.

I begin to feel the heat from her body, and her scent drifts around me.

Closing my eyes, I focus on how it feels to hold her.

It's comfortable, and she fits perfectly on my lap and in my arms.

She flattens one of her hands over my side, and I feel the tension drain from her body.

After a few minutes, she admits, "This feels really nice. I like it."

"Good," I murmur.

I hold her for a while longer before she lifts her head and sits upright on my lap.

I bring my hand to her face and brush my fingers along the curve of her jaw. "You're beautiful, Gabriella."

"Thank you."

When I remain quiet, just staring at her, she asks, "Should I climb off your lap?"

I shake my head.

When she begins to look awkward because I'm just staring at her, I say, "I like silence. It helps me recharge."

"I'll remember that," she whispers before she leans into my chest again.

The corner of my mouth lifts, and I close my eyes as I get used to the feel of her body against mine.

Chapter 20

Gabriella

Lying in bed, I struggle to fall asleep, my mind filled with the past two days' events.

I saw another side of Damiano today. When he held me on his lap, I actually felt safe.

I felt more than safe.

Whenever I'm near him, there's a constant fluttering in my stomach and my heart beats a mile a minute.

I'm becoming more and more aware of how attractive he is. The way he moves. The domineering air he carries himself with. The brisk way he talks.

Even the silence.

It feels like he says so much without him saying anything at all.

He held me tight, which means he does have a caring side. He hasn't hurt me since the incident where he slammed me down on the floor.

He pressed kisses to my hair like he does with Aunt Aida, and it felt indescribably good.

For the first time in my life, a man has shown me kindness. I never in a million years expected it to be Damiano Falco.

My eyes start to burn with tears because now that I've felt some form of affection, it shines a glaring light on the cold and lonely childhood I had to endure.

It hurts.

I suck in a slow breath, trying to force the negative feelings down.

I never have to go home again.

I'll never see my parents again.

They'll never hurt me again.

Slowly, I start to feel calmer, and my thoughts turn to when Damiano kissed me.

It felt like he wanted me, and he made emotions I've never experienced burst in my chest.

A smile curves my lips, and I snuggle into my pillow.

The kisses were perfect.

While thinking about the upcoming shopping trip, I finally drift off to sleep.

My mother's nails dig into my skin as she drags me to the living room. I hear voices rumble, and when we enter the room, my eyes dart over the men.

My father stands next to Santo, and they're both looking at me with sneering smiles.

Stefano steps closer to Damiano, who doesn't even look at me.

"Will you give your blessing, cousin?"

My heart thunders in my chest.

Mother shoves me forward, and I fall to my hands and knees.

Damiano pours himself a tumbler of bourbon before he turns to face me.

His eyes sweep over me with disgust, then he mutters, "Yes."

The single word, sealing my fate, echoes around me.

Stefano closes in on me, and before I can scramble to my feet, he's on top of me.

Suddenly, my parents pin my arms to the floor while Stefano crawls over my body.

"No!" I scream as I thrash against their hold.

When Damiano crouches beside us, I cry, "You were supposed to say no."

His voice is a low rumble of thunder as he says, "You're not strong enough to survive by my side."

"No!" I sob as Stefano's hands tear my clothes from my body. Everywhere he touches me, awful bruises appear, and blood starts to seep from my pores.

I scream, the taste of blood filling my throat.

Waking up with one hell of a start, I scramble off the bed, and running to the closet, I crawl into the farthest corner.

Wrapping my arms around my shins, I sit in the dark. I hold still as I try to stop the breaths from rushing over my lips.

Hiding in the closet is something I used to do to escape my parents. It's been years since I've done it, but it's the only thing I can think of while the nightmare's still fresh in my mind.

A sob sputters over my lips, and I quickly press a hand to my mouth.

Shh…

What doesn't break you makes you stronger.

Shh…

I can still feel Stefano's hands on my body, and it makes my stomach churn.

"Gabriella!" Carlo's voice cracks like thunder through the room.

Shh…

"Christ," I hear him snap.

"Where is she?" I hear Damiano ask, his tone sounding very aggressive.

"No fucking idea," Carlo mutters. "I heard her scream, and when I came into the bedroom, she was already gone."

Suddenly, light fills the walk-in closet, and I let out a panicked sound. I desperately try to squeeze tighter into the corner, covering my mouth with both hands so I don't make another sound.

"Fuck," I hear Damiano growl. "You can go. I've got this."

When my eyes fly up, I see Damiano towering in front of the closet with his gun in his hand. He's only wearing sweatpants, but it doesn't take away from how dangerous he looks right now as his eyes burn on me.

I start to shake my head and suppress the sob that's threatening to choke me.

I struggle to get air into my lungs, and when he crouches beside me, my heart almost stops.

His tone is much gentler than I expect when he murmurs, "Breathe, *principessa.*"

198

Reaching for my hands, he pulls them away from my mouth. "You're fucking smothering yourself."

When he pulls me out of the closet, panic flares hot in my chest.

"No!" Instinct takes over and like hundreds of times before, I start to fight back.

My fists connect with bare skin, and I strain to get free, but strong arms wrap around me. I'm pinned to a solid chest, and it rips a cry from me.

"It's okay, Gabriella. I'm here. You're safe. No one can hurt you anymore," I hear Damiano repeat over and over, and at some point, the words get through to me.

The fight drains from my body, and I sag against him as I suck in desperate breaths of air.

His hand brushes over my hair, and I feel him press a kiss to the top of my head. "I'm here."

He didn't say yes.

It was just a nightmare.

When my breathing starts to slow down, he asks, "Feeling better?"

Nodding, I push away from him, and as I climb to my feet, a wave of intense embarrassment floods me.

Why did I react like that?

Dio. Damiano's going to think I'm weak.

199

"I...I..." I stammer, my eyes flitting over the walk-in closet, the doorway to the bathroom, and just about everywhere but Damiano.

"What happened?" he asks, his tone deceptively soft.

Unable to avoid him, I lift my eyes to his face. His features are tense with anger, and it makes my heart sink.

Caro Dio.

"It was a nightmare," I whisper. Disappointment trickles into my chest. "I'm sorry for waking you."

"I wasn't sleeping."

He moves closer, and taking my hand, he pulls me into the dark sitting area in my suite. He sets his gun down on a side table and takes a seat on the floral-print sofa.

He pats his thigh. "Come."

I brace my knee beside his thigh as I climb onto his lap and place my hand on his shoulder. He grips hold of my hips and tugs me flush with his body.

When the heat of his muscled chest seeps through the satin fabric of the cami I'm wearing, it sinks in that Damiano's not wearing a shirt.

Holy crap.

My cheeks heat up, but I still manage to meet his eyes.

"What was the nightmare about?" he asks.

Once again, I feel embarrassed, as I admit, "You said yes." My stomach churns when the awful remnants of the nightmare shudder through me. "You gave your permission for Stefano to marry me. My parents held me down, and he…he…" I can't finish the sentence and just shake my head.

Damiano lifts his hand to my face, and when his palm cups my cheek, it feels so comforting my eyes drift shut.

His hand moves to the back of my head, and he nudges me to rest my cheek against his chest.

Silence wraps around us, and it soothes me.

For the second time today, I find safety in his arms, and it makes it so much harder not to cry.

Chapter 21

Damiano

Slowly, the trembling eases in Gabriella's body.

My mother's had so many panic attacks I've lost count over the years. In the beginning, they were bad, to the point where she'd pass out. But not once has my mother fought me while she had an attack.

I had to restrain Gabriella before I was able to calm her down.

Even during a panic attack, she still fights.

I press another kiss to the top of her head.

A nightmare about me giving my permission for Stefano to marry her had her hiding in a fucking closet.

"What did Stefano do to you?" I ask my tone too rough from the anger skirting around the edges of my mind.

Not wanting her to misunderstand and think I'm talking about the nightmare, I add, "Before I brought you to New York."

"Nothing I couldn't handle."

Anger pours into my chest, and I clench my jaw as I snap, "Tell me!"

Gabriella jerks in my hold, and when she climbs off my lap, I don't stop her.

"He just hit me a few times." She pauses for annoyingly long seconds before adding, "My hair used to be really long. And black. He would grab my hair and call me his black beauty, so I cut it all off and changed the color."

My defiant little spitfire.

Wanting to know everything about her past, I ask, "And your parents?"

She pulls her knees up to her chest and wraps her arms around her shins, looking fucking small next to me.

It's impossible for me to just watch, and I reach for her, pulling her back onto my lap.

When I have her straddling me again, I take hold of her chin and lock eyes with her. "Tell me everything."

Her tongue darts out to wet her lips, then she lets out a shaky breath. She again tries to avoid the topic when she says, "There's too much to tell. I'll keep you up all night."

"Don't make me repeat myself," I warn her.

Her features tighten, then she finally murmurs, "They hit me a lot, and I was locked in my bedroom for days at a time without food."

My anger multiplies with every word from her, and knowing it's not the worst she's had to endure has my muscles tightening.

"A month before the marriage with Stefano was arranged, my father tried to kill me."

My tone is filled with rage as I demand, "How?"

"He beat me before throwing me over the balcony," she replies. Then she lets out a weird-sounding chuckle. "Surprisingly, I didn't break any bones."

Christ.

"What else?" I growl.

When she folds her arms around her middle, I take hold of her wrists and pull them open again. My fingers wrap around her slender ones, and I have to focus to keep my touch gentle.

"They hurt me every day. I don't want to go through the whole list," she mutters, her tone tense.

When I just stare at her, she lets out a sigh, then says. "Once, Santo beat me so badly, he dislocated my jaw. My father has broken my ribs countless times. I was starved and mostly stayed in my bedroom. The only attention I got from my family was violent." I feel a burst of energy from her right before she yanks her hands free from mine and climbs off my lap. "I don't want to talk about this!"

When she walks toward the doorway, I snap, "Stop!"

I get up from the sofa and close the distance between us. Taking hold of Gabriella's arm, I turn her around so she's facing me.

Her eyes lock with mine, her expression completely blank.

"Don't ever walk away while we're talking," I mutter the order.

Gabriella just nods.

More anger pours into my chest. "And don't wear that fucking mask in front of me."

Confusion flutters over her face. "What mask?"

"The one where nothing can touch you." I lean a little down, my eyes burning into hers. "Don't hide your vulnerable side from me."

Her eyes narrow as she says, "Showing any kind of vulnerability is being weak."

I shake my head. "Not when it's just the two of us. Around other people, you can be a little spitfire, but with me, you'll be raw and honest. I need to know what kind of trauma you suffered so I know how to deal with it."

Worry darkens her eyes. "You won't think less of me?"

"No." I lift my hand and wrap my fingers around the back of her neck. "You're my fiancée, and I need to get to know every part of you, Gabriella."

The defiance in her eyes lessens a bit.

With the light from the walk-in closet and the bedroom, I'm able to see every inch of Gabriella, her pajamas barely covering her body. Her nipples strain against the satin fabric, and the shorts … *fuck her shorts*.

Desire bleeds through my veins, and it makes me grab hold of her hips. I lift her from her feet, and as my mouth takes hers prisoner, I stalk to her bed, where I slam her down onto the rumbled covers.

A shocked breath explodes from her, and I drink it like the sweet nectar it is.

When my body covers hers, Gabriella's hands press against my shoulders. I grab her wrists and pin her arms down on either side of her head, and she has no choice but to spread her legs so she can accommodate my hips.

I fucking feast on her mouth, my mind quickly clouding with a hunger I've never felt before. It's fucking insatiable and dangerous.

Dangerous because this woman already has a hold on me I can't shake. She's beneath my skin and crawling into my chest where my heart is supposed to be.

My tongue lashes against hers, memorizing her mouth and her sweet, sweet fucking taste.

My hands move down her arms and over her sides. When my palms find her ass, I rub my aching cock against the scorching heat coming from her pussy.

We both groan, and I almost lose my fucking mind.

The kiss turns wild, and with zero control, I start to thrust against her pussy, my hard-on rubbing her clit through the fabric.

"*Dio*," she moans into my mouth. She brings her hands to my jaw, and then my little spitfire starts to kiss me back with so much passion stars explode behind my eyelids.

My hips continue to move, and I rub her pussy raw, my cock fucking desperate for every bit of friction I can get.

When Gabriella lifts her hips, and she begins to meet my thrusts, gasps spill from her lips. "*Dio…Dio…Dio.*"

Her body strains against mine, and I break the kiss to watch her face as she comes apart beneath me.

She looks fucking angelic, her swollen lips parted, and her eyes clouded with pleasure.

There's no stopping me as I move down her body. Grabbing her shorts, I rip them down her legs.

"Take off your top," I order, my tone way too fucking harsh with impatience.

My eyes burn over every inch of her skin as she carries out the order, and when my fiancée lies naked on the white covers, something shifts in my chest.

She's fucking perfect.

I shove my sweatpants down, and Gabriella's eyes widen when they land on my cock.

She's a virgin.

The words drift somewhere in the back of my mind as I crawl back over her sweet little body that's trembling from the pleasure she's just experienced.

Was it her first orgasm, or has she made herself come before?

The thought is fleeting as I press a kiss to the valley between her breasts before my mouth finds her nipple. I suck it into my mouth while my hands feast on her soft as fuck skin.

My touch grows rougher as my palms burn a path from her sides to her breasts.

I kiss my way up her throat before taking her mouth again.

Gabriella wraps her arms around my neck, and when I feel her fingers twisting in my hair, my body shudders with satisfaction.

My hands move down, and I position my oversensitive cock at her soaked entrance.

Fuck, it's been too long since I've had sex. I'm not going to last long.

I free her mouth and lock eyes with her.

As I stare down at Gabriella, her hands slip over my shoulders and down my chest before moving back up to settle on the sides of my neck.

I should be gentler. I should ask if she's ready.

There's a lot I should do, but I have zero self-restraint.

My hips move, and I'm met with absolute resistance by her virgin pussy.

I brace a forearm beside her head, and my free hand grips her hip tightly. I thrust again, managing to force myself a couple of inches into her wet heat.

Christ, she's too fucking tight.

Gabriella's back arches, and her muscles tighten, pain rippling over her beautiful face.

I feel her breasts against my chest as I thrust deeper, and this time, she clenches her jaw to keep from making a sound.

Not wanting to torture her, I brace her leg over my ass to open her wider. When I slam into her, she pulls her arms away from me to cover her mouth as a cry is torn from her.

209

Fuck.

Fuck.Fuck.Fuck.

Being fully sheathed by her way-too-tight pussy feels fucking incredible.

Letting go of her thigh, I bring my arm up and pull her hands away from her face.

"Breathe," I grind the word out.

She gasps, and when tears spiral from her eyes, she tries to wipe them away, but I take hold of her wrists and pin them on either side of her head.

I kiss a tear away from her temple, and not able to keep still for much longer, I push an arm beneath her and hold her to me.

"Mine," I growl right before I start to move.

The pleasure of being inside her becomes an inferno that engulfs my entire being. I feel like a possessed man as I hammer into her, and I can't control the pace at all.

Fuck.

I hear the sounds of our bodies colliding as mine claims hers.

I hear her gasps and pain-filled whimpers, and I seal my mouth to hers because each one belongs to me.

Chapter 22

Gabriella

I can't stop the tears from falling, the pain something I've never experienced before.

I knew it would hurt losing my virginity, but not this much. With every thrust, it feels like Damiano's trying to tear me open, and it burns like hell everytime he pulls out.

His arm around me tightens, and I cling to him for dear life as he thrusts harder and harder.

Breaking the kiss, his eyes keep mine imprisoned as he claims me, and even though it hurts, I don't look away.

I watch as his features tighten, then he jerks once before all his weight bears down on me. His face transforms from brutal to the hottest sight I've ever seen.

As Damiano orgasms, and I feel the strength drain from his body, I realize in this moment, he's as vulnerable as he'll ever be.

I wrap my arms tightly around his neck, and he practically engulfs me before he plunges into me twice more.

When his body stills, he doesn't pull out.

The pain starts to ease a bit, and as we just hold each other, the gravity of the situation sinks in.

Damiano just took my virginity.

We've consummated our union, and nothing will be able to tear it apart.

I belong to him.

And he belongs to me.

My eyes widen as I stare up at the ceiling.

Holy shit.

The *Capo dei Capi* belongs to me.

I wear his ring.

I'll bear his children.

I'll stand by his side for the rest of our lives.

Damiano lifts his head, and again, his eyes lock with mine.

I bring my hands to his jaw, and lifting my head, I press a kiss to his mouth before whispering, "I paid with blood for you. You now belong to me."

When I lie my head down again, his gaze burns into mine with so much intensity I feel it in my soul.

Damiano

Gabriella's words fill my chest, and with my cock buried deep in her body, she takes ownership of me.

I stare into her light brown eyes, the green flecks brighter from the tears she cried.

And. I. Fall.

Fucking hard.

The longer I stare at Gabriella, the more emotions pour into my chest until my heart races like a horse caught in a wildfire.

The possessiveness I felt before spirals out of control. The protectiveness becomes a living force.

I'm so fucking obsessed with her I can't stop staring, not wanting to miss a breath from her lips.

And she holds my gaze.

My voice is hoarse as I murmur, "My queen." I press my mouth to hers and whisper, "*La mia regina.*"

"*Il mio re.*"

Hearing her call me her king fills me with intense satisfaction.

I press another kiss to her mouth, then say, "Your virgin pussy took me so well."

Her cheeks turn pink, and I love the sight of her blushing.

When I pull out of her, the color drains from her face until she's pale from pain.

"You okay?" I ask.

She nods as she sits up.

My eyes land on the blood coating her pussy and inner thighs.

Worried, I ask, "Should you bleed so much?"

I glance down at myself and see my pelvis and cock are covered in her blood.

"I'm sorry. I'll clean everything quickly," Gabriella says as she climbs off the bed.

She only takes two steps before she sinks to the floor.

In a split second, I dart off the bed and haul her into my arms.

She lets out a breathless chuckle. "My legs are numb."

Seeing all the blood, the pain on her face, and that she's not even able to fucking walk, regret pours hot and fast into my chest.

I was way too fucking rough with her.

Climbing to my feet, I carry her to the bathroom before I set her down on the counter.

I switch on the faucets in the shower, and the moment the water is warm enough, I move her into the shower.

"Lean against me," I order.

Her hands grip my sides, and her breasts press against my stomach.

I use my hands to rinse her blood from our bodies, and when my fingers gently brush over her pussy, she lets out a gasp.

"Almost done, my little spitfire," I murmur.

When I'm finished, I switch off the faucets and grab a towel. I dry her body, and after wrapping a towel around her, I lift her to sit on the counter again so I can dry myself.

I wrap another towel around my waist before I pick my woman up bridal style.

Walking out of the bathroom and through the walk-in closet, I stop in the sitting room and lean down so she can reach the side table.

"Grab my gun."

Gabriella picks up the weapon, then I walk through her bedroom and head to my suite.

Not even bothering to switch on a light, I take Gabriella to my bed and carefully lay her down.

Grabbing the gun from her, I set it down on the bedside table before I stalk to my bathroom, where I keep a first aid kit and painkillers for when I get hurt.

I grab the Tylenol and get a bottle of water from the mini-fridge in my private sitting area, then head back to the bed.

"Take two," I order as I hold the water and painkillers out to Gabriella.

I grab the remote control from the bedside table and push the button to turn on the lights, then watch as she takes the medication.

When she's done, I ask, "How do you feel?"

"I'm okay."

When I reach for the towel around her body and pull it open, her eyebrows fly into her hairline.

The moment I nudge her legs open so I can see if the bleeding has stopped, she gasps, "Are we going to have sex again?"

I let out a chuckle. "No. Just checking whether I should call a doctor."

"Don't call a doctor, and don't look down there," she snaps, clamping her legs shut while trying to slap my hand away.

My eyes flick to hers, and bracing my hands on either side of her ass, I mutter, "Your pussy belongs to me, and I will fucking look all I want."

"It's embarrassing," she argues.

She fucking argues.

With me.

I blink at her a couple of times, then force her legs open and make sure she's not bleeding to death. Once I'm happy, I grip her chin and lean in close to her face.

"There's no space for embarrassment between us. The sooner you get comfortable being naked around me, the better."

There's a stubborn look in her eyes. "It's not going to happen overnight."

I sit down beside her, and with my eyes locked on hers, I pull the towel completely away from her and toss it on the floor.

Slowly, I let my gaze drift down to her fucking amazing breasts and over her stomach before settling on her pussy that's barely visible with her legs so tightly squeezed together.

"Open," I demand.

"*Dio*," she mutters before opening her legs slightly.

"More."

"Damiano," she hisses my name.

When I just stare at her, she lets out a sigh, and with a dark frown on her face, she spreads wide fucking open for me.

My cock hardens at the erotic sight, but I try to ignore the desire burning through my veins because she needs time to recover.

"You're so fucking beautiful," I murmur, my tone hoarse from wanting her.

I lift my eyes back to her face. "I like it best when you're only wearing my ring."

She moves onto her knees, and when she reaches for the towel around my waist, I lift my ass so she can pull it away from my body.

She brings a hand to my chest, and as her palm brushes down to my abs, she sucks in a trembling breath of air.

"You're the first naked man I've seen," she admits.

"First kiss?" I ask.

She nods as her hand moves lower.

"First orgasm?" I demand.

"Yes."

Her fingers brush over my cock, and my soul almost ups and leaves my shuddering body. My cock jerks for more attention from her.

Compared to other men in my profession, I've had a quiet sex life. I've only been able to tolerate six women, and the sex wasn't near as good as it was tonight.

I only kissed the first woman I was with. I thought I didn't like it, so I never did it again until Gabriella.

Turns out I love kissing.

"Wrap your fingers around my cock," I order.

Gabriella scoots closer until her knees press against the side of my leg. When her hand closes around me, I let out a harsh breath.

Having a woman's hand on my cock for the first time feels out of this fucking world.

"Stroke me, *mia regina.*"

She starts to pump my cock, and when my ass lifts off the bed to thrust into her fist, she tightens her hold on me, and I slump back onto the mattress.

So fucking good.

Her free hand rubs over my abs and chest while she keeps pumping my cock eagerly.

Christ, I love her hands on me.

"That's it," I praise her, my breaths coming faster and faster. "Make me come."

Her eyes feast on my body as she picks up speed, and when her fucking tongue darts out to lick her lips, pleasure shoots through me.

Gabriella watches as I come for her, my release shooting over her hand and my abdomen.

My fiancée is a little too eager, and I have to wrap my hand around hers to stop her from stroking my sensitive cock.

When her eyes fly to my face, I explain, "I'm very sensitive after an orgasm."

She climbs off the bed, and a frown forms on my forehead as I watch her walk to the bathroom. She comes back with a washcloth and proceeds to wipe the cum from my abdomen, but then she pauses, and only when I nod does she carefully clean my cock.

That's another first for me.

Taking the washcloth from her, I toss it near the towel and say, "Get in bed."

"I'm sleeping here?" she asks.

"Yes." I get up and pull the covers back. "Your bed looks like I massacred your pussy."

"That's because you did," she sasses me as her sexy ass crawls beneath the covers.

I lie down beside her, and reaching for her, I pull her tightly to my side. "How's the pain?"

"Bareable."

"How was your first time having sex?"

She snuggles against my chest, and the position hides her face from me.

"Look at me," I order.

She tilts her head back, and when her eyes meet mine, she answers, "Even though it was painful, it was a million times better than I thought it would be."

"Christ." I frown at her. "How much pain did you expect?"

"I'm not talking about the pain." An emotion I can't quite place tightens her features. "It was a million times better because it was you."

When I keep frowning at her, she adds, "It wasn't Stefano."

Finally on the same page as her, I rub my hand up and down her back before holding her tighter.

"Thank you for saying no," she whispers.

We lie in silence as I think about everything that's happened from the moment I laid eyes on Gabriella.

I took her for Dario. At least, that's the lie I told myself.

Honestly, I took Gabriella because when our gazes locked for the first time, I saw the most beautiful woman I've ever laid eyes on.

I tried to fight the attraction, but somehow, she walked past all my defenses and demanded I face the truth.

I fell in love with Gabriella at first sight.

I press a kiss to her hair, then whisper, "Saying no was the best thing I ever did."

She lifts her head to look at me again, and I bring my free hand to her face. As I brush my fingers over her cheek and jaw, I admit, "You were mine the moment you refused to break eye contact with me."

She scoots up and presses a kiss to my mouth. "It's a good thing I'm stubborn."

Gabriella relaxes beside me again, and I pick up the remote control, turning off the lights.

Staring into the darkness, I enjoy the feel of her body pressed against mine.

The peacefulness of being in my private space wraps around us, and for the first time ever, the presence of another person doesn't bother me.

Chapter 23

Gabriella

When I wake up, it takes a moment to make sense of my surroundings.

I become aware of Damiano's arms wrapped tightly around me, my back pressed to his chest. He's holding me the same way I hold my pillow when I sleep.

With his face pressed to the back of my neck, his breaths warm my skin. One of his legs is thrown over mine, and his manhood is hard and big against my butt.

I had sex with Damiano.

After the first memory hits, they all pour into my mind.

The shooting lessons.

Damiano hugging me.

The nightmare, and him comforting me.

Experiencing my first orgasm.

My thoughts stop on the memory, and my lips curve up.

When Damiano kept rubbing his cock against me, it made me feel so much pleasure it was overwhelming.

I remember everything when he took my virginity. The look on his face. The way his body moved. The pain as he kept thrusting until he found his own pleasure in my body.

Even though it hurt a lot, I'd do it a million times to see that hot look on his face as he orgasms. To feel his weight bear down on me.

For a couple of seconds, I was stronger than him.

Damiano's arms tighten more around me, and it makes my stomach flutter.

Suddenly, he yanks away from me. Within a couple of seconds, his hand grips my neck, I'm flat on my back, and once again, I have a gun pressed to my forehead.

Dio.

As I gasp, his eyes focus on my face, then letting go of my neck, he sags back while exhaling a harsh breath.

"Fuck," he mutters while putting the safety back on his gun. "I'm sorry."

Lying still, I just stare at him, wondering why he reacted that way.

"This is new to me," he explains.

"What?" I whisper.

"Waking up next to a woman." His eyes find mine. "I'm used to sleeping alone."

My eyebrows fly up. "You've never slept next to a woman before?"

He shakes his head, and lying back down, he lets out a deep sigh.

Knowing I'm the first woman to sleep in his bed, a smile spreads over my face.

I turn my head, and when my eyes land on the clock on the bedside table, I notice it's already past ten in the morning. I dart up off the bed and hurry into Damiano's closet to grab the first shirt I see.

I hope Martha hasn't been to my bedroom yet.

"What are you doing?" he asks.

"I need to get rid of the bedding and clean up the blood," I say as I drag the shirt over my head.

"I already took care of it," he mutters.

Surprised out of my mind, I stop to blink at him. "You cleaned my room?"

He nods and pats the space where I slept. "Come back to bed."

When I crawl onto the mattress, he takes hold of me and settles me against his side.

"I didn't want anyone to see your virgin blood. It's for my eyes only," he explains.

Damn, the man is possessive as hell.

225

Still, my heart melts.

My body relaxes, and I hesitate before I place my hand on his chest.

My eyes drift over his golden skin, the muscles that look like they've been carved into him, and his sheer size.

Everything about him is intimidating and too much.

He's too aggressive. Too domineering. Too impatient. Too attractive. Too powerful.

The list is endless, but when all is said and done, he's mine.

"Take off the shirt," he orders, drawing me out of my thoughts.

I sit up, and even though I feel a little self-conscious, I do as I'm told.

He shifts into a more comfortable position, adding a pillow behind him.

When I drop the shirt onto the covers, his hands grip my hips, and he pulls me over him. I'm forced to straddle Damiano, and the position puts me face-to-face with him.

I feel his hard length near the sensitive valley between my legs.

"Let me look at you," he murmurs.

His eyes lower to my breasts, and when I feel his cock harden even more beneath me, there's one hell of a tightening sensation in my abdomen.

Damiano's hands lift to my chest, and when his palms cover my breasts, a tremble moves through my body.

His eyes flick to my face before he focuses on where his fingers massage my breasts and nipples.

It makes the tightening sensation in my abdomen so much more intense, and needing to touch him, too, I flatten my hand against his abs.

My lips part as my fingertips brush over the hard ridges, and when he leans forward and sucks one of my nipples into his mouth, a moan drifts past my lips.

I never knew being intimate with a man would feel so good. I always feared it or, at the very least, worried about having to have sex with the man I was forced to marry.

As Damiano sucks and bites my nipples, alternating between my breasts, I wrap one of my hands behind his neck while my other one grips his bicep.

Before I know what I'm doing, my hips roll, and the needy spot between my legs searches for his cock.

Damiano frees my nipple, and his eyes lock on my face before he asks, "How do you feel?"

Tender, but in desperate need of the pleasure he gave me last night.

Not wanting to lie, I avoid answering his question and say, "I want you."

His eyes narrow on me. "How do you feel, Gabriella?"

"Just tender," I mutter, my tone unhappy because the intimate moment is fading at the speed of light.

Frustration pours into my chest.

Damiano tilts his head as the corner of his mouth lifts, and I scowl at the hot grin on his face.

"My woman needs my cock," he says, his voice filled with satisfaction.

He leans closer, and his lips brush over my jaw. When he reaches my ear, he growls, "Ride my cock, *mia regina*."

He grips my hips, and when he shows me how to rub myself against his hard length, a powerful wave of tingles makes my body shudder.

"Christ, is my little spitfire desperate for her orgasm?"

I nod, and tightening my hold on his neck, I slam my mouth to his as my hips begin to gyrate. I rub my pussy desperately against his cock to massage my clit.

I kiss Damiano the way he's kissed me, but I don't have control for long. He grabs hold of my hair and pulls my head back. With my throat exposed to him and my hips moving faster and faster, my lips part as gasps spill from me.

His dark gaze burns over my face and body as I keep riding him, desperate to feel the same pleasure from last night.

My back arches, and I grab hold of his forearm. The next second, I'm completely overpowered as ecstasy seizes my body.

When I feel Damiano jerk beneath me, I pull his hand away from my hair and look down between us. Seeing him shooting his release over his abdomen intensifies my pleasure, and I let out a throaty moan.

Caro Dio. Watching him come is one hell of a turn-on.

I slow my movements, and as the orgasm fades, Damiano swipes a finger through his release.

When he brings his finger to my mouth, my eyes jump to his.

His tone is harsh as he demands, "Open."

My lips part, and his finger enters my mouth. I suck his cum off, surprised when it tastes salty, manly, and slightly bitter.

His expression grows darker until he looks like the merciless capo that took me away from my parents.

Slowly, he pulls his finger out of my mouth.

I lift my hands to the sides of his jaw where his dark stubble scratches my palms.

Leaning forward, I kiss his mouth softly before asking, "Why do you look angry?

"I hate not having control," he grumbles.

"You feel you don't have control right now?" I press another kiss to his mouth, hoping to soothe his temper.

"Not with you naked on my cock."

Pulling back, I meet his eyes. Slowly his expression softens, and titling his head, he just stares at me for a long while.

"What are you thinking about?" I whisper.

"I have to go to work, but all I want to do is stare at you."

His words make my mouth curve into a smile, then my stomach rumbles.

"I suppose I have to let you go so you can eat," he mutters as he lifts me from his lap. "And I have to get back to work."

He climbs off the bed, and my eyes glue themselves to his hot-as-hell ass when he walks to the bathroom.

I get up and grab the shirt I wore earlier. Putting it on, I glance at the closed bathroom door.

When I hear the water running in the shower, I leave Damiano's suite and quickly sneak back to my own.

Chapter 24

Damiano

Dressed in black cargo pants, a long-sleeved shirt, a coat, and boots, I tuck my Glock behind my back as I leave my suite.

As I take the stairs down to the first floor, my phone starts to buzz like crazy.

I dig the device out of my pocket, and a dark frown forms on my forehead as I answer, "What?"

"The hotel is on fire!" Emilio shouts, sirens blaring in the background.

Anger explodes in my chest, my fingers tightening around the phone.

"Fuck," I mutter. "I'm on my way."

"Carlo!" My voice thunders through the foyer.

He comes running out of my mother's sitting room. "What?"

"The hotel is on fucking fire," I relay the message to him as I stalk toward the French doors. When I step out onto the veranda, I mutter, "You'll have to fly."

"On it." He runs ahead of me to start the helicopter.

When I climb inside, I glance at the house and see Gabriella standing on her balcony. She's only wearing a bathrobe, and it's freezing outside.

I yank my phone out, but not remembering the number Gabriella used to call me last week, I send a text to Gerardo.

Get Gabriella off the balcony. She's not allowed out in the cold until she has warmer clothes.

We lift into the air, and I keep my eyes on her. She glances behind her, and I see Gerardo pulling her into the room before shutting the door.

As Carlo turns the aircraft in the direction of Manhattan, I shove my phone back into my pocket.

During the flight, ice pours into my veins, and the soft spot Gabriella carved out in my heart hardens again.

Twenty minutes later, Carlo sets us down on the helipad, and I shove the door open.

"Wait for me," he says as he switches everything off.

Impatient to get to the hotel, I order, "Hurry the fuck up."

"It's a helicopter, not a fucking car," he mutters.

I clench my jaw, and by the time he joins me, I'm ready to kill someone.

We take the elevator down to the basement and rush to the SUV.

I climb into the passenger seat while Carlo slides behind the steering wheel. When he starts the engine, he says, "Hopefully, there isn't too much damage to the hotel."

"Hmm," I grumble.

The roads are fucking busy, and as we get closer to the area where the hotel is and I see the plumes of dark smoke, rage shudders through me.

I'm going to kill whoever's responsible for the fire.

The road is closed, and Carlo has to park two blocks away. I climb out of the SUV, and pushing my hand beneath my coat, my fingers curl around the handle of my Glock as we begin to walk in the direction of the hotel.

Carlo's tense beside me, and we both keep glancing around us. He stays between the road and me.

Rounding the corner, we're met with fire trucks and police cars.

"It's a fucking shit show," I growl as I look up at the flames licking from the windows. "Christ."

"Boss!" I hear Emilio shout.

He comes running toward us with Vito right behind him.

When they're closer, I ask, "How did it start?"

"Don't know yet," Emilio answers.

Vito moves in behind me, covering my back.

My eyes lift to the burning hotel, and I watch as months of work, and a fuck ton of money goes up in smoke.

"Go to the club, boss. I'll stay and clean up the mess," Emilio says. "It's too dangerous for you out in the open like this."

He's right.

Nodding, I order, "Pay off whoever you have to. I want complete control of the situation."

"I'll handle everything," he assures me.

I turn around, and when I stalk back to the SUV, Vito comes with us to offer extra protection.

Once we're back in the safety of the armored SUV, Carlo asks, "Do you think it's arson?"

"We won't know until the inspection's been done," I reply, my tone harsh with anger.

If it's arson, then someone's attacking me.

Probably Miguel because I sent men to wipe out his family after the fuckers took Eden.

Fuck.

I pull my phone out and quickly dial Gerardo's number.

It only rings once before he answers. "Boss?"

"Cancel the shopping trip for the women. I don't want them leaving the house at all."

"Okay."

"Get Aunt Greta to contact her personal shopper to bring warm clothes for Gabriella."

"Will do."

"Keep my women safe," I order.

"With my life, Mr. Falco."

I end the call and stare at the device for a moment before I bring up the last number Miguel called me from. I press dial, and I'm not surprised when it says the number is not in service.

When we reach the club, I stalk inside and head straight for my private lounge. I gesture for Carlo to pour me a tumbler of whiskey.

I dial Tommy's number, and when he answers, I mutter, "I want all available men in the streets. Kill every fucking drug dealer you can find."

"Everyone?" he double-checks. "Not just Miguel's men?"

"Every-fucking-one," I grind the word out.

Even if Miguel is not behind the hotel burning down, I'm done waiting for Dario to find the fucker. I'll work my way up from the bottom. Eventually, we'll find someone who'll lead us straight to Miguel.

Carlo holds the tumbler out to me, and taking it, I toss the whiskey down my throat.

The past week has been fucking tiring. It's been one fucking problem after the other, making the anger in my chest reach boiling point.

Tommy and his men were attacked, and I lost six good soldiers, the alcohol delivery to the club was hijacked, and the senator I had in my pocket was found floating in the Hudson.

When my phone rings, I'm in a piss-poor mood and bark, "What?"

"They said the fire was started on the fourth floor. It was arson, boss," Emilio gives me the news I've been waiting for.

Uncontrollable rage pours like hot lava through my body as I mutter, "We're definitely under attack. Put everyone on high alert."

237

"Okay. I'm on my way to the club," he informs me.

I end the call and immediately phone Dario.

"Miguel was last seen in South America," he answers.

"I want the fucker found, Dario," I order, my tone low and deadly. "Stop fucking around and make it happen."

He must hear I'm at the end of the little patience I have because he doesn't try to crack a joke.

"Hold up," he says. "The whereabouts of Miguel's uncle just came in."

"Send it to me."

"Okay."

"Be extra careful out there," I mutter. "Miguel is attacking."

"Thank God I have Eden at my penthouse," he breathes.

I end the call, and when the uncle's details come through, I forward it to Carlo.

"I just sent you a message," I say. "Have men bring him to me."

"On it," he replies, getting to work.

I start a group video call with the other heads of the Cosa Nostra, and when they all answer, I say, "Miguel's attacking. He burned down the new hotel and took out six of my men. Be extra vigilant while I deal with the problem."

"Christ," Angelo mutters. "Anything I can help with?"

"Be on standby. The second Dario finds out where the fucker is hiding, we're attacking."

"Okay."

When I end the call, I have to suppress the urge to throw the fucking phone.

"We'll find Miguel," Carlo says. "He can't hide forever."

"We better," I snap.

Carlo pours me another drink, and while I take a sip of the whiskey, my thoughts turn to Gabriella.

I haven't been home the past week, and I'd give anything to ease some of the tension by sinking deep into her sweet pussy.

Suddenly, Emilio rushes into the lounge, and it draws my attention back to work.

Chapter 25

Gabriella

With my lips parted, I watch as bag after bag of clothes is carried into the foyer.

Holy crap.

"Did we really order so much?" I ask.

"I added a couple of items I thought you might like," Mrs. Accardi says.

Caro Dio.

"Should I take the clothes to your suite, Miss di Bella?" Martha asks. "Or do you want me to wash them first?"

"They've already been dry cleaned," Savannah, Mrs. Accardi's personal shopper, informs us. "My team can pack the clothes in your closet. Just show them the way."

Martha leads the team up the stairs, and all I can do is shake my head.

"Damiano is going to lose his shit when he sees how many clothes I got," I whisper under my breath.

"No, he won't," Aunt Aida says. "As his fiancée, you always have to look your best."

Still.

My thoughts turn to Damiano, who hasn't been home in over a week.

"I'll be right back," I say before I head up the stairs.

Walking into my bedroom, I hear the staff work in the closet. I grab my phone and quickly leave so I don't interrupt them.

I head to Damiano's suite, and when I shut the door behind me, I type out a text.

Thank you for the clothes. I hope you're getting some rest.

I hesitate before I press send.

I watch as it shows he's read the text, then realizing he might not have my number, I quickly send another message.

It's Gabriella.

He reads it, but it shows he goes offline again.

I worry my bottom lip before I decide to send a final text.

Keep safe.

He comes online, and when it shows he's typing, the corners of my mouth lift.

241

When the message appears on my phone, my smile grows.

Dress warm.

My fingers fly over the keypad.

I will. I miss you.

His reply comes quickly.

Miss you too.

I stare at the messages for a while before I let out a sigh. Wishing he was here, I glance around his bedroom.

I open the door, and heading back downstairs, I find Aunt Aida, Mrs. Accardi, and Savannah in the sitting room.

"There you are," Mrs. Accardi says when her eyes land on me. "Savannah brought photos of wedding dresses."

"Wedding dresses?" I ask as I take a seat.

"Have you forgotten you're getting married?" Aunt Aida asks with a playful tone.

"No…ahh…I didn't."

Savannah hands me a heavy book and a pad of sticky notes. "Just mark the ones you like, and I'll bring them next week for you to try on."

I open the book, and when I see the first wedding dress that's a cloud of white chiffon, I'm hit with a wave of emotion.

I'm planning my wedding.

To Damiano.

I page through all the photos before I start over, picking my favorites.

When I look at a photo of an off-the-shoulder, satin dress with long sleeves, I pause for a while. There's a slit that comes up very high, and a train of satin makes the model look like royalty.

"Which one are you staring at?" Mrs. Accardi asks.

Savannah gets up and peeks over my shoulder. "Oh, that one will look stunning on you. It's our winter wonderland theme."

Mrs. Accardi climbs to her, and I turn the book so she can see the dress.

"It's gorgeous, *cara*." Her eyes jump from the photo to me. "Do you want this one?"

I begin to nod before I've even made up my mind, then let out a chuckle. "Yes. I love the design."

"It's an off-the-shoulder satin dress with a high slit, Aunt Aida," I say so she'll know what it looks like.

"You're going to show some leg on your big day?" she teases me.

"Definitely," I laugh before I stare at the dress again.

Yes, this is the one. I'll look like a queen.

I hand the book back to Savannah and say, "Only bring this dress. I don't think I'll change my mind."

"Okay. Let's take your measurements quickly."

I stand up, and while Savannah moves around me, Mrs. Accardi says, "I've arranged for a wedding planner. He'll be here tomorrow at ten."

I give her a soft smile. "Thank you. I wouldn't know where to start to plan the wedding." Remembering what Damiano said, I mention, "Damiano is only inviting fourteen people."

"Angelo and Torri. Franco and Samantha. Renzo and Skylar," Aunt Aida names some of the guests. "Dario and whoever he's dating. That makes eight."

"Me and you. Carlo," Mrs. Accardi adds. "Who are the other three?"

"Gerardo, Emilio, and Vito," Aunt Aida answers. "Unless they won't attend, and it's your parents and brother?"

"No!" The word explodes from me. Clearing my throat, I say with finality in my tone, "They won't be at my wedding."

The silence following my words is tense, then Aunt Aida murmurs, "Whatever you want, *cara*."

"I'm happy with the fourteen guests you've mentioned," I say, and when Savannah's done taking my measurements, I give her a thankful smile.

"I'll have the dress adjusted." She collects her belongings. "Thank you, ladies. I'll call to make an appointment for next week. I hope you all have a lovely day further."

"Drive safely," I murmur.

"Thank you for coming to us. Let me walk you out," Mrs. Accardi offers.

I sit down again and glance at Aunt Aida. To ease more of the tension left behind by my strong reaction, I ask, "What are you going to wear to the wedding?"

"I have no idea. I have a closet full of gowns that I've never worn. I'm sure we can find something."

"Oh." My eyebrows lift. "Should we go look now?"

"Why not." She chuckles as she holds her hand out to me.

I get up and hook her arm through mine.

Walking to the elevator, I say, "I really love it here at the mansion."

"I'm happy to hear that, *cara*. This is your home now."

I press the button, and when the doors slide open, we step inside. My eyes land on Mrs. Accardi, and I quickly stop the doors from closing.

"Why are we going up?" she asks as she joins us.

"To decide what Aunt Aida's going to wear to the wedding," I bring her up to speed.

"*Caro Dio*," Mrs. Accardi gasps. "I haven't even thought about what we would wear." She lets out a sigh. "If we don't find anything in our closets, Savannah will just have to arrange gowns for us."

The elevator stops on the second floor, and I follow them to Aunt Aida's suite. When I walk into the room, I curiously glance around, seeing as it's my first time in her private space.

The décor is soft pink and creams with paintings of cherry blossoms on the walls.

"Gosh," I whisper. "Your room is pretty."

"I've always loved cherry blossoms." A sad expression tightens her features. "Before I lost my sight, I visited Japan during springtime. I'll never forget how beautiful all the cherry blossom trees looked."

My heart.

Taking her hand, I give her a squeeze before I tug her toward her walk-in closet. "Let's find you a gorgeous dress."

"Here are the gowns," Mrs. Accardi says.

She starts to look through them, and when I see a pink, floral-print, A-line gown, I gasp, "That one."

Moving forward, I grab the hanger and pull it out of the closet. "Wow. This dress is stunning." Turning to Aunt Aida, I rush closer and take hold of her hand. I brush her fingers over the fabric as I say, "It's pale pink silk with floral-print lace." When her fingers slide over the sleeves, I say, "They're three-quarters."

"Gabriella's right," Mrs. Accardi agrees. "You'll look so beautiful in this dress."

A soft smile tugs at Aunt Aida's mouth. "Then I'll wear it."

On impulse I hug Aunt Aida, then feeling awkward, I quickly pull back. "Sorry. I got overexcited."

She lets out a chuckle. "You can hug me anytime. I don't mind."

"Are you going to put on the dress so we can see if it still fits?" Mrs. Accardi asks.

"Yes."

I wait in the walk-in closet while Mrs. Accardi takes Aunt Aida to the bathroom. A few minutes pass before the door opens, and then I stare in wonder at my future mother-in-law.

"How does it look?" Aunt Aida asks.

"So pretty," I murmur, the awe clear in my voice. "You're breathtakingly beautiful."

"Thank you, *cara*," she says, a pleased smile on her face. "Okay, let's get me out of the dress so we can find you something to wear, Greta."

When they walk back into the bathroom, I press my hand to my happy heart.

Even though I miss Damiano, I'm enjoying every second I get to spend with Aunt Aida and Mrs. Accardi.

It feels like I'm gaining two mothers who actually care about me.

Chapter 26

Damiano

My phone starts to ring, and seeing Dario's name on the screen, I answer, "You better have good news for me. My men killed the fucking uncle."

"Miguel's in Miami." I can hear the relief in his voice, and it finds an echo in my chest.

"Wheels up in thirty minutes," I order. "Let the others know we're meeting at the airfield."

"On it."

Ending the call, I lock eyes with Carlo. "Dario found Miguel. The fucker's in Miami."

Climbing to his feet, he says, "Let's go."

As I walk out of the lounge, I signal for Vito and Emilio to join us.

When they catch up to us, I mutter, "Get a group of men to meet us at the airfield. I want them heavily armed. We're attacking Miguel."

"Got it, boss," Emilio says, immediately pulling out his phone to make the call.

We hurry out of the club, and once we're all in the SUV, Carlo starts the engine. "Fucking finally."

"You can say that again," I mutter, more than ready to put an end to Miguel.

I haven't been home in two weeks, and I'm exhausted.

Fuck, it feels longer than two weeks.

The drive to the airfield takes forty minutes, and by the time Carlo stops the SUV, I have zero patience for the three-hour flight to Miami.

Hopefully, the fucker doesn't disappear before we get to him. I'll lose my fucking shit if that happens.

I climb out of the SUV and stalk to where Angelo, Dario, and Renzo are waiting.

"It's a good day," Dario says. "We know where Miguel is. Why aren't you happy?"

"I am," I growl.

"Sure as fuck doesn't look like it."

"Dario, I'm not in the mood for your shit today. Let's get this over with so I can take some time off to deal with–" I catch myself before mentioning Gabriella and our upcoming wedding.

I can feel everyone's eyes on me, and losing my temper, I shout, "Get on the fucking plane."

When I enter the cabin, I take my seat. Angelo sits down beside me and gives me a questioning look. I shake my head so he won't start asking questions.

I just want to focus on killing Miguel. That's my main priority right now.

Once all the men have boarded, Dario says, "Franco's babies are sick. They all have the shits."

"Christ, poor man," Angelo mutters. "I'd rather go to war than deal with three babies who all have diarrhea."

"Can we not talk about shit," I growl.

"Seriously, who pissed you off?" Angelo asks me.

"Just focus on the mission," I snap.

The other men know not to push me any further, and after the private jet's taken off and we're in the air, Dario inspects the weapons we always keep onboard.

Once he's done, he takes a seat again and checks his phone.

My thoughts turn to the past two weeks. The hotel burning down.

The attack on my men.

The attack on my men has been bothering me. Tommy said it wasn't drug dealers but trained men.

251

If it wasn't Miguel, then who would have the guts to gun down my men?

Dario lets out a sigh, then Renzo asks, "What?"

"Miguel hasn't been spotted again."

Fuck.

With my eyes locked on the oval window beside my seat, I ask, "Where was he last seen?"

"A set of traffic lights near one of his clubs."

"He'll probably be there until late," Renzo says. "Which means we'll have to wait him out."

"Or we go in." Looking at the other heads of the Cosa Nostra, I mutter, "I want this done as quickly as possible. We've wasted enough time on this fucker."

"How do you want to do this, Damiano?" Angelo asks.

I play out a couple of scenarios in my head before answering, "We'll all go into the club. Our men as well. We'll walk up to the fucker as a family, and I'll kill him in front of everyone. It will send a message not to fuck with us."

Just in case someone else is behind the fire and killing of my men.

"And the witnesses?" Renzo asks.

I wave a careless hand in the air. "Let them talk."

When we finally touch down in Miami, I feel fucking moody from the flight.

We head to the SUVs Emilio arranged for us and pile into the vehicles.

During the drive, I tap my fingers impatiently on my thigh, and when we pull up to the club, it's quiet because it's still early.

We climb out of the SUVs, then Renzo asks, "What do you want to do?"

"Let's go knock on the door," I mutter.

"You think they're just going to open for us?" Renzo asks another question.

All the fucking questions are starting to aggravate me, and I growl, "Of course not. I'm not fucking stupid."

Lifting my arm, I signal for my men to move closer.

I look at Tommy, who's carrying a grenade launcher, and order, "Blow the door."

I can feel Angelo, Renzo, and Dario staring at me, but ignore them.

Tommy launches the grenade, and I watch with satisfaction as it blows a hole in the front of the club.

When I stalk toward the hole, my men follow. I pull my Glock from behind my back and take off the safety.

Carlo shoves an extra magazine into my hand before he takes the lead while ordering, "Stay behind me."

The air is filled with smoke, and I glance over my shoulder, finding Angelo right behind me.

Our eyes meet momentarily, then we reach the end of the hallway. When Carlo sets foot in a dance area, gunfire erupts around us.

"Move!" Carlo shouts, and when he ducks to the left, I follow him, my arm lifting as I return fire to the second floor, that must be the VIP area.

Miguel is definitely here.

We duck into a hallway that leads to a restroom, and with the meager cover, Carlo and I try to pick off the enemy one by one.

When Angelo tries to move forward to help out, I mutter, "We've got this."

There's a lone fucker with a submachine gun hiding behind the pillar.

Not knowing the whereabouts of the rest of my team, I shout, "Where the fuck are you?"

"DJ's booth," Renzo yells.

Fuck, they don't have a clear shot of the bastard.

Suddenly Carlo darts out from behind our hiding place, and my heart fucking stops as I watch him slide across the floor before he ends the fucker with a kill shot to the head.

When he climbs to his feet, I nod at him with pride filling my chest, then I shout at the others, "Get your asses out here."

Carlo catches up to me as I head for the stairs, and when we're heading up them, I mutter, "Good job."

"Thanks," he breathes as he reloads his gun.

Halfway up, I glance behind me where Angelo and Big Ricky are, then I see Dario running toward us while Renzo keeps an eye out for any stragglers.

This is too fucking easy.

As soon as the VIP area comes into view, my eyes lock on Miguel. He's seated at a table, with his men forming a half circle around him.

What the fuck is he playing at?

"Did you really have to go to all this trouble?" Miguel asks, his eyes locked on me.

"Yes," I mutter as I pull out a chair and take a seat at the table. Looking at Carlo, I nod toward the bar.

I turn my gaze back to Miguel, and staring at the fucker, I let out a sigh. "All you had to do was listen, but no, you had to be stubborn and come into our territory."

"There's a lot of money to be made in New York," he says. "The deal still stands."

I notice the sweat beading on his forehead.

Carlo places a tumbler of whiskey down on the table, and picking it up, I take a sip.

When I set the tumbler down again, I murmur, "As good as a thirty percent share sounds, I have to decline."

My eyes narrow on the fucker, and unable to hold back a second longer, my arm flies up, and I pull the trigger. I watch as the bullet hits him right between the eyes. His head snaps back, and his mouth drops open.

Intense satisfaction pours into my chest as I watch him drop dead to the floor.

As the bullets start to fly, Dario plows into me, and the fucker tackles me off the chair. Hitting the floor, his knee slams into my thigh.

The gunfight doesn't even last a minute, and when the last of Miguel's men drops dead, Dario moves off me and slumps down on the floor beside me.

"Christ," he mutters.

I lift my hand and hold my thumb and pointer finger an inch apart. "You came this close to kneeing me in the balls, fucker."

Dario lets out a burst of laughter, then says, "I'm pretty sure I took a bullet for you."

"What?" I snap, and darting up, I check him for gunshot wounds.

Just as I see the blood on his side, he says, "Flesh wound on my back."

I shove him before climbing to my feet, "That's not taking a fucking bullet." I glance around the area, then ask, "Everyone okay?"

"Yeah, just need to visit the clinic," Vincenzo, one of Renzo's men, mutters. "I took a bullet in the leg."

One of his friends moves closer to help him down the stairs.

I glance at Miguel's body.

He won't be the last enemy I have to face, but I'm taking today as a win.

"Let's go," I mutter.

"Someone going to give me a hand?" Dario asks where he's still lying by my feet.

I glance down at him, and shaking my head, I grab hold of his hand and haul him to his feet.

As my friends and men head down the stairs, I reach for the tumbler of whiskey Carlo poured before I killed Miguel and down the amber liquid.

"One down. God only knows how many to go," Carlo mutters.

I pat his shoulder. "Let's go home."

Chapter 27

Gabriella

I startle awake when I'm picked up off the bed.

Grabbing hold of broad shoulders, it takes me a few seconds before I realize Damiano's carrying me out of my room.

"You're home," I say, my voice hoarse with sleep.

"Hmm…" he grumbles.

He stalks into his suite and places me on the bed before he goes to shut the door. The room is dark, but I can see as he comes back to bed.

He lies down beside me, then orders, "Turn on your side. Back to me."

I do as I'm told, and when his arms wrap around me, and I feel his face press against the back of my neck, a wide smile spreads over my mouth.

I hear him take a deep breath before he lets it out slowly, then his body shudders. An intense energy pours from him, filling the air with tension.

"Are you okay?"

Not saying anything, he only nods.

Needing to hold him, I turn around, and wrapping my arms around his neck, I nudge him to tuck his face beneath my chin.

Brushing my hand over his hair, I press a kiss to his temple.

His arms tighten around me, and he presses closer to me.

I throw my leg over his and try to engulf him with my smaller body.

With one of my hands in his hair, I let the other gently brush up and down his back.

He shudders again, and I feel how the tension in his body eases a little.

He just needs to decompress from whatever hell he faced the past two weeks.

In the darkness, I become a safe space for him, and it makes a new emotion fill my chest.

It's feral, an instinct to protect what's mine.

I press another kiss to his temple and hold him as if he's my most precious possession.

It takes almost an hour before the tension in the air fades away. Damiano presses a kiss to my throat, and lifting his head, his eyes meet mine.

I reach for the remote control on the bedside table and switch on the lights. After dimming them slightly, I set the remote down again.

My eyes lock on Damiano's, and I say, "Let me look at you."

"I'm fine," he murmurs.

"Hmm…" I grumble at him.

My eyes flit over his chest, and when I don't see any wounds, I look at his face.

Lifting my hand to his jaw, I say, "You must be so tired."

He turns his head and presses a kiss to my palm, then his body pushes mine back as he crawls over me.

I have to open my legs to accommodate his hips, while my hands settle on either side of his neck.

For a moment, Damiano just lies down on top of me, his eyes drifting over my face with an emotion I haven't seen before.

The look in his gaze finds an echo in my chest, and not wanting to disturb the moment, I whisper, "What are you thinking about?"

"You."

The corners of my mouth lift slightly. "What about me?"

"I hate people."

A frown forms on my forehead from the sudden change in topic, but then he says, "Usually, I need to be alone so I can recharge," he shakes his head, "but not with you."

My smile widens again, and lifting my head, I press a soft kiss to his lips. "I'm happy to hear that."

His eyes just drift over my face, and I realize he's looking at me with wonder.

As if I'm a miracle.

Damiano's features are always expressionless or angry, but as I stare up at him, I watch as emotion after emotion plays out on his face.

My heart starts to beat faster when his dark eyes fill with a tenderness that makes me want to cry, then he whispers, "At fucking first sight."

"What?"

"I fell for you the moment I saw you," he admits. "So fucking hard." His features grow serious again. "Don't use it against me."

I quickly shake my head, and thinking he needs to hear the words, I say, "You're safe with me." I lift my head again, giving him another tender kiss. "I'll never betray you."

Because I know he'll kill me if I do. Whether he cares about me or not. It's the code we live by.

Our eyes lock, then he says, "I hope I'm the first."

"First to what?" I whisper.

"To say the words to you."

"Which ones?"

He braces his arm beside my head, and his other hand brushes over my cheek.

For the longest moment, his eyes burn into mine. My heart beats faster and faster.

"I love you, Gabriella."

My eyebrows draw together because it's the last thing I expected to hear from him. I thought he was just going to say he cares.

But love?

So quickly?

He must see the questions on my face because he explains, "It was instant for me. I tried to ignore it, but we both know that didn't work."

I let out a chuckle.

Then it sinks in hard and fast – Damiano loves me.

My voice trembles as I ask, "Can you say it again?"

The corner of his mouth lifts. "I love you, *mia regina*."

The words soak into my bones, filling me with a warmth I've never experienced before. It feels safe and as if I've finally found a place where I truly belong.

I've found my home.

"Am I the first?" he asks.

I nod, not trusting my voice right now.

"Good," he sighs before he lowers his head to claim my lips.

The kiss starts out slow as if Damiano's taking his time to show me how he feels. But as the seconds pass, the need grows between us, and he becomes impatient.

His tongue lashes at mine, and when his teeth tug at my bottom lip, his hand moves away from my face, and he suddenly ends the kiss.

He crawls down my body, and taking hold of my shorts, he tugs them off of me.

I quickly remove my cami while he shoves his sweatpants down.

When we're both naked, he pushes my legs open. I still feel self-conscious, but the emotion quickly turns to surprise when Damaino kisses the inside of my thigh.

"Time to taste you, *mia regina*," he groans right before his tongue sweeps over my clit.

My body jerks from the foreign sensation as I gasp.

Then he starts to suck and lap at me as if I'm the best ice cream he's ever tasted.

My eyes almost roll into the back of my head from the incredible pleasure he creates between my thighs.

Somehow, my hands find his hair, and my hips start to swivel. I keep gasping through the amazing sensations, my abdomen tightening and tightening until it feels like fireworks explode through my body.

"Damiano!" I cry, my body convulsing as the orgasm tears through me with a relentless potency.

His mouth leaves my clit, and soon I feel his cock press against my entrance.

I don't have any time to prepare before he enters me partially. Another hard thrust buries him so deep inside me that I feel impossibly full.

Damiano braces his forearm beside my head again and lets out a groan as he grinds his pelvis against mine.

There's a mixture of pain and pleasure, and it's overstimulating.

Breaths explode over my lips, and our eyes meet.

"Christ," he whispers. "You feel so good."

I wrap my arms around him and let my palms brush over his broad shoulders, loving the feel of his muscles.

Surprisingly Damiano keeps his hips still with his cock buried inside me. His head lowers, and he peppers my jaw and throat with kisses.

His hand cups my breast, and his touch quickly grows rougher, then he ducks his head and sucks my nipple into his mouth.

My back arches, and my fingers dig into his skin as a moan slips from me.

Lifting his head, his eyes search mine. "You good?"

I nod quickly. "Yes." When his hand brushes down my side, I breathe, "More than good."

His fingers grip my hip, and as he pulls out, I feel a slight burn from the friction.

Damiano slams back into me, my body jerking from the force, making air explode over my lips.

When he thrusts impossibly hard into me again, I whimper, "*Dio*."

"You can handle me, *mia regina*," he growls. "I know you can."

I nod quickly, and needing to hold onto him, I wrap my arms and legs around him.

Somehow, he sinks even deeper into me, and he snaps, "Christ!"

He sucks in a desperate breath, and his eyes find mine, intense need burning in them.

"I'm okay," I assure him. "You don't have to hold back."

His mouth slams against mine, and he pulls out slowly before slamming into me again.

I feel the moment Damiano loses control. The kiss turns wild as hell, and he starts to move fast and hard, claiming me with the violent power that makes him the most feared man in our world.

He's rough, and his features are carved from stone as he breaks the kiss, his eyes locking on my face.

The pain keeps mixing with pleasure, and my hips instinctively begin to move, meeting him thrust for thrust.

A savage expression fills his eyes, and there's a split second where it makes fear ghost through my chest before my abdomen tightens and pleasure dances just within my reach.

"Mine." The word rumbles deep from his chest, and when I nod, he hammers into me until his body suddenly loses all strength, and he slumps down on me.

"*Dio*," I whimper as my hips keep moving, my clit desperately working to reach my orgasm.

Damiano pulls out and enters me at a different angle, and I lose all control of my body.

When a cry tears from me, he hits the same spot three more times, and I cling to him as the most intense pleasure I've ever experienced completely overwhelms me.

Holy crap. So good.

I can only sob against his neck, and it takes longer than before for the pleasure to start fading.

When my senses return, Damiano's holding me so tight, it borders on painful.

Only our rushed breaths fill the air, his cock still buried deep inside me, his body pushing mine into the mattress.

Unexpectedly, a sob bursts from me as emotions fill my chest.

Once again, I realize Damiano Falco belongs to me, and no one will ever dare to hurt me again.

He peppers my face with kisses, his lips catching the single tear that escapes before I'm able to regain control over my emotions.

And I realize it's safe for me to care about him.

Chapter 28

Gabriella

When Damiano pulls out of me, I flinch, and it has his eyes snapping to mine.

"You okay?"

I nod quickly. "Yes. Just sensitive."

He lies down on his back, and when I climb off the bed, his gaze follows me to the bathroom.

I quickly clean myself before wetting a washcloth. When I walk back into the room and crawl onto the bed, he takes the washcloth from my hand and throws it on the floor.

My eyebrows draw together, then he says, "I don't want to clean you off me yet."

His possessive tone makes my stomach flutter.

Damiano pulls me closer, and when I lie down beside him, his arms wrap around me, and he buries his face in the crook of my neck.

Just like earlier, I throw my leg over his and hold him tightly to my body.

My fingers trail up and down his back, and I press a kiss to his temple.

He lets out a heavy sigh and melts into me.

I keep caressing his back, and not even minutes later, his breaths even out as he falls asleep.

He smells like rough sex and danger, and I keep taking deep breaths of him while the night replays in my mind.

Even though Damiano's all sharp edges and anger, there are times when a gentler side peeks through the darkness.

I live for those moments.

He's harsh, controlling, and takes no shit, but I'm starting to grow accustomed to it.

The only thing I have a problem with is how little time we spend together. I want to get to know him better.

Slowly, I drift off to sleep, and when I wake up, my eyes focus on Damiano's dark ones.

"How long have you been awake?" I ask, my tone groggy.

"A while."

"Do you need to go to work?"

He surprises me by shaking his head. "I'm taking a break for a few days so we can spend some time together."

My eyes widen and the sleepiness ups and vanishes. "Really?"

Pulling away from me, he stretches while nodding.

I sit up, a wide smile spreading over my face.

Damiano's gaze drifts over my body, then he moves fast, and I'm tackled back to the mattress, face down.

His hand squeezes my buttcheek before he shoves my legs open. Gripping my hips, he hauls my butt into the air, and I quickly brace myself on my hands, so I don't faceplant into the covers.

"Fuck, your ass is perfect," he mutters, his tone rough around the edges.

He starts to massage my buttcheeks, then his hand slips between my legs, and he thrusts a finger inside me.

My hands fist the covers, and I glance over my shoulder. Damiano's on his knees behind me, his eyes focused on the spot where he's fingering me. His other hand brushes up and down my thigh before squeezing my buttcheek again.

His finger curls every time he pushes it inside me, and it feels so good heat floods my core.

"So fucking wet already," he groans, a satisfied expression tightening his features.

He pulls his finger out of me, grabs my hips, and yanks me backward. My butt slams into his cock, and I feel the impatience rolling off him while he aligns himself with my entrance.

I'm yanked backward again as he thrusts inside me.

A cry rips from me because he hits so much deeper than before.

"That's it, my little spitfire. Let me hear your cries while you take every inch of me," he orders, his tone low and brutal.

Damiano wraps an arm around my front, and my back hits his chest. I grab hold of him as he thrusts roughly into me again.

His pace doesn't quicken. He keeps it slow and hard, my breasts bouncing with every thrust.

"Am I not fucking you hard enough?" he asks, sounding angry.

"You are," I gasp.

"I'm not hearing your screams!"

He shoves me forward again, and just as my hands hit the covers, Damiano slams so hard into me that I faceplant with a cry.

His cock is too thick. Too big.

And way too rough as he fills me with brutal thrusts.

I start to sob against the covers from how intense it feels, and my emotions spiral into chaos right before an intense orgasm tears violently through me.

I hear myself scream.

"So fucking good," Damiano praises me.

He slams into me twice more, then he pulls out of me, and I feel his release hit my lower back and butt in warm spurts.

My body slumps to the bed, and I gasp and twitch as if I was electrocuted.

Holy crap.

When I feel Damiano's hands rub his release into my skin, my eyebrows fly up.

"You're fucking sexy wearing my cum," he murmurs, his voice hoarse.

A tremble rushes through me from his possessiveness.

He crawls over me, and I feel his breath by my ear as he whispers, "Your pussy is fucking addictive, my little spitfire. I'm going to fuck you raw."

I'm very surprised when my pussy clenches with need.

Pushing myself up, I turn around and shove Damiano onto his back. "Not if I don't fuck you raw first."

His mouth curves up at the corners, and the man looks downright devilish when I straddle him.

I reach down and curl my fingers around his thick length. As I start to stroke him, I watch with wonder how he hardens for me.

I position myself over him and carefully sink down on his cock.

"Oh," I gasp because I'm still sensitive from him fucking me hard.

"Need help?" he asks.

I shake my head, and bracing my hands on his chest, I say, "I want to fuck you."

"Hmm…" he grumbles, his eyes dark with desire as he watches me.

It takes me a minute to find my rhythm, and as I begin to move faster and faster, Damiano grabs my hips, his muscles straining from holding back so he doesn't take over.

Looking hot as hell and breathless, he asks, "You like that?"

I nod, a moan floating from me as I rub my clit against his pelvis while his cock fills me perfectly.

I never knew sex could feel this good.

My nails dig into his skin, and my body tenses. My lips part, and when I start to orgasm, Damiano takes over and forcefully thrusts inside me.

His body strains beneath me, his muscles rippling as he hurries toward his own orgasm.

I can barely hold on by the time he comes with a groan. He yanks me down on top of him, and his arms lock around me before he plunges into me again, his body jerking with each thrust.

When he stills beneath me, we're both breathless, and I can feel his heart racing where my cheek is pressed to his chest.

"Christ," he gasps. "You might just kill me."

I let out a chuckle, and when my inner walls squeeze his cock, he lets out a sharp breath before his body shudders.

I press a kiss to his racing heart, then let out a happy sigh.

His hand pats my butt, then he orders, "Up before I end up fucking you the whole day."

As I climb off him, his cock slips out of me. My body jerks because I feel raw and sensitive from all the sex.

I let out a chuckle. "I'm going to need time to recover."

Damiano moves off the bed. "Get your sexy ass in the shower."

I scoot off the mattress and follow him into the shower.

Once we're both beneath the warm spray of water, Damiano starts to wash my body.

I feel a little self-conscious again, but it quickly fades, and when he lets me rub soap over his skin, it feels more intimate than sex.

"I love feeling your hands on me," he admits.

My eyes dart up, and standing naked with him with our hands on each other, I start to fall in love for the first time in my life.

The emotions are a bit overwhelming, but I enjoy feeling them.

When we're both clean, Damiano switches off the faucets while I climb out of the shower. I grab a towel, and drying myself, my eyes keep roaming over his muscled body.

The man is built like a god.

"You keep looking at me like that, and we won't leave the bedroom today," he warns me.

I quickly wrap the towel around myself before walking out of the shower so I can put on my discarded pajamas.

After drying himself and brushing his teeth, Damiano uses his fingers to comb his hair while walking to the closet.

The sight is hot, my gaze dropping to the muscles carved into his hips.

Holy crap.

Sitting down on the bed, I pull my knees up and wrap my arms around my shins, watching as he gets dressed in tan-colored chinos and a brown sweater.

After putting on boots, he grabs a coat and shrugs it on, then comes to grab his gun from the bedside table.

As he shoves the weapon into the waistband of his chinos behind his back, his eyes flick over me.

"Let's get you dressed, *mia regina.*"

Hearing the pet name, a smile spreads over my face.

He bends over me and picks me up. I quickly wrap my arms and legs around him before he carries me to my room.

Dio. I'm so happy.

Damiano picks a polka dot pencil dress and black high heels for me to wear.

After I've put the clothes on, he takes a seat on my bed and watches as I go through my skincare routine.

When I apply my makeup, he murmurs, "I love the way you move. It's relaxing to watch you get ready for the day."

More happiness pours into my chest, and I fall a little harder for him.

Once I'm ready, Damiano gets up and takes hold of my hand. He links our fingers as we leave my bedroom, and for the first time, we head hand in hand downstairs.

We feel like a couple.

Chapter 29

Damiano

Even though I want to spend the entire day in bed with Gabriella, I don't. The women have been cooped up in the mansion for over a month, and it would be selfish of me not to take them out.

Especially now that Miguel's been dealt with.

When I walk into the dining room with Gabriella beside me, Aunt Greta grins at us.

Carlo's sitting where Gabriella used to sit, so she can take the chair to my left.

I pull out the chair and wait for her to take a seat before I press a kiss to the top of her head. Walking around the table, I place my hand on Mamma's shoulder then kiss the scar on her temple.

"Morning, everyone," I murmur as I take my seat.

When we're all done greeting each other, I announce, "We're going out after breakfast."

Carlo lets out a groan. "Where?"

"Wherever the women want to go," I mutter.

"Shopping?" Mamma asks, excitement in her tone. "Christmas is only two weeks away."

Fuck. I forgot about the festive season.

"Shopping it is," I agree.

"Forget breakfast," Aunt Greta mutters as she climbs to her feet. "Come, Aida, let's go get ready."

Gabriella smiles as she watches the women rush out of the dining room then turns her attention to me. "I still have your credit card."

"It's yours to keep."

Martha comes in with the breakfast, and she sets an omelet and bacon down in front of me.

"Thank you," Gabriella murmurs when she receives her food. "It looks delicious."

"What can I bring you to drink, Mr. Falco?" Martha asks.

"Coffee."

"I'll have coffee, too," Gabriella says. She pats my thigh beneath the table, then adds. "Please."

I stare at her for a moment before I realize she expects me to thank Martha.

My eyes flick to the housekeeper, and I mutter, "Thank you, Martha."

Startled, her eyes widen. "Oh...ah...of course, Mr. Falco. You're welcome."

I watch my housekeeper flee from the dining room before picking up my utensils and cutting into the omelet.

Silence falls around us while we enjoy the meal, and when I'm done, I sip on my bitter coffee while I watch Gabriella pour two sugars into her beverage.

No wonder she tastes so sweet.

Carlo climbs to his feet. "I'll get the guards ready."

I nod, and when Carlo and Gerardo leave the dining room, I reach for Gabriella's free hand.

"Is there anything you need to get?"

She nods, and after swallowing the sip she just took, she replies, "Just toiletries."

Wanting no misunderstandings, I say, "You'll use the credit card for everything."

She nods again.

"Is your bank account in Sicily?" I ask.

She shakes her head. "It's a dollar account with Payoneer."

"We'll have to open one for you in New York so I can transfer money to you."

Her eyebrows lift. "For what?"

"For whatever you need."

"Oh…but I have the credit card," she argues.

I let out a sigh. "You're mine, Gabriella, which means I'm going to provide for you. You need an investment in case of an emergency."

"What…" she doesn't finish her question, and her features tighten when she whispers, "In case you die."

I nod because, contrary to popular belief, I'm not indestructible.

Her fingers tighten around mine, and she glances away from me.

"It won't happen easily," I say to put her at ease.

She sets her coffee cup down as she lowers her head. "I really hope not."

"Come here," I order as I scoot my chair backward.

She gets up, and I pull her onto my lap. Taking hold of her chin, I nudge her face so she'll look at me.

"I'm not going anywhere anytime soon."

"Okay," she whispers before wrapping her arms around my neck.

I hold her tightly while it sinks in that it upsets her a lot to think of me dying.

More love pours into my chest, and I press a kiss to her shoulder and another to the side of her neck.

"Look at me." She pulls back, and when her eyes lock with mine, I say, "I have the whole Cosa Nostra behind me. It will take one hell of an army to overthrow me."

She brings her hand to my jaw and presses a soft kiss to my mouth. "I just don't want to lose you. You're the first place that feels like home."

Christ. My heart.

I close the distance between our faces and kiss her tenderly, but then we're interrupted when Mamma and Aunt Greta come rushing into the dining room.

"We're ready … oh dear … we can wait," Aunt Greta says before pushing Mamma back to the door.

There's a confused expression on my mother's face as she asks, "Why?"

"They're kissing," Aunt Greta whispers.

I let out a chuckle as I lift Gabriella off my lap. We get up, and taking her hand, I head to the doorway. "Let's go."

When we walk out of the house, five SUVs are waiting out front.

"We're in the third SUV," I say.

Aunt Greta climbs into the second one, and as Gerardo leads Mamma to the fourth one, I feel a twinge in my heart.

Now that I'm engaged to Gabriella, she takes precedence over my mother. I wish I could have them both with me, but the risk is too high.

With us separated, some of us might survive during an attack.

I let Gabriella climb into the backseat before I slide in beside her.

"Why are your mother and Mrs. Accardi taking different cars?" she asks.

"It's a precaution," I explain.

Carlo gets in behind the steering wheel, and Dante, one of my other guards, takes the passenger seat.

With fourteen guards to protect us, the convoy of SUVs drives toward the gates. When they open, we head down the narrow road that's lined with trees.

"Where are we?" Gabriella asks.

"Shelter Island. We have to take a ferry to get to Long Island."

She lets out a burst of laughter. "Still don't know where I am."

I pull out my phone and bring up a map of the area to show her. "We're here."

"It looks far from Manhattan," she mentions.

"That's why I take the helicopter."

Relaxing into my side, she glances out the window. "It's quiet out here."

"That's the plan," I mutter.

She glances up at me. "Do you ever host parties at the mansion?"

"The other four heads of the Cosa Nostra come over for a poker game occasionally. Mostly, we meet in Manhattan. I have another house and a penthouse there."

"Is that where you stay when you're not with us?" she asks.

I nod, my eyes searching through the trees as we drive toward the ferry.

"Only a few people know where the mansion is situated," I mention.

"Who?"

"The other heads. The guards. My aunt on my father's side and Stefano."

A frown forms on her forehead. "Will Stefano be at the wedding?"

I shake my head. "No. The last thing I want is family visiting when I marry you."

"Me too," she agrees.

"After the wedding, I want all the guests gone as soon as possible," I mutter.

So I can be alone with my wife.

My wife.

I wrap my arm around her shoulders and pull her tightly to my side.

"We're getting married before Christmas," I announce.

"That's less than two weeks," she gasps.

"Two weeks too fucking long," I mutter.

I'll have to invite the other heads over to introduce them to Gabriella.

So much for resting.

"What the hell was I thinking," I growl to Carlo.

"You tell me," he mutters before letting out a sigh. "You're the one who decided to bring them shopping."

We're following the women like two lost fucking puppies as they move from one store to the next. The guards keep taking turns carrying the parcels to the SUVs, and I start to worry there won't be enough space.

"*Dio!*" I hear Gabriella gasp, and my eyes flick to the outfit she's staring at.

I walk closer, taking in the sheer body suit the mannequin is wearing. There are meager strips of fabric covering the breasts and pelvic area.

It's fucking sexy.

My eyes flick back to Gabriella's face, and I start to shake my head. "Over my dead body."

She takes my hand and gives me a pleading look. "I'll pair it with a jacket. All the important parts will be covered."

Christ.

Letting out a sigh, I give in and nod.

"Thank you!" She wraps her hand around the back of my neck, and standing on her toes, she pulls me down so she can kiss me before rushing into the store.

Carlo lets out a chuckle, and when I shoot him a glare, he stops and pretends to search the area for any threats.

By the time we leave the mall, I'm fucking tired and it's already dark.

But my women are happy.

When I'm back in the SUV with Gabriella beside me, I ask, "Did you enjoy the trip?"

"So much!" She rubs her hand up and down my thigh, and I revel in how good it feels. "Thank you."

"You're welcome, my little spitfire," I murmur before I relax against the seat and close my eyes.

Gabriella links our hands together and wraps her other arm around my waist as she leans into my side.

She doesn't try to make conversation as we drive home but just holds me, and like the night before, I find a sense of peace having her next to me.

Somehow, she has the power to help me recharge after an exhausting day.

Chapter 30

Gabriella

With the wedding date scheduled for next Saturday, we've been super busy.

Mrs. Accardi's been an enormous help. Honestly, she's done most of the work.

I got to spend some time with Damiano, but tonight, the other heads of the Cosa Nostra and their partners are coming over, and I'm nervous as hell.

I've just put on the sheer body suit and high heels when Damiano comes into my walk-in closet. His eyes land on me, and he stops dead in his tracks.

"No," he growls as he slowly starts to shake his head, his expression darkening by the second. "There is no fucking way you're wearing that in front of the other men."

"Hold on before you burst a vein," I mutter.

I grab the cream jacket out of my closet and put it on. When I fasten the belt, and the fabric spreads out like a short skirt, I say, "See. Everything's covered."

He stares at me for a while before he says, "Fine. But the fucking jacket stays on at all times."

I walk closer to him, and wrapping my fingers behind his neck, I pull him a little down. Against his lips, I whisper, "It will only come off when you take it off."

His hands settle on my hips, and our eyes lock.

"Keep tempting me, and I'll cancel the poker game."

My features tighten with nerves. "Do you think they'll approve of me?"

He lifts a hand to my face and cups my cheek. "Only my approval matters, *mia regina*. They have no choice but to accept you."

When he pulls away, I say, "I'm just going to do my makeup. I'll be down soon."

"Take your time," he murmurs before leaving the room.

I remove the jacket, so I don't get powder on it, and sitting by my dressing table, I get to work.

I take extra care with the eyeshadow and highlight my cheekbones.

When I'm done, I put on the jacket again before adding a black choker with a single diamond around my neck.

Looking at my reflection, I lift my chin.

You've got this.

Leaving my bedroom, I head down the stairs. When I reach the second floor's landing, I see Damiano greeting a group of men, their women standing near them, but not touching my man.

One of the men glances in my direction, and shock flashes over his features as he says, "Now it makes sense."

"What?" Another man asks before he sees me. "Holy fuck."

Damiano's eyes lock on me, and he walks to the bottom of the stairs. His tone is soft as he orders, "Come, *mia regina*."

My heart beats a little faster as I take the stairs down to him, and when I place my hand in his, I lift my chin higher and look at the other men.

"Introduce me," I say with the same tone Damiano uses when issuing a demand.

Damiano gestures at each of the men. "Angelo Rizzo and his wife, Vittoria. Franco Vitale and his wife, Samantha. Renzo Torrisi and Skylar. And last but not least, Dario La Rosa and Eden."

I don't reach my hand out and nod at them instead. "It's nice to meet you."

Looking stunned, Angelo shakes his head, then he glances at Damiano, who says, "This is Gabriella di Bella. My fiancée."

"Holy fuck," Renzo mutters again. "You got engaged? When?"

"Doesn't matter," Damiano replies.

"Just nod if you need to escape," Dario says, his tone playful.

Damiano lets go of my hand and wraps his arm around my lower back.

His voice is dark as he growls, "Don't start with me, Dario."

Pulling away from him, I glance at the women. A smile tugs at my mouth as I say, "Care to join me in the sitting room?"

"Yes, please," Samantha says.

As we walk to the sitting room where Aunt Aida and Mrs. Accardi are waiting, Vittoria murmurs, "I love your outfit."

"Thank you." I offer her a grateful smile. When we walk into the room, I say, "Our guests are here, Aunt Aida."

While the women greet Aunt Aida and Mrs. Accardi, I take a moment to look at the women.

They're all beautiful, but it doesn't escape my attention that I'm the shortest.

I lift my chin higher as I take a seat on an armchair.

As soon as everyone is comfortable, Samantha looks at me. "So…you're engaged to Damiano? We weren't aware he was dating."

"We didn't date," I answer honestly.

"It's an arranged marriage?" Vittoria asks. When I nod, she says, "It was the same for me and Angelo." My eyes lower to her pregnant belly, then she adds, "We're very happy."

"When are you due?"

"Soon." She lets out a chuckle. "But not soon enough."

My eyes drift to Skylar and Eden, and noticing Eden looks a little uncomfortable, I say, "Eden, you must be feeling out of sorts, having just met everyone as well?"

"You have no idea," she chuckles. "It's a little overwhelming."

"We'll get used to everything together," I assure her.

"Ahh, here's the tea and cake," Mrs. Accardi says as Martha pushes a cart into the sitting room.

There's also wine with a cheese and crackers platter, catering for those who prefer something salty.

I glance at Aunt Aida, and reaching over, I place my hand on hers. "Would you like some cake?"

She nods. "Just a small piece, *cara*."

Everyone waits for me to get tea and cake for Aunt Aida before they start to help themselves.

I place the tea on the side table and guide Aunt Aida's hand to the plate. "It's carrot cake. I know you don't like the icing, so I took it off."

"Thank you, *cara*," she murmurs.

I get some tea for myself, and sitting down, I keep an eye on my future mother-in-law in case she needs help.

"Seeing as everyone's here," Mrs. Accardi says. "The wedding is on the twenty-first."

"Of which month?" Skylar asks.

"This month," I answer. "It's next Saturday, and you're all invited. The invitations will be delivered on Monday."

"Wow, Damiano isn't wasting any time," Samantha murmurs.

I let out a chuckle. "No, he isn't."

"Do you need help with the arrangements?" Vittoria asks.

"Mrs. Accardi has everything under control," I reply. "Thank you for the offer, though."

"Call me Aunt Greta, *cara*," she says, a frown forming on her forehead. "I didn't even realize you were still calling me Mrs. Accardi."

"*Aunt Greta* has arranged everything for the wedding," I repeat, giving her a playful look.

"That's much better," she mutters.

"The catering as well?" Skylar asks.

Aunt Greta has a proud expression as she says, "Thank you, but it's all taken care of. All you have to do is come and enjoy the celebration with us."

The conversation hovers around the topic of the upcoming wedding, and soon, all the women relax, and we're talking as if we've known each other for years.

———————

Damiano

"You're engaged," Dario mutters for the tenth time since we started the game.

"I'm going to fucking kill you if you mention it again," I growl as I throw down the shitty hand I was dealt.

Carlo sets a tumbler of whiskey down beside me before he takes a seat on one of the armchairs in my private lounge.

"When did you meet her?" Angelo asks.

"The trip to Sicily," I reply.

"To give Stefano your blessing?" he asks, then his eyes widen. "You took her from your cousin?"

I nod, then order, "I'm done talking about Gabriella."

"All jokes aside," Dario says. "Is she okay marrying you?"

"What the fuck is that supposed to mean?" I growl at him.

He holds my stare. "You're not the easiest person to get along with."

I can see he's actually worried about her, and letting out a sigh, I mutter, "Gabriella is much stronger than she looks. She knows how to handle me, so back the fuck off."

Dario nods, knowing not to push me any further.

"Did you find out who started the fire at the hotel?" Angelo asks, changing the subject.

I shake my head. "I think it was Miguel. There hasn't been any trouble since I killed him."

"That's good news," he mutters as he places a card on the table. "You better give me a good card," he tells Renzo.

"Don't shoot the dealer," Renzo chuckles as he places a card in front of Angelo.

"I need two," Franco says.

"I'm good." Dario grins.

"Fucker," Franco mutters, and not even looking at the two new cards, he bows out of the game.

"Let me see your hand," Renzo demands.

"You first," Dario taunts him.

They all put their hands down, and Dario smirks at his royal flush. "Pay up."

"I swear, if I ever catch you cheating, you're dead," Franco grumbles as he pushes his stack of cash toward Dario.

"If you're good, you're good," Dario brags.

"How's business?" I ask.

"Good," Angelo answers. "I'm going to open another club."

"I just completed a big arms deal," Renzo mentions.

"Where and with who?" I ask.

"Filippo Vero. He's based in Italy."

When I don't recognize the name, I ask, "What does he do?"

"Just buys and sells arms," Renzo answers.

I glance at Franco. "And you?"

297

"Business is good as usual."

"How are the triplets?" Dario asks Franco.

The conversation turns to the kids, and letting out a sigh, I take a sip of my whiskey.

I wonder how long it will take for Gabriella to get pregnant.

Picturing her pregnant with my child has the corner of my mouth curve up.

"He's smiling," Dario gasps.

I quickly school my face and glare at the fucker.

"You have to tell us what you were thinking about," Renzo says, a broad grin on his face.

"Nothing that concerns you," I mutter. "Deal the next hand."

Chapter 31

Gabriella

I'm busy doing Aunt Aida's makeup for the wedding when Aunt Greta rushes into the room, looking frazzled.

"You need to take a break," I tell her while I swipe some mascara onto Aunt Aida's lashes.

"I'll take a break after the wedding," Aunt Greta says as she sits down on the side of my bed. She glances around the room. "Are you going to stay here or move to Damiano's suite?"

I already spend every night in Damiano's bed, and half of my stuff is in his bathroom, but I'm not telling them that.

"I'll move everything tomorrow," I reply.

"Has he told you where he's taking you for the honeymoon?" Aunt Aida asks.

"No. He only said we'll leave after New Year's," I answer before sitting back to check her makeup. "There we go. You're ready."

She glances in Aunt Greta's direction. "How do I look?"

"Very beautiful and ten years younger." Aunt Greta gives me a pointed look. "You better work your magic on my face. These wrinkles are taking over."

Aunt Aida and Aunt Greta swap places, and I start by cleaning Aunt Greta's skin before putting on moisturizer.

"Are you excited?" Aunt Greta asks, her eyes drifting over my face.

"I am." A smile tugs at my mouth. "It's a great honor to become a member of the Falco family."

"Is that the only reason?" Aunt Aida asks.

"No." My cheeks warm a little before I admit, "I'm excited because I can't wait to share my life with Damiano."

"Do you love him?" Aunt Greta asks.

I let out a chuckle. "Enough with the questions. You'll find out soon enough."

When I'm done with Aunt Greta's makeup, she looks in the mirror, and a happy smile spreads over her face. "You have performed a miracle, *cara*. Thank you."

Hoping to get a few minutes to myself, I say, "Go get dressed while I do my makeup."

I watch as they leave my bedroom before I look at the ring on my finger.

I'm marrying Damiano today.

"Christ," he says, appearing in the doorway as if my imagination conjured him up, "I thought they'd never leave."

"Did you see your mom's makeup?" I ask.

He nods as he shuts the door. "She looks beautiful and happy. Thank you for all the attention you're giving her."

I stand up, but when a serious expression tightens his features, I freeze.

"Is something wrong?" I ask.

He shakes his head, and taking my hand, he drops to his knee in front of me.

Holy crap.

Looking up at me, he says, "I gave you no choice when I took you, and I don't regret it." His thumb brushes over the engagement ring on my finger. "You have a hold on me I can't shake, Gabriella. You've crawled into my heart, and I've become fucking obsessed with you."

A lump forms in my throat, and I'm so glad I haven't put on my makeup yet.

"I love you." His tone grows softer. "I hope you'll learn to love me."

Damiano Falco is mine.

I have the most powerful man kneeling at my feet.

Knowing he'll never hurt me and it's safe to be vulnerable, I admit, "I have."

His eyes darken as he stares at me.

"I love you, Damiano," I say the words out loud for the first time in my life.

He shoots to his feet, his hands cup my cheeks, and his mouth takes mine in a feverish kiss.

When his body tries to push mine toward the bed, I place my hands on his chest and break the kiss.

"No sex. I have to get ready, and so do you," I say sternly.

He lets out an unintelligible sound, then sighs. Brushing his palms up and down my sides, he mutters, "I can't wait for this day to be over."

I lift my hand to his jaw, and he presses a kiss to my palm.

"Go get ready and wait for me at the altar."

"Don't make me wait long," he orders before he walks to the door. He looks at me one last time then leaves.

Feeling like a queen, I look at my reflection in the mirror.

Aunt Aida and Aunt Greta have gone to take their seats, and everyone's waiting for me.

There's a knock at the door, and when I glance over my shoulder, I see Carlo.

"Ready?" he asks.

I nod, and turning around, I walk toward him.

"Did Damiano send you to make sure I don't run away?" I ask.

He lets out a chuckle. "Something like that."

As we wait for the elevator, he clears his throat. "You look beautiful, Gabriella."

"Thank you."

The doors open, and we step inside. Carlo has to help me with the dress so it doesn't get caught in the doors.

When we step out onto the first floor, Carlo says, "Good luck."

I suck in a deep breath and walk down the hallway toward the sunroom.

Damiano refused for the wedding to be held outside. He didn't want me out in the cold wearing only a dress.

I stop a couple of feet before the doorway, and Carlo heads inside to give the signal that I'm ready.

The notes slowly start to fill the air as 'Pachelbel Canon in D' begins to play.

I close my eyes and suck in a desperate breath.

Don't cry.

Slowly, I start to walk, and when I enter the room, my eyes search for Damiano. Finding him, I keep my gaze locked on my groom, and with my head held high, I walk toward the man I'll spend the rest of my life with.

When he sees me, it looks like he takes a physical blow to the stomach, even staggering a step back, and tears jump to my eyes.

His jaw clenches, but then he shakes his head, and emotions tighten his features.

"Christ, you look breathtaking, *mia regina*," he says when I'm halfway down the aisle.

My eyebrows draw together, and I almost let out a sob, but I swallow it down, my body trembling from all the effort it's taking not to cry.

I come to a stop in front of Damiano, and seeing how emotional he looks, I can't stop a tear from escaping.

He reaches for my face and wipes the tear away, then looks at the priest.

"Damiano and Gabriella, have you come here to enter into marriage without coercion, freely and wholeheartedly?" the priest asks.

"I have," Damiano answers.

My voice is hoarse when I say, "I have."

"Since it's your intention to enter into the covenant of Holy Matrimony, join your right hands, and declare your consent before God and His church."

Damiano grabs my right hand before I can even lift it, and I let out a chuckle.

My impatient man.

"I, Damiano Custanti Falco, take you, Gabriella di Bella, for my lawful wife, to have and to hold from this day forward, for better, for worse, for richer, for poorer, in sickness and in health, until death do us part. I will love and honor you all the days of my life."

Hearing the words from Damiano makes it impossible for me to keep the tears back, and as they start to fall, my voice is shaky as I vow, "I, Gabriella di Bella, take you, Damiano Custanti Falco, for my lawful husband, to have and to hold from this day forward, for better, for worse, for richer, for poorer, in sickness and in health, until death do us part. I will love and honor you all the days of my life."

Damiano takes a deep breath as if he's trying to inhale my words, then the priest says, "What God joins together, let no one put asunder." He glances between us. "Exchange wedding rings."

Carlo steps forward, holding out a satin pillow with two wedding bands resting on top of it.

I take the bigger one while Damiano picks up the small one.

He takes my left hand, then orders, "Look at me."

A smile spreads over my face as I meet his eyes.

"Gabriella, receive this ring as a sign of my love and fidelity, in the name of the Father, and of the Son, and of the Holy Spirit."

I feel how he pushes the wedding band onto my finger, then he adds, "It's you and me forever, *mia regina*."

I nod before I look down to position the wedding band by his ring finger, then glance up again as I say, "Damiano, receive this ring as a sign of my love and fidelity, in the name of the Father, and of the Son, and of the Holy Spirit." I push the ring onto his finger. "You and me, until the end, *mio re*."

"In the sight of God and these witnesses, I now pronounce you husband and wife. You may kiss the bride."

Damiano lifts his hands, and framing my face, he presses a tender kiss to my mouth. He pulls back an inch, and when our eyes meet, he says, "I love you, my wife."

I wrap my arms around his neck and whisper, "I love you, my husband." Then, pulling him back to me, I seal my mouth to his.

Chapter 32

Damiano

With every passing second, where the guests are drinking champagne and enjoying the reception, I grow more and more impatient for them to leave.

"Stop scowling at everyone," Gabriella whispers, where she's sitting beside me.

"How much longer?" I mutter.

"We only get one wedding," she says, "try to enjoy it."

"I am, but I also want to be alone with you."

She pats my chest and smiles at Samantha as she walks by the table.

"You look stunning, Gabriella," Samantha says, not even daring to look in my direction.

"Thank you," my bride accepts the compliment like the queen she is.

Aunt Greta rushes toward us and says, "It's time to open the dance floor."

"Dance floor?" I mutter. "No one said anything about dancing."

"Do it for me," Gabriella whispers before standing up.

Unable to refuse her anything, I climb to my feet and follow her to the middle of the floor.

A song starts to play, and as I take Gabriella into my arms, I ask, "Which song did you pick?"

"Anyone by Tommee Profitt and Fluerie." She wraps her arms around my neck, her fingers playing with my hair as she smiles up at me. "It says everything I feel."

Not giving a fuck what everyone else thinks, I stand on one spot and sway from side to side as I listen to the words.

The lyrics make emotions trickle into my chest, and I tighten my arms around her.

Christ, I love Gabriella with everything I am.

My eyes lock with my wife's, and seeing how happy she is, I pull her hands away from my neck. Wrapping an arm around her back, I tug her flush with my body while I hold her right hand in mine.

When I start to move her across the floor, her lips part.

"You made it sound like you couldn't dance," she chastises me.

"No. I said I don't like it," I correct her. "But for you, I'll do it."

When the song speeds up, I twirl Gabriella away from me before bringing her back to my arms.

Laughter explodes from her, and it makes the corners of my mouth lift.

I do it again just so I can hear her laugh, and when she looks up at me with the green flecks shining brightly in her light brown eyes, I know I'll never love another as much as I love her.

I'm so fucking thankful I kept her for myself.

I notice Emilio leading Mamma to the floor, and when he dances with her, I give him a thankful nod.

Carlo grabs Aunt Greta, who hasn't stopped running around for one second, and drags her protesting ass to the dance floor.

I glance at everyone having fun and needing to be alone with my wife, I take Gabriella's hand and order, "Come."

I drag her out of the room and head for the elevator.

"What about the guests?" she asks.

"Let them enjoy the night," I mutter.

I pull her into the elevator and growl at the fucking fabric of her dress when we struggle to get it all into the small space.

"You're so impatient," she chuckles.

"You have no fucking idea."

I lift my hands to her face and keep her in place as I claim her mouth.

I fucking devour my wife as we ride to the third floor, and when the doors open, I don't stop, and we stumble into the hallway.

We somehow make it across the landing before I break the kiss and unfasten my belt.

"On your knees, my little spitfire."

She sinks down and helps me unbutton my pants. When she pulls the zipper down, I free my cock, and order, "Open your mouth."

When her lips part, I step forward. The moment I feel her mouth wrap around my cock, I grab hold of her hair.

"Take me deep."

Her cheeks hollow out as she sucks me into her mouth, and feeling her tongue brush against the side of my cock, my legs go a little numb from how good it feels.

"It's the first time a woman has her mouth on my cock," I tell her.

Gabriella grabs hold of my ass and starts to suck as if her fucking life depends on it, a possessive light in her eyes.

"Christ," I grind the word out through clenched teeth as I watch my wife rock my fucking world.

When I thrust too deep, she gags and tears jump to her eyes. The sight is downright erotic, and within seconds, I come.

Pleasure zips through my body like a current of electricity, and Gabriella swallows every drop of my cum.

I pull out of her mouth, and grabbing hold of her, I haul her over my shoulder. I shove the fabric of her dress out of my face and carry her into my bedroom, only pausing a second to kick the door shut behind us.

Throwing Gabriella onto the bed, I mutter, "How the fuck do I get you out of this dress?"

Laughter bursts from her, and sitting up, she turns her back to me. "Help me with the zipper."

I pull it down, and then it's surprisingly easy as Gabriella shoves the dress down her body, exposing white lace lingerie that makes her look like a porn star.

"Jesus Christ, you are so fucking sexy," I say as I pull the bowtie loose from my neck. While I undress, my eyes drink in the sight of my wife as she lies down on the bed.

She watches me with hooded eyes, and when I'm naked, she murmurs, "You're so handsome. I'll never get tired of looking at you."

Taking hold of her legs, I yank her to the edge of the bed, and leaning over her, I bite her nipple through the lace.

"Are you fond of the lingerie?"

"No, I got it for you."

"Good," I mutter as I take hold of the lace, and without much effort, I rip it open so I can get to her skin. I drop kisses all over her breasts, and it only makes my desire for her burn hotter through my veins.

I yank the lace off her, and aligning my cock with her soaked pussy, I enter her in one hard thrust.

"Christ, your pussy is getting used to taking all of my cock," I groan as I grip hold of her hips, and then I fuck my wife until she's crying my name as she comes apart for me.

When I slump over her, I gasp for air, my heart thundering in my chest.

Pleasure spasms through my body while I look deep into her eyes where I see my entire future.

Chapter 33

Gabriella

While Martha carries the clothes between my old suite and Damiano's room, Aunt Greta helps me pack everything into my side of the closet.

Aunt Aida's sitting on a chair we brought into the room for her, keeping us company.

"Did you enjoy the wedding before Damiano dragged you away?" Aunt Aida asks.

"Yes." I let out a chuckle. "Thank you for everything you did to make it a perfect wedding, Aunt Greta."

"You're welcome, *cara*."

"Oh, I just remembered," Aunt Aida says. "You can call me mamma or mom. Whichever you prefer."

I stop what I'm doing and drop the hanger on the floor.

"Really?"

When she nods, I rush to her, and leaning down, I wrap her up in a hug. "Thank you."

"No need to thank me," she chuckles as she pats my back. "We're family now."

Letting go of her, I get back to work.

Damiano comes into the closet, then glances over the clothes. "Is it all going to fit?"

"Yes." I shoot him a smile. "I'll make it fit."

"You can always leave your summer clothes in the other bedroom and just change it every season," Aunt Greta mentions.

"That's too much work," I reply.

Damiano's phone starts ringing, and I watch as he takes the call.

"What?" As he listens to whatever the other person is saying, a dark frown forms on his forehead. "I'm on my way."

My shoulders sag, and when he ends the call, he says, "I have to go to Manhattan. I'll try not to be long."

I walk to him, and wrapping my hand around the back of his neck, I lift myself on my tiptoes. I press a kiss to his mouth. "Be careful."

"I will." He gives me another kiss then pulls away to press a kiss to Mamma's temple. "Have fun while I'm gone."

"Fun?" Aunt Greta huffs. "We're working hard, and he calls it fun."

Laughing, we continue to work, and when I hear the helicopter take off, I hope the call wasn't anything too serious.

"I need a break," Aunt Greta says thirty minutes later. "Let's have some tea before round two."

"It's almost done. Martha and I can finish. Go rest."

"You sure?" she asks while helping Mamma to her feet.

"Yes. I'll be done in a few minutes."

Martha comes in, and when she sees Mamma and Aunt Greta leave, she says, "Go with them, Mrs. Falco. You've done more than enough."

Mrs. Falco. Sigh.

Tired, I don't put up a fight and give her a grateful smile. "Thank you, Martha."

I walk out of the walk-in closet and leave the suite. I take the stairs down to the first floor, and as I step into the foyer, there's a loud explosion, and the entire mansion shudders.

"*Dio!*" I scream with fright, pins and needles spreading over my body from shock. "What the hell was that?"

There's another loud explosion that's followed by gunfire erupting outside.

Shit!

My mind is still racing to catch up to what's happening as I run to the sitting room. Debris starts to fall around me like missiles aiming to kill me.

"Mamma!" I scream, my heart threatening to pound right out of my chest.

"Gabriella!" Gerardo shouts from the kitchen. "We're here."

I change direction and run toward the kitchen, and as I rush inside, the mansion groans before there are loud crashing sounds. It sounds like it's collapsing on top of us.

"*Caro Dio*," Mamma cries. "We need to call Damiano."

Gerardo grabs my hand and yanks me down beside the island.

"Stay down," he orders, his breaths bursting over his lips.

Seeing Mamma and Aunt Greta, I crawl closer to them and wrap my arm around Mamma.

"We have to call Damiano," she cries again.

My breaths rush over my lips as I say, "I don't have my phone. It's up in the bedroom."

"My phone is charging," Gerardo spits out.

The gunfire grows louder, and terrified of what might happen, I pull Mamma to her feet. "Come."

317

"Where are you going?" Gerardo snaps from where he's standing guard by the doorway.

"I'm finding a hiding place!" I hiss at him.

I open the pantry door and shove Mamma inside. "Sit down and make yourself as small as possible," I order before I pull boxes of coffee and sugar in front of her.

Luckily, we buy enough supplies to last us a couple of months, and I'm able to cover her partially.

"Stay here until one of us comes for you," I order before shutting the door.

As I take a step away from it, Gerardo starts to fire one bullet after the other.

"Out the back door!" our guard shouts, panic lacing his words. "Get to the armory and lock yourselves in the building."

"*Caro Dio!*" Aunt Greta sobs.

Just as she runs to me, Gerardo staggers back as bullets slam into him, and a second later, men pour into the kitchen.

Not thinking, I dive for Gerardo's gun as it skids across the floor, and as I lift my arms to fire the weapon, horror crashes through me as I see a bullet hit Aunt Greta in the chest.

"Noooooo!" I let out an agonizing scream, pulling the trigger until the gun clicks in my hand. I manage to hit two attackers, but there are too many.

A shocked silence buzzes in my ears as I try to make sense of what's happening. It's all too sudden, and I struggle to cope.

"Is that the fucking mother?" One of the men asks.

"The mother is blind," another replies.

I scramble to my feet and run to Aunt Greta. Pulling her into my arms, I press my hand to the wound.

As if it will help.

An intense feeling of acceptance spreads through my body as I look into Aunt Greta's eyes.

At least I got to experience some happiness before I die.

She lifts her hand to my cheek. "Tell Carlo I love him. It was an honor being his mother."

"I will," I lie while waiting for the bullets to hit me.

"Such a good girl," she gasps. "Love you."

My voice is thick with sorrow as I say, "I love you too."

I'm grabbed, and as they haul me away from Aunt Greta, she stretches her arm out to me as she gasps for air.

"No!" I cry, and I manage to yank free.

Instead of bullets riddling my body, I'm grabbed again. When I'm dragged out of the kitchen, I start to fight with all my strength, hitting, scratching, and kicking until I'm thrown onto the floor in the foyer.

"Fucking bitch," a man growls before a gun is pressed to my head. "Where is Mrs. Falco?" he demands, his tone aggressive.

My heart slams against my ribs, and I don't know where the strength comes from, but I glare at the man as I bite the words out, "You're looking at her." Holding my left hand up, I say, "I'm Mrs. Falco."

I know they're either going to take me or kill me right here, but hopefully, they won't look for Mamma.

One of the other men talks into a radio, "We have a young woman claiming to be Mrs. Falco."

'What does she look like?' I hear a familiar voice, but I can't place where I know it from.

His eyes roam over me. "Light brown hair. Pretty."

'Bring her.'

I'm hauled to my feet, and the gun remains trained on my head.

"What about the mother?" the one in charge asks.

'We have the wife. She'll do.'

If I let them take me, they might do much worse things to me.

With panic and fear swirling in my chest, I swing around, and my fist connects with the bastard behind me. I break out into a run toward the sunroom, but debris blocks my way, so I dart into Damiano's private sitting room.

Wildly, I glance around, but with no way of escaping, I turn to face the men as they follow me into the room.

The one who was talking on the radio stalks right at me, and when I try to put up a fight, he slams something hard against my head, and everything grows dark.

Chapter 34

Damiano

Carlo lands the helicopter on top of the building, and I wait for him to switch everything off.

"Who would attack the warehouse?" Carlo asks as he joins me

"I have no fucking idea," I mutter while sending Emilio a text demanding an update.

Anger vibrates in my chest as we walk toward the elevator.

When my phone vibrates, I read the message from Emilio.

Three men dead. Nothing was taken. It's weird. I don't feel it's safe for you to come here. Go to the club. I'll meet you there.

Letting out a sigh, I mutter, "We're going to the club. Emilio will meet us there."

The news of the attack was unexpected. Sure, an enemy can crawl out of a fucking hole at any time, but usually, things are quiet over the festive season.

We take the elevator down to the basement and head to the SUV, and soon, Carlo steers the vehicle in the direction of the club.

A couple of blocks from our destination my phone starts ringing while it buzzes with message after message.

"Jesus fucking Christ," I growl as I yank the device out of my pocket.

The words '*under attack*' catch my attention before I answer the call. "What?"

"We're being attacked!" Dante shouts, the noise of gunfire filling the background. "Fucking missiles hit the mansion! Four helicopters," he relays as much information to me as possible while I hear him fire his weapon.

"The mansion!" I shout at Carlo. "It's under attack."

Carlo makes an illegal U-turn in the middle of the road, the tires screeching, before he floors the gas to get us back to the helicopter.

My heart stutters in my chest as the harrowing news sinks in, and for a couple of seconds, I feel completely lost.

I hear Dante suck in harsh breaths. "I don't recognize anyone. Too many. It's an army."

Uncontrollable rage hits me hard, my body trembling from the violent emotion.

"Dante," I bark. "Where are my women?"

"Don't..."

I hear the phone hit something and listen as automatic gunfire continues to erupt in the background. It sounds like a fucking war zone.

Christ.

Gabriella. Mamma. Aunt Greta.

"What's happening?" Carlo growls, drawing my attention to him as he brings the SUV to a sudden stop in the parking area.

"The mansion is being attacked," I mutter, my tone dark as I shake my head. "It's all I know."

The elevator opens, and we rush inside. Carlo presses the button for the roof.

I still have the phone to my ear and listen as the gunfire dies down.

Who won?

Are my women safe?

"Move out," I hear a man shout, authority in his tone.

No.

"Is that the mother?" someone asks.

I grip the fabric over my heart as intense worry fills me.

"No–" I don't hear the rest of the reply as the sound of helicopters comes over the line.

They don't have Mamma.

Ice pours through my veins because there's only one other person they would take to hit me where it will hurt most.

Gabriella.

I suck in a harsh breath as intense worry and anger fills every inch of my body.

"Damiano!" Carlo snaps, the same worry I'm feeling etched onto his face. "What do you hear?"

"I think they just took Gabriella," I growl as I listen to the sounds of the helicopters fading away.

I'm stunned that someone would even dare to take me on.

Only those closest to me know where the mansion is.

This is an attack by someone I trusted.

I end the call with Dante and dial Emilio's number.

"I'm almost at the club, boss," he answers.

"Get every fucking man we have to the mansion. They hit my home." The words rumble from me as an avalanche of emotions crashes over me.

"Jesus, boss. We're on our way."

I end the call, and as I walk out onto the roof, I bring up the group chat for the other heads of the Cosa Nostra.

The moment Angelo's face appears, I don't wait for the others to answer and say, "They hit my fucking home."

"What?" he gasps, shock tightening his features.

Franco, Renzo, and Dario join the call.

"Someone attacked the lake mansion," I say, the words that are still hard to believe. "I need you. Meet me at the mansion."

"We're coming," Angelo replies, anger brimming in his voice.

As I climb into the helicopter, I bring up Gabriella's number, and even though I know she won't answer, I press dial.

The call instantly goes to voicemail, and I dial Gerardo's number.

As the helicopter lifts into the air, Gerardo's phone just rings, and desperation pours into my chest.

I start trying one number after the other, but they all either go straight to voicemail or go unanswered.

"I can't reach anyone," I growl.

"We'll be there soon," Carlos says, but I hear the dread in his voice.

Not soon enough.

We're already too late.

Someone fucking attacked me. Attacked my home. My women.

Just as I start to process the initial shock, the mansion comes into view, and my heart is ripped from my chest by the devastating sight.

"Christ," I whisper.

Smoke billows from the right wing, and there's a huge hole where my suite should be.

My suite.

That's where I left the women.

The bodies of all my guards and the enemy's men lay strewn over the yard.

Carlo sets the helicopter down, and I shove the door open. Jumping out of the aircraft, I break out into a run as I draw my gun from behind my back.

I have to jump over debris and bodies to get to the veranda.

When I run into the mansion, more bodies lie scattered over the floor. I recognize some of my men.

Carlo catches up to me. "Gerardo would've taken the women to the armory."

We rush toward the front door, but as I glance at the kitchen, I see Gerardo's body.

327

"Fuck!"

No! Christ. Please.

I change direction, and as we storm into the kitchen, Carlo lets out a wounded cry, "Ma!"

My eyes land on Aunt Greta, who's lying in a pool of blood.

Christ, no.

"Ma," Carlo cries again as he drops to his knees beside her. He checks her vitals, and when he begins to shake his head, my heart aches.

This is our worst nightmare.

"Ma," he whispers before he pulls her into his arms.

"Carlo?" I hear Mamma's frightened voice.

I hear boxes fall from the direction of the pantry and hurry to open the door.

Seeing my mother trying to stand up between boxes of coffee and sugar, the relief hits me so hard I can barely breathe.

"Mamma!" I grab hold of her, and lifting her out of the panty, I hug her fucking tight to my body. "Thank God."

"I'm sorry. I couldn't do anything," she starts to cry, her body trembling hard from the shock she suffered.

I glance at Carlo and see how he lays Aunt Greta back down before brushing his hand over her cheek.

"We'll find who's responsible for this and get our revenge," he whispers to her, then he gasps through his pain, "Jesus, Ma."

I take Mamma to where Carlo is and hate as the words fall over my lips, "Aunt Greta is gone. Stay with Carlo while I check the rest of the mansion."

Mamma lets out a sob as she carefully lowers herself to the floor. Her hand bumps against Carlo's arm, then she pulls him into a hug.

"I'm so sorry," she cries. "*Caro Dio.* We had no warning."

Sorrow hangs thick in the air as I walk to the doorway, but before I can leave, I hear Mamma say, "Gabriella! I think they took her. I couldn't hear everything, but when they asked where I was, she told them she's Mrs. Falco. It got quiet after that."

Dread shudders through me as Mamma confirms what I already knew deep down.

As I stand between the kitchen and the foyer, my eyes drift over all the destruction and bodies.

Pulling my phone from my pocket, I dial Dario's number.

"I'm thirty minutes out," he answers.

I can hear his R8 roaring as he pushes the sports car to its limits.

"Whoever attacked took Gabriella. Get facial recognition going and search the fucking globe for her."

"On it."

I end the call and stare at Mamma and Carlo as they mourn losing Aunt Greta.

I shove all the shock and grief to the back of my mind, and a deadly thirst for vengeance bleeds into my soul.

"Get up," I order. "We have work to do."

Chapter 35

Gabriella

My body jerks as I regain consciousness. My shoulders strain, and rope bites into my wrists as I jerk again from being hauled into the air.

A headache starts to pulse behind my temple, and when I crack my eyes open, I see a concrete floor beneath me.

Shit.

The memories of the attack pour through my mind.

I remember the mansion shuddering from loud blasts.

Gerardo falling.

Aunt Greta gasping for air.

Aunt Greta.

Dio, I hope she survives the gunshot.

I lift my head, and seeing two men in a room with me, horror ripples through me.

One of them secures the rope so it will keep me hanging in the air.

My shoes are gone, and the pencil dress I'm wearing is pulled up high on my thighs.

Shit.

"She's awake," one of the men mutters. "Get the boss."

Boss?

My mind starts racing, flashes of the attack hitting me while I worry about what's going to happen.

I hope Mamma's okay.

Maybe Damiano found out about the attack, and he got to her in time.

Damiano.

Suddenly, Stefano walks into the room, and my heart almost stops beating.

It was his voice I heard over the radio. Dio.

He stops a couple of feet away from me and just stares me up and down. Then, a smile slowly spreads over his face.

"Mrs. Falco," he sneers. "When did you get married?"

I lift my chin and lock eyes with him. "Yesterday."

One of his eyebrows lifts. "My invitation must've gotten lost in the mail."

"You weren't invited," I bite the words out through clenched teeth.

I can't believe he attacked us.

"Why?" I demand.

"Why not," he chuckles. "Damiano's not the only one with Falco blood in his veins." His features tighten with anger. "I'm older. I've watched him run the Cosa Nostra for far too long. It's my birthright to sit at the head of the table."

I shake my head. "Damiano's the *Capo dei Capi*."

"Not for long," Stefano hisses. "Once he's dead, I'll take over."

What reality does this man live in?

"The other four heads won't allow it," I argue.

Stefano steps closer to me until I feel his breath on my face. "They'll have no fucking choice but to follow me once I kill Damiano."

Dio. Is he insane?

We no longer live in the eighties where you can kill the *Capo dei Capi* and take over the family.

I've seen how close the five heads are.

"Good luck," I mutter. "You're going to need it."

He lets out a chuckle. "No, Gabriella, you're going to need it."

Shit.

He signals something to his men, and I watch as they bring a camera closer. They set it down on a metal table, and a red light comes on.

No.

I start to strain against the ropes, but it only makes them cut deeper into my wrists.

Stefano turns to his men while ordering, "Filippo, take off her dress."

NoNoNoNoNo!

As I begin to struggle again, my body swings, and one of the men grabs hold of me.

The man that Stefano called Filippo comes closer, and using scissors, he starts cutting my dress from the hem upward.

When I hear Stefano let out a bark of amused laughter, I force myself to stop fighting. Sucking in a deep breath, I find a spot on the wall to look at.

You will not cry.

You won't beg.

You're Damiano's wife. Don't give them anything.

The fabric is ripped off my body, and hanging in only my underwear, I keep repeating the words to myself.

What doesn't kill you makes you stronger.

You're Gabriella Falco. The wife of the Capo dei Capi.

They will not break you.

Stefano picks up an A4 piece of paper, and I get a glimpse of the words written on it before he walks closer to me.

Step down or she will die.

When Filippo picks up some kind of gun, horror pours through me, and I clench my jaw tighter.

Dio.

My breathing speeds up when Stefano pushes the piece of paper against my stomach.

Filippo presses the gun to the paper, and I brace myself for a lot of pain, but all I feel is a pinch as if I'm getting an injection.

I slowly let out a breath of relief.

"Send the recording to me," Stefano orders before walking out of the room.

That's it?

My eyes flit to Filippo, and I watch as he works on a laptop. The camera is still trained on me and recording.

With Stefano gone, I begin to feel the pain in my shoulders and wrists from hanging for so long.

Filippo nods at the other man who I forgot about, giving him a silent signal.

The men don't taunt me or show any emotion, and for some reason, it worries me more.

What's going to happen now?

I hear the man move in behind me, and suddenly, I feel an intense pain, and my body convulses violently. Every muscle locks into pace, cramping horribly.

The pain stops as quickly as it started, and I press my lips tightly together, staring at the wall again as I try to breathe through the shock of being electrocuted.

"Again," Filippo orders.

Dio. No!

Whatever they're using to shock me presses against my back, and my muscles instantly tighten, the pain spasming through me.

I'm unable to breathe, and on the fourth shock, an agonizing sound escapes my clenched teeth, and I instantly regret it because I don't want to give these men anything.

"One more," Filippo mutters.

What doesn't kill you makes you stronger.

My body shakes violently as the electric currents zaps through me, and when it stops, it's hard to lift my head as I suck in desperate breaths of air.

My mind is frazzled, and I struggle to process what just happened.

"Turn her around so her back is to the camera," Filippo instructs.

When the bastard takes hold of my hips and turns me to face him, I manage to shoot a glare at him.

"Step down, Falco," Filippo demands. "Or we will tear her apart."

Damiano will never do that.

"Got the burns for the recording," Filippo says. "You can let go of her."

The other guy's hands drop from me, and my body swings back into its original position.

Filippo works on the laptop, his features expressionless.

Dio, they're going to torture me.

This won't be a quick death.

My eyes find Filippo again, and with every ounce of strength I possess, I say, "Damiano will never submit."

He shrugs as he keeps working. "For your sake, I hope he does."

He won't. Never.

Chapter 36

Damiano

I'm standing in the armory with Angelo, Franco, Renzo, and Dario.

Dario's set up a working station for himself by my systems where he's searching for anything that can help us find out who's behind the attack.

My phone starts ringing, and letting out a growl, I pull the device from my pocket.

"What?" I snap.

"The club," Pippa, the manager of my club, says. Panic laces the words. "There was a car bomb, Mr. Falco. It blew the side wall away. We won't be able to open."

"Motherfucking Christ," I shout. "Deal with the shit. I'm busy."

"Yes, sir."

I end the call, and before I can throw my phone against the wall, Carlo grabs it from me.

"We need the phone," he reminds me. "In case the fucker calls."

The fucker, being the person who's attacking me.

I let him keep the phone as I stalk a few steps away before turning to face the men.

"Who is behind the attacks?" I bark.

"We took out Miguel's entire family, but maybe it's one of his men," Angelo says.

"No. The person knew where the mansion was. Who else?"

"Besides us, who knows the location of the mansion?" Franco asks.

"My men." My eyes flick over the other four heads. "Your men and women."

"It wasn't one of us," Renzo mutters, cautiously watching me.

"My aunt on my father's side and my cousin." My eyes narrow as I glance at Carlo. "Would Stefano have the balls to attack me?"

He shakes his head. "He doesn't have the manpower or weapons to launch such a big assault on us."

"I have the footage of the attack," Dario says. "Well, part of it. They wiped out some of the surveillance cameras as they entered."

I stalk to where Dario's sitting and stop behind him. My eyes latch onto the screens, and I watch as the four helicopters approach.

"Those are black hawks," Renzo mutters from next to me.

"No fucking shit," I grumble.

I watch as the attack begins, and it makes my rage burn a million times hotter.

My men didn't stand a chance.

"Pause!" I snap when a man stalks out onto the veranda with Gabriella draped over his shoulder.

My fucking heart breaks seeing her in the enemy's clutches, but I forcefully shove the emotion down and focus on his face.

"Find out who that fucker is. I want a name!"

"On it," Dario says, immediately getting to work.

Within seconds he has the information for me.

"Filippo Vero. He's a mercenary for hire," Dario murmurs. "Fuck, Damiano. He has the best team out there. Why the hell would he attack you?"

"Jesus fucking Christ," Renzo hisses. When our eyes flick to him, he shakes his head as he takes a step backward. "That's the big arms deal I completed last week. He's the buyer I told you about."

Fuck.

"I remember you mentioned it at the poker game," Franco says.

Renzo's eyes lock with mine. "I didn't know it would be used against you."

"Someone hired him," Angelo says. "Someone who knew where to hit so it would hurt you most."

Stefano.

Fuck. It can only be Stefano.

Is he really that fucking insane to come for me?

I look at Carlo. "Does Stefano have enough money to hire mercenaries?"

Carlo's features are drawn tight with grief, and I can see he's struggling to think before he replies, "I have no fucking idea."

"Give me Stefano's full name, and I'll find out," Dario says.

"Stefano Falco Ferraro," I mutter.

"Seriously?" Dario asks. "Falco is his second name?"

"Yes. It's the way his mother wanted it," I reply.

Just as Dario starts to type, Carlo says, "There's a message from Stefano on your phone."

As I walk to Carlo, I tell Dario, "Trace the following number." I ramble the number to him before grabbing my phone from Carlo.

Opening the message, there's a video. I press play.

Intense pain shudders through me when I see Gabriella hanging from a ceiling. She's straining against the ropes around her wrists, then I hear Stefano say, "Filippo, take off her dress."

Christ.

No.

Don't force me to watch the fuckers rape her.

Gabriella tries in vain to free herself, and it makes my fucking heart bleed.

A man grabs hold of her to keep her still, and Filippo starts to cut the dress from her body.

Amused laughter sounds up from Stefano, but I can't see him.

I'm going to fucking tear him apart.

I watch as the emotionless mask settles over Gabriella's face, and she stops struggling. She just stares ahead at something I can't see.

They rip the dress off her, then the stubborn defiance that made me fall for her begins to burn in her eyes.

She lifts her chin higher, not giving them anything.

Christ, my little spitfire.

"Damiano?" Carlo asks, stepping closer.

"Stay back," I bark as I move away from him so he can't see the screen.

I watch as Stefano presses something to her stomach, and then Filippo fucking staples it to her.

Step down or she will die.

The recording stops, and I lock the screen of my phone before I toss the device at Carlo.

The rage pouring into my veins burns hotter than the sun.

The footage of Gabriella hanging helplessly in a fucking cold room where men are going to torture her pushes me to my limits.

I stalk out of the armory and keep going until I walk into the lining of trees.

Only when I'm sure I'm alone, and no one will see me, do I suck in a shuddering breath before letting out a heartbreaking groan.

Gabriella.

I close my eyes as wave after wave of pain hits, and it feels like someone's trying to claw my heart out of my chest.

La mia regina.

My entire body trembles, and it takes more strength than I have to push all the pain down.

I suck in a desperate breath, and tilting my head back, I stare at the treetops.

You're the Capo dei Capi.

The responsibility for the family rests on your shoulders.

I take another deep breath.

There's no stepping down. You will face this head-on.

Whatever happens, you will stay strong.

I shake my head because, for the first time in my life, I'm faced with an impossible situation.

Gabriella or the family.

"Damiano," Angelo calls.

I glance over my shoulder and watch as the four capos walk toward me.

Squaring my shoulders, I turn around so I can face them.

They stop in front of me, and Angelo says, "An attack on you is an attack on all of us. We are a family. Tell us what you want us to do so we can bring Gabriella home."

I stare at them, and lifting my chin, I focus on Dario. "Find out where Stefano is hiding."

I look at Angelo and Franco. "Get every available man ready for war. Take my mother, your women, and the children and place them in a safe house. We don't need anyone else being taken."

Lastly, I turn my attention to Renzo. "I want every weapon you can get your hands on."

They all nod, and turning around, they walk away to carry out the orders.

I head back to the armory, and when I step inside, I hear my phone buzz.

Christ.

My eyes touch on Carlo's before I take the device from him.

Sucking in a deep breath, I brace myself for the worst before I open the message.

There's another video, and I press play.

I watch as a man steps in behind Gabriella. I take in every single fucking detail about him.

He's shorter than average. Brown hair in a buzz cut. The usual combat uniform. Gloves.

When I catch glimpses of a cattle prod, my fist tightens around my phone.

Fuck.

When he presses the prod to her back, I'm forced to watch as every muscle in Gabriella's body strains while she convulses horribly.

When it stops breaths explode from her before she presses her lips tightly together and lifts her chin.

Jesus, she's so fucking strong.

"Again," I hear someone order.

She's electrocuted three more times, and when a wounded sound escapes her, my heart fucking shatters.

"One more," the order comes again.

No. Jesus, stop.

It hurts more than anything I've ever endured to watch as Gabriella convulses and pain tightens her features. When it stops, her head falls forward, and I hear her gasping for air.

Christ, I wish I could swap places with her.

"Turn her around so her back is to the camera," the other fucker says.

He turns Gabriella until I see her back where the five burn marks mar her skin.

"Step down, Falco," the unknown man, who I assume is Filippo demands. "Or we will tear her apart."

"Never," I growl.

"What is it?" Carlo asks.

346

"Videos of the fuckers torturing Gabriella," I mutter, my tone filled with the promise of death. "They want me to step down, or she dies."

He sucks in a deep breath before letting it out slowly. "What are we going to do?"

Locking eyes with my second-in-charge, I growl, "We're going to war."

Chapter 37

Gabriella

When I startle awake, my entire body aches so badly, I let out a gasp before groaning.

Dio.

They left me hanging overnight, and the room is freezing. The extreme chill in my body makes the pain so much worse.

There's complete silence as I glance around the room.

Yesterday, I was too shocked by the attack and torture to take in anything.

I see a metal table and various tools and knives. There's also a stick with prongs, which they used to electrocute me with. The laptop is still on the table, and the camera's pointed at me. It looks like I'm in a basement.

Knowing I'm being recorded, I lift my head and school my face into an emotionless expression.

What doesn't break you makes you stronger.

With nothing to do but think, my thoughts turn to the attack.

Aunt Greta. Gerardo. Martha.

Sorrow pours into my chest.

Please let Aunt Greta be okay. Dio. I hope they got to her in time.

When a lump forms in my throat, I try to swallow it down.

Before I'm able to process my sorrow, it sinks in hard that I've been taken captive. I've been stripped to my underwear, and the piece of paper is still stapled to my stomach.

My harrowing situation fills me with immense dread, the realization that I won't get out of here alive shuddering through me.

My first thought isn't about where I'll go when I die but about everything I'll miss out on.

There was so much I wanted to do.

I'll never become a mother.

I won't get to go on my honeymoon with Damiano.

Damiano.

I won't see him again.

The heartache tearing through me is too much to handle, and my mind scrambles to shove all the emotions into the darkest corner of my soul.

It was so much easier when my parents used to abuse me because I didn't know any different.

Now that I've felt loved and have so much more to lose, it's unbearable.

I don't want to die.

Not now.

Not like this.

I hear the lock turning, and my chin lifts higher. I suck in a fortifying breath and find the spot on the wall to stare at.

Whatever happens, don't show them any emotion.

Don't break.

You're a mafia queen.

You're Gabriella Falco.

"Morning," Filippo greets me as he walks into the room. "Did you get some sleep?"

What?

I don't bother answering the bastard.

He types something on the laptop, and when the other man from yesterday enters the room, Filippo says,

"Morning, Manny. Give her a bathroom break before we get started."

Manny unwinds the rope from the hook, and I'm lowered to the floor. The strain in my arms relents when I'm finally able to bring them down, but then a sharp pain shoots through my shoulders.

Jesus.

I can't stop a gasp from escaping my lips.

The rope remains around my wrists, and Manny uses it as a leash while shoving me forward so I'll start walking. My legs feel numb, but I manage to put one foot in front of the other.

Even though pins and needles are spreading through my arms, I grab hold of the piece of paper and rip it away from my stomach. Crumpling it, I throw it to the floor.

Bastards.

Lifting my chin high, I walk out of the room.

"Go right," Manny orders as he shoves me from behind, making the burns on my back sting.

I clench my jaw and walk down a dimly lit hallway.

"Up the stairs," he snarls.

It's so cold my body trembles uncontrollably, but I don't want to show them I'm freezing and resist the urge to wrap my arms around myself.

351

Once I reach the top of the stairs, he again orders, "The door on your left."

I walk into a small restroom that reeks as if it's never been cleaned.

Dio. I hope I don't catch an STD from the seat.

When I turn around to close the door, I mutter, "The rope."

Manny shakes his head.

Stubborn as hell, I shove the door until the rope stops it, but at least it offers me some cover.

I struggle to move my underwear down, and keeping myself braced over the seat so my butt doesn't touch it, I quickly relieve my bladder.

There's no toilet paper, so I try to pull up my underwear as quickly as possible.

While I'm glancing down, I take in my matching black lace underwear set, and I feel a flicker of panic. It's the first time in my life I regret not wearing granny panties.

If they really want to hurt Damiano, they'll rape me.

It's inevitable.

Dio.

I suck in a quivering breath and shut my eyes as the fear of being raped creates a tense knot in my chest.

"Hurry up!" Manny snaps.

Yanking on the rope, he makes the door shudder open.

I quickly flush the toilet, then lifting my chin, I force my features not to show any of the fear I feel and step out of the restroom.

Walking back to the basement I try to brace for whatever they're going to do to me today.

How long will they keep trying to force Damiano to step down?

A few days?

Hours?

How long do I have before they kill me?

Entering the room where I'll be tortured and killed, panic flares hot in my chest.

Just reacting, I swing around and slam my tied hands into the side of Manny's neck before I try to make a run for it. He yanks the rope back, and it rips me off my feet. My side slams into the cold, hard floor, and air wooshes from my lungs.

Manny pulls at the rope and starts to drag me across the floor before hauling my body into the air once more.

He fastens the rope around a hook on the wall, then shoots me a glare.

"Let's start with the cattle prod," Filippo orders, seemingly unbothered by my pathetic escape attempt.

Dio.

I suck in deep breaths of air, and finding the spot on the wall, I do my best to focus on it as I brace for the pain.

Chapter 38

Damiano

With Mamma and the other women and children safe, we all focus on getting everything ready for the attack.

Impatient as fuck, I glance at Dario, who hasn't stopped working since I gave the order. "Do you know where Stefano is?"

"His phone signal is bouncing off three towers. I have the area but not a precise location."

"Where?" I bark.

"Somewhere near Manorville. Just over an hour away by car."

My phone buzzes, and I rip the device out of my pocket. Unlocking the screen there are more messages from Stefano.

I haven't tried to call him, because then I'd be playing straight into his hands.

They've had Gabriella for twenty-four hours now, and I try to brace for the worst as I open the text.

You're quiet, cousin. I hope you don't think you have any other option than to step down.

I suck in a deep breath before pressing play on the attached video.

It shows Gabriella still hanging from the ceiling by a rope.

She must be in so much fucking pain.

"Let's get started," the same man from the other recordings orders.

Again, they use a cattle prod to electrocute her, and by the time they're done, Gabriella breathes heavily through the pain.

Her eyes flick to the camera, and I want to reach through the fucking phone and yank her to me, but instead, I'm forced to feel as my heart is pulverized to dust.

For a moment, she looks directly into the camera lens, and I know she's speaking to me when she whispers, "Don't surrender."

The fucker behind her presses the prod to her back again and keeps it there until she loses consciousness.

Christ.

"We're heading out," I roar. "Right fucking now!"

My phone starts to ring, and seeing Stefano's name, I accept the call and wait for him to speak first.

"Cousin," he snarls, "do you have good news for me?"

"Just how fucking stupid are you?" I say, my tone as deadly as it's ever been.

"Careful. I have the upper hand."

I almost fucking laugh. "You do? Let's say a miracle happens, and you get rid of me. Do you really think the other four heads will call you their capo?"

"They will have no choice. When I overthrow you, they must accept me as their new capo."

Has he lost his fucking mind?

"This isn't the nineteen-eighties. You don't get to just kill me and take over."

Dario gestures excitedly that he has Stefano's location.

"Step down, or Gabriella dies," he hisses.

I just need enough time to get to her.

Fuck.

I hear myself suck in a harsh breath, and then I lie through my fucking teeth, "I'll step down."

I never thought those words would leave my mouth, but I'm willing to say anything to protect Gabriella and the family.

I'm not prepared to lose either of them.

Stefano lets out a burst of laughter. "You made the right choice."

"What now?" I ask.

"You have one hour to send me a video of the other four killing you, and I'll let Gabriella go."

I shake my head because it's fucking hard to believe that Stefano is so stupid and arrogant to think his plan will work.

I end the call, and dropping the phone, I grab the nearest cabinet and rip it from the wall. Glass shatters as it hits the floor, and it does nothing to calm the violent storm in my soul.

When I stop and suck in a harsh breath, it's to find Angelo, Renzo, Franco, and Dario all staring at me.

"It was a fucking lie," I roar at them, my entire body vibrating with rage. "I'll never step down."

When they see the vengeance on my face, they seem to relax.

"Dario, send photos of Stefano and Filippo to everyone. I want them taken alive." I stalk toward the door. "Let's end this fucking war."

When I walk out of the armory and see Emilio, Vito, Tommy, and the rest of my army waiting for their orders, I shout, "You will receive photos of two men. You can wound, but don't kill. Move out!"

Carlo falls into step beside me as we walk to one of the SUVs at the front of the line, and I climb into the passenger seat.

Breathe, Damiano. You need a clear head for the attack.

Once you have Stefano and Gabriella's safe, you can lose your fucking mind.

Carlo shoves a bulletproof vest at me. "Put it on right now."

Letting out a frustrated growl because every second is precious, I get out of the SUV and put on the fucking vest before climbing back in and yanking the door shut.

"Go!" I order.

Dario slides into the back with Angelo, who drops a heavy bag of weapons on the floor between the seats.

"I've sent the GPS coordinates to everyone," Dario informs me.

I watch as Carlo brings up the map on the GPS screen, and after starting the engine, he steers the SUV away from the mansion.

"How do you want to handle this?" Angelo asks.

"We attack and get Gabriella out alive."

"The property is nestled between trees," Dario begins to give us a rundown of what to expect. "We'll head up North

Road until it becomes Mill. There aren't many houses, and it's a fucking long stretch of road."

My eyes flick to the map, and I hate that it will take another hour and five minutes to get to Gabriella.

"Faster, Carlo," I growl. "We need to make it to Gabriella in fifty minutes." Glancing over my shoulder, I look at Dario and ask, "Can you get plans for the property?"

"I can try," Dario mutters before he gets to work.

Silence falls between us, and when we're twenty minutes out, my phone buzzes.

I unlock the screen, and seeing another video from Stefano, the blood chills in my veins.

Did he call my bluff?

My thumb hesitates over the video because I won't be able to handle watching Gabriella die.

"Damiano," Carlo says to get my attention. My eyes flick to his. "Let Angelo watch the video."

I shake my head hard. "No."

She's my wife. The love of my fucking life. No one but me will see these videos.

I turn my gaze back to the screen and press play.

I see Stefano come into view as he moves closer to Gabriella.

360

"Damiano surrendered," he sneers. "Two months with you, and he turned so fucking soft he'd die for you."

She starts to shake her head. "No! Damiano will never surrender."

"I should hear of his death within the hour," Stefano says. "Or you die."

She clenches her jaw, her eyes burning with rage on the bastard.

He moves closer, and reaching out a hand, he trails a finger from between her breasts to her navel.

His tone is low as he says, "You'll be a widow soon."

Fucking fucker. Get your hands off her!

Gabriella lifts her chin, and she stares ahead of her, the expressionless mask I fucking hate back on her face.

But this time, I'm thankful for it.

Don't show any emotion, mia regina. Stay strong. I'm coming.

"Faster!" I roar as if I can change what's about to happen by getting there sooner.

Stefano walks out of sight, and when he comes back into view, he's holding a knife.

No.

Christ, please. Don't do this to me. Don't make me watch my wife die.

"But I don't want Damiano's leftovers," Stefano says as he drags the blade over her stomach.

My breathing speeds up, my eyes locked on the screen.

Every muscle in my body tenses until it feels like I might snap.

Slowly, he pushes the knife into her right side, and I see every single excruciating inch of the blade sinking into her.

"Motherfucker!"I roar as I slam my fist into the dashboard.

No.

Fuck.

Gabriella's body twitches, and for a moment, her eyebrows draw together as pain flashes over her face. But then she fucking schools her face into a neutral expression again as she lets out a breath.

Jesus, she's stronger than me.

"Let's see who dies first. You or Damiano." Stefano turns around to face the camera, "You're running out of time, cousin. The sooner you die, the quicker she'll get medical attention. Miss the hour mark, and I'll slit her throat."

My eyes flick to the GPS, and I see we're ten minutes out.

"What time did we leave?" I ask.

"We have nineteen minutes," Carlo answers. "We'll make it in time."

"We better," I growl. Glancing over my shoulder, I order, "Give me a submachine gun and knife."

Angelo opens the bag and begins to hand out weapons as our convoy race down a dirt road that looks like it's heading into the woods.

Chapter 39

Damiano

Dirt shoots into the air as we come to a screeching stop in the lot at the front of the property. The house is medium-sized and looks like it hasn't been painted in the last decade.

There are a dozen armed men scattered around the property, and they open fire on the SUVS while they try to find cover against the sides of the house.

I shove the door open and order, "Launch the fucking grenades!"

Tommy sends a grenade flying into the side of the house where a group of men are taking cover, and bodies fly into the air.

Using the door as a shield, I open fire on the fuckers that are shooting from inside the house, and I have to reload the magazine before I'm able to move away from the SUV. With the submachine gun held in position, I run toward the house while shooting every fucking man I lay eyes on.

364

My vision tunnels on the front door, and I riddle it with bullets before my body slams into the wood. It gives way easily, and I keep going, taking out target after target until I'm out of fucking bullets.

As I drop the submachine gun so I can reach for my Glock, a body plows into me. I grab the knife from my belt, and before my back even hits the floor, I plunge the knife repeatedly into the side of his neck.

Blood spurts over me, and I slam into the floor with a grunt. Shoving the dead fucker off of me, I quickly dart back to my feet. I move the knife to my left hand and rip the Glock from behind my back.

Carlo and Angelo join me, and while they take out the rest of the men, I hear Renzo shout from outside, "I have Stefano!"

"Keep the fucker alive," my voice thunders through the house as I hurry from room to room, searching for Gabriella.

When I open a door with stairs leading down to a basement, a bullet slams into my bulletproof vest, forcing me a couple of steps backward.

My arm swings into the air, and I pull the trigger as I move forward.

Another bullet zips past my head just as Carlo grabs hold of the back of my vest, yanking me to crouch on the stairs.

"Stay the fuck down while I take care of the asshole," Carlo mutters, breathless from all the action.

Reluctantly, I stay crouched as Carlo creeps down the stairs, and when he reaches the bottom, a short gunfight ensues before he takes out whoever's down there.

"Clear," he shouts. "Gabriella's not here."

"Fuck!" I snarl, and turning around, I run back into the hallway.

"Damiano!" Carlo calls, wanting me to wait for him, but I need to find Gabriella before it's too late.

Entering a kitchen, I see a back door and head outside. With my gut telling me to head for the trees, I break out into a run.

Don't let me be wrong. Christ. Please.

My breaths explode over my lips as I run into the woods, and every few steps, I pause to listen for any movement, hoping for confirmation that Filippo's out here with Gabriella.

Fuck. Am I wrong?

"Move!" I hear a man hiss, and intense relief and anger swirl into a potent mixture in my chest.

Carlo catches up to me as I run in the direction I heard the voice, and I finally catch sight of Filippo as he forces Gabriella to run barefoot through the fucking woods.

"Stop," she gasps, clutching her side where blood is coating her hand.

Motherfucker!

Letting out a growl, I lift my arms, and training my barrel on the fucker's shoulder, I pull the trigger.

The bullet hits, and he spins to the side, his hand coming up as he opens fire on me.

"No!" Gabriella screams, and forgetting about her own safety, she fucking throws her body at Filippo and tries to fight him for control of his gun.

"Gabriella!" I shout as I run toward them.

Another shot echoes through the woods, and the blood in my veins chills with fear.

Filippo throws Gabriella off him and trains his gun on her, and Carlo and I open fire as we rush toward them, one bullet after the other slamming into the fucker. His body jerks with each shot before he falls backward, gasping through the shock and pain.

Coming to a stop beside Filippo, I train my barrel on his head and lock eyes with him before I pull the trigger again.

As Gabriella climbs to her feet, my eyes snap to her.

She's alive.

The amount of relief flooding through my soul paralyzes me for a few seconds, and I can only suck in desperate breaths of air as I stare at her.

Then my eyes drift over her shivering body, and not seeing any gunshot wounds, I dart forward. My arms lock around her, and I squash her to me.

A painful gasp from her has me instantly easing my grip, and I quickly crouch down so I can check the stab wound to her side. I've stabbed enough people in my time to know whether the wound is serious or not, and I let out a breath when I see it's not too serious.

I straighten up again, and there are no words to say what I feel as I see the breaths rushing over her lips. The fight and life shining from her eyes ease the tension in my chest.

She's alive.

The realization shudders through me again, and I thank all that's holy that I got to her in time.

"You're bleeding," she says as she reaches her bloody hand to my face.

"It's not mine," I mutter while I grip hold of her hand. Feeling how fucking cold she is, I'm hit by another wave of anger.

"Damiano!" I hear Dario shout.

Taking a step back from Gabriella, my eyes flick over the lace bra and panties, and I quickly take off the bulletproof vest so I can get the long-sleeved shirt off my body.

Once I have the shirt covering my wife, Carlo hands me his coat, and I quickly wrap it around her.

I hate that Carlo saw her half naked, but I'm too relieved to feel any anger.

When I bend to pick her up, she shakes her head. "No. I can walk."

"The fuck you can," I snarl.

"Damiano," she snaps at me.

Our eyes lock, and she lifts her chin. "I will walk out of here. I need your men to see I haven't been broken."

Holy fucking Christ.

As much as I hate the idea of her walking barefoot, I relent because this is important to her.

She wants to show them she's their queen, and that no matter what's thrown her way, she will survive. Nothing can break her.

Standing in the middle of the fucking woods on an icy winter's day with blood soaking into the ground, I fall in love with Gabriella all over again.

Needing to touch her, I wrap my arm around her shoulders before we walk back through the trees.

When Dario and Angelo come into sight, I drop my arm from around her and take hold of her left hand where her blood is drying and link our fingers.

"Is everyone okay?" Dario asks as we reach him.

"Yes," I reply.

When we break through the trees, all the men of the Cosa Nostra, one by one, look in our direction.

Gabriella tightens her grip on my hand, and I hear her suck in a trembling breath before she pushes through her pain and walks toward the nearest SUV.

Once I have her safely inside the vehicle, I wrap my fingers around the back of her neck and press my forehead to hers. "I'm so fucking proud of you, *mia regina.*"

She nods, her skin way too fucking pale.

Letting go of her, I turn to face my men.

"Clean up the shit and go home to your families," I order.

"Yes, boss," the chorus sounds up.

Glancing at the other four heads, I nod my thanks to them before locking eyes with Angelo. "Keep my mother with you until I come to get her."

"Take your time," he replies. "Vitorria will love the company."

Only then do I lock eyes with Stefano, where he's being restrained by Emilio and Vito.

"Take the fucker to the warehouse. I'll deal with him later."

They nod before shoving him into an SUV.

Looking at Tommy, I order, "Take a team of men and go to Sicily. Bring me Cettina Ferraro and the di Bella family alive. Make them think they're coming for the wedding."

I want to break the news to them in person that they're going to die. I want to savor their fear before they're killed.

With all the orders out of the way, I climb into the backseat and pull Gabriella into my arms.

She's shaking like a leaf in a fucking shitstorm, and I struggle not to hold her too tight.

Carlo slides behind the steering wheel, and Renzo takes the passenger seat.

"I've let the clinic know we're coming," he informs me while tossing a first-aid bag at me.

I quickly open the bag, and taking out antiseptic wipes, I move the clothes out of the way so I can get to the stab wound on Gabriella's side.

Once it's as clean as it can be in the backseat of the fucking SUV, I grab some gauze and pressing it firmly against the wound, I order, "Hold it in place."

She does as I instruct while I dig out an adhesive dressing, and when I have it stuck to her skin, I take a few seconds to clean the puncture marks from where they stapled the fucking paper to her stomach.

"I'm fine," she mutters. "I can hold out until we get to the clinic."

I only nod as I take hold of Gabriella's chin, nudging her face up so she'll look at me.

Our eyes lock, and I stare at my woman with so much fucking pride pouring into my chest.

In this moment, where I get to touch her, I realize Gabriella is the most dangerous person I've ever met because she has the power to control me.

"*Ti amo, mia regina*," I whisper, so fucking thankful I get to say the words to her again.

"*Ti amo, mio re.*"

I can see she's struggling to keep it together and it takes a swing at my heart.

"It's okay," I murmur. "You don't have to be strong anymore. I'm here."

She shakes her head and shoots a glance at Renzo and Carlo, and once a-fucking-gain, she somehow shoves all her trauma away and holds her head high, refusing to break in front of them.

Chapter 40

Gabriella

I was allowed a very quick shower before a nurse tended to my wounds.

I sit on the side of the hospital bed, and clench my jaw while I watch as Damiano talks with a doctor.

I just want to be alone with my husband.

Somehow, I manage to keep my expression neutral as I struggle to keep all my emotions from spiraling out of control.

Finally, the nurse leaves, and I slip off the bed. Even though my feet are raw and ache from running barefoot through the damn woods, I walk to the window and pull the blinds shut.

"I'll take her home first thing tomorrow morning," I hear Damiano tell the doctor while I gingerly move back to the bed.

I brace my right hand on the white sheets and suck in a desperate breath of air.

I hear the door shut, and I glance at Damiano to make sure we're alone.

I suck in another breath of air, then all the trauma I've been forced to endure shudders through my body.

Damiano moves closer to me, and when his fingers wrap around the back of my neck, I can't keep the sobs back any longer.

The floodgates open, and every degrading moment, the pain, the cold, the fear – it all creates a chaotic mess in my chest, forcing a broken cry over my lips.

Damiano gently pulls me into his arms, and he tries to avoid the burns on my back as he holds me to his chest.

I smell his familiar scent.

I feel the heat from his body.

And finally able to let go of being strong, I break in his arms.

"I've got you, *amore mia*," the words rumble from him.

I bring my hand up and clutch his shirt in a fist as I struggle to breathe through the sobs.

He just holds me, giving me a safe place to cry over what was done to me.

They didn't break you. After everything you were forced to endure, you're stronger.

Damiano presses a kiss to my temple, then murmurs, "I'm here, my little spitfire. You're safe."

Once I manage to calm down, I whisper, "I was so scared I'd never see you again."

He pulls a little back and tilts his head so he can meet my eyes. Using his thumbs to brush the tears off my cheeks, he says, "I'll always come for you."

Seeing the blood splatters on his face and neck, I take his hand and pull him toward the bathroom. I find a washcloth and wet it beneath the spray.

When I bring it to his neck and start to clean the blood off him, he mutters, "Don't worry about it. I'll shower while you're resting."

"Let me do this," I whisper, my voice hoarse from crying.

Once every last drop of blood has been wiped from his skin, I toss the cloth into the sink.

With my head bowed, I ask, "Did Aunt Greta make it?"

Damiano lets out a slow breath. "No."

Dio.

My hands fly up to cover my face as intense grief seizes my heart in a relentless grip.

No.

Damiano pulls me back to his chest as a heavy blanket of sorrow falls over my shoulders.

Unable to accept she's gone, I choke the words out, "No. *Dio*. Not Aunt Greta."

She was so full of life and love.

How am I supposed to process that the first person to hug me, to show me any kind of love, is gone?

We'll never feel her warmth again. We'll never hear her laughter.

"We lost Gerardo and Martha as well," Damiano says.

I start to cry again, the losses we've suffered too much to bear.

Damiano gently picks me up, and carrying me back into the room, he sits down on an armchair.

His arm brushes over the burns on my back, making me flinch.

"Straddle me," he orders.

I do as I'm told, and pressing my face to his chest, I mourn the loss of the people I got to love for such a short while.

"Shh, *amore mia*," he whispers. "I'm here."

I feel feverish when the tears stop, and I just lie still against his chest.

This is the world we live in. We'll love, and we'll lose.

Somehow, I manage to dose on and off for a while.

The door opens, and I hear Carlo say, "I brought you some clothes from the house in Manhattan."

"Thanks," Damiano murmurs. "Have Emilio come to the clinic so you can get some rest."

I glance over my shoulder and see Carlo shake his head. "I'm not leaving. I'll be right outside the room."

"Carlo," I say as he starts to turn around. When he looks at me, I continue, "I'm so sorry for your loss."

He nods before pulling the door shut behind him as he leaves.

"Want to move to the bed so you can sleep while I shower?" Damiano asks.

I nod and climb off his lap. He picks up the bag Carlo brought, and when I follow him to the bathroom, he gives me a questioning look.

"I just want to brush my teeth."

Damiano sets the bag down on the closed toilet lid and digs out a toothbrush and toothpaste for me.

I take it from him, and while I clean my teeth, he switches on the faucets in the shower.

I watch as he strips out of his clothes before I rinse my mouth. Checking the bag, I'm surprised to see Carlo packed a satin robe for me. I quickly take off the hospital gown before putting on my robe. I don't find any underwear but refuse to put on the weird-looking granny panties of the hospital.

Feeling a little better with my own robe on, my eyes scour Damiano's body, and when I'm sure he hasn't been hurt in any way, I walk back to the bed and sit down on the side of the mattress.

I listen to Damiano moving in the bathroom while I stare at the red abrasions around my wrists.

I'm so lucky Damiano got to me in time.

I've survived so much in my life, and it's the reason I don't take anything for granted.

But this is the closest I've come to dying.

They could've done so much worse to me.

I send up a thankful prayer that I wasn't raped.

Once Damiano's finished in the bathroom, he comes back into the room, his eyes instantly locking on me.

"You're not going to sleep?"

"I can't lie on my back or right side," I say. "Can I sleep on your lap?"

"Of course, *amore mia*."

I wait for him to sit down on the armchair before I climb on top of him again. Straddling him, I pull my arms up between us and rest my cheek against his chest.

I lie still for a little while before lifting my head and asking, "Can you remove your shirt?"

Damiano tugs the fabric over his head, and when I open my robe, he mutters, "You're in no condition to have sex."

"I just want to be as close to you as possible." I lean against him again, and when the heat from his skin soaks into my chest, I let out a sigh.

Much better.

I press a kiss to his chest and take a deep breath of his clean, woodsy scent.

I feel Damiano's cock harden beneath me, then his hands settle on my hips, and he lets out a sigh.

"You okay?" I ask.

"I can feel the heat of your pussy through the sweatpants," he grumbles.

I move a little back, and reaching down, I push down the fabric of his pants to free his cock.

"What are you doing?" The words rumble from him.

I position him at my entrance and slowly sink down on his cock. When he's buried to the hilt inside me, I say, "I just want to feel you everywhere."

"You're warming my cock, *mia regina*?"

"Hmm…" I relax against his chest. "Warming my pussy. It was so cold without you."

380

Damiano places a hand behind my head and presses a kiss to my hair.

He doesn't try to fuck me, but instead, lets out a satisfied groan as he relaxes beneath me. "I can get used to sleeping like this."

The corner of my mouth lifts slightly. "Me too."

The heat from Damiano's body chases the chill from mine, and closing my eyes, I manage to drift off to sleep.

Chapter 41

Damiano

I got little to no sleep with my cock buried deep inside Gabriella. Not fucking her is impossibly hard, but she needs the rest, so I power through.

I deserve a fucking gold medal for the sweet torture I'm forced to endure.

Then she fucking stirs against my chest, and her pebbled nipples brush over my skin.

Christ.

When her inner muscles clamp around my cock, I let out a harsh breath, sweat beading at the back of my neck.

Before I can ask if she's awake, Gabriella slowly starts to swivel her hips.

I let out a groan, my fingers digging into her ass cheeks. "You're killing me."

"Hmm…"

She rubs her clit against me, the movements quickly pushing me toward an orgasm.

"*Amore mia*," I grunt. "You're going to make me come."

"That's the plan," she moans before starting to press kisses to my pecs. "You feel so good." Her teeth tug at my nipple. "You taste even better."

I don't stand a chance against my wife, and I thrust up once before shooting my release into her wet warmth.

My body shudders from the extreme fucking pleasure after being tortured for hours.

"Christ," I gasp through ragged breaths, my cock jerking inside her while my body loses all strength.

Gabriella curls against my chest, her muscles tensing before I feel her orgasm hit. Her quivering breaths explode over my skin, and I bury my hands in her hair to pull her head back so I can claim her lips.

The moment I kiss her, a peaceful feeling fills my heart.

My mouth worships hers for long minutes before I finally end the kiss so I can stare into her beautiful eyes.

"You okay?"

"Yes." She nods, then her pussy frees my cock as she climbs off my lap.

Getting up, I follow her to the bathroom, where we clean ourselves.

I check the bag for chinos, a sweater, and shoes, and getting dressed, I glance at the satin robe that's the only thing covering my wife's body.

I dig in the bag again, and when I find leggings and a warm shirt, I mutter, "Just fucking great."

"What?" Gabriella asks, moving closer to me.

"Carlo packed leggings for you."

"Oh. He did? Let me have them."

Not happy, I hand the clothes to her. She pulls on the fucking tight leggings, and when she struggles with the shirt, I help her to ease the fabric over the burns on her back.

"Put on the robe as well," I order. "I want you covered as much as possible."

"My possessive man," she chuckles and the sound eases more of the tension from my body.

When she's done, I take hold of her chin and tip her face up so she'll look at me. "How do you feel?"

"Mostly just tender where they shocked me. The stab wound is surprisingly okay." She glances down. "I don't think I can put on shoes today. Do we have socks in the bag?"

I check quickly, and let out a breath of relief, thankful that Carlo thought to pack socks for Gabriella.

Crouching down by her feet, I say, "Grab hold of the counter."

Gabriella lifts her left leg, and I carefully pull the sock onto her foot. We repeat the same process with her right foot, and after I'm done, I look up at her.

Our eyes lock, and as my wife stares down where I'm kneeling by her feet, I admit, "It was hell without you."

She places her hand against my jaw, and I press a kiss to her palm.

"Thank you for not surrendering and coming to get me."

"Always, *mia regina*. It's you and me forever."

"Forever," she whispers as I climb to my feet so I can press a tender kiss to her mouth.

Lifting my head, I say, "You ready to leave?"

She nods, then asks, "Where's Mamma?"

"Angelo has her. We'll pick her up on the way home," I reply while throwing everything into the bag.

"Is she okay? She didn't get hurt?"

"She's fine. I found her in the pantry where you hid her." Looking at my wife, I add, "Thank you for protecting her."

Gabriella lets out a breath of relief. "I'm glad to hear she's okay…well, as okay as she can be after losing Aunt Greta and the fright of the attack."

I pick up the bag, and taking my wife's hand in mine, I walk out of the bathroom.

When I open the hospital room's door, I find Carlo sitting on a chair with a coffee forgotten in his hand.

"Let's go," I say.

He gets up and places the cup on a counter.

"You're leaving, Mr. Falco?" the nurse asks.

I notice her nametag says 'Bianca' before I nod.

"Instead of bringing Mrs. Falco in for a follow-up, I can come to your house," she offers.

Knowing Bianca is a part of the family, I nod.

"Thank you," Gabriella murmurs.

Carlo takes the bag from me, then he waits as I pick Gabriella up bridal style before we leave the clinic that's been set up for the Cosa Nostra.

———————————

When Carlo pulls the car up to Angelo's mansion in Long Island, I glance at Gabriella. "Wait in the SUV. I won't be long."

She nods before glancing at Angelo's home.

I climb out and give Emilio and Vito a chin lift where they've parked behind us.

When Carlo climbs out of the SUV, I shake my head. "Stay with Gabriella."

I walk toward the front door and see Angelo's already waiting for me.

Shaking his hand, I say, "Thank you for everything."

"Anytime," he replies.

Entering the house, I see Mamma standing with Vittoria, and as I close the distance between us, she reaches an arm out in my direction.

The second I touch her, her face crumbles, and I quickly pull her against my chest.

"I was so worried," she sobs.

"I'm fine," I say to reassure her.

"Gabriella?"

"She'll be fine." I wrap my arm around Mamma's shoulders and steer her toward the front door. "Let's go home."

"Home?" she asks.

"The house in Manhattan."

Stopping by Angelo, I give him a thankful nod before heading back to the SUVs.

I get Mamma settled in the SUV with Emilio and Vito, then order, "Straight to the Manhattan house."

"Yes, boss."

I press a kiss to Mamma's temple. "I'm riding with Gabriella."

"Of course, *mio figlio*."

Shutting the door, I walk to the other SUV and climb in beside my wife.

"We're taking separate cars again?" she asks.

I nod. "We'll always ride in separate cars."

"Okay."

The drive to Manhattan feels like it takes forever, and when Carlo finally parks the car at the back of the mansion, I let out a breath of relief.

Gabriella glances over the estate as we climb out, and I say, "It will be home until all the repairs have been done to the property on Shelter Island."

"Are there clothes here for Mamma and me?" she asks.

"Yes."

I watch as Gabriella walks to Mamma.

"*Dio*. I was so worried about you?" she sobs as she wraps Mamma up in a tight hug.

Before Mamma can return the hug, I say, "Careful of Gabriella's back and side. She's hurt."

"*Mia cara!*" she exclaims, taking hold of Gabriella's shoulders. "What happened to you? Are you okay?" She lets out a sob. "I'm so sorry I couldn't help you."

"It's okay," my wife coos to my mother. "I'm fine. I'll heal in no time."

"Let's go inside," I say, gesturing for Emilio to unlock the door while I go to pick up Gabriella.

"I can walk," she protests. "It doesn't hurt so much."

"You'll stay off your feet until I say otherwise," I mutter.

"So bossy," she sighs as she rests her head against my shoulder.

I walk to the living room and set Gabriella down on the nearest couch. The mansion isn't as big as the one on Shelter Island, and it doesn't have an elevator.

Mamma's bedroom is on the first floor, whereas mine is on the second one.

"You should all try to get some sleep," I say.

Carlo takes hold of Mamma's arm. "I'll help you to your bedroom, Aunt Aida."

"Thank you." Her tone is filled with sorrow as she hooks her arm through Carlo's.

I turn my attention to Emilio and Vito. "Make sure all the fallen men's families receive their payments for their sacrifice."

"Yes, boss," Emilio replies. "Tommy let me know they're on their way back from Sicily."

"Good," I mutter.

"We'll stay here while you get some rest," Vito says before walking to the front of the house.

When Carlo comes back into the living room, I can see he's struggling with losing his mother.

I close the distance between us, and placing my hand on his shoulder, I lock eyes with him. "You'll have your revenge soon."

His jaw clenches as he nods.

"You going to try and sleep?" I ask.

Letting out a sigh, he replies, "Yes. Tomorrow's going to be one hell of a day."

"I'm here," I murmur.

His eyes meet mine again before he nods.

When I turn around, Gabriella's standing behind me. Her eyes flit between Carlo and me, then she asks, "Can I give Carlo a hug?"

"It's okay," Carlo replies. "Thanks, though."

I pick my wife up, and walking out of the living room, I head for the stairs.

"I just wanted to offer him some comfort," she explains.

"If he needs a hug, Mamma will give him one," I mutter.

I walk into the bedroom and kick the door shut. After I set Gabriella down on the bed, I draw the curtains to block out the light.

Instead of staying on the bed, she follows me into the walk-in closet, then asks, "Where did you get my clothes?"

"I had Aunt Greta's personal shopper purchase an extra set of everything and bring it here. There's also clothes at the penthouse. I like to travel light."

"*Grazie a Dio*," she murmurs as she takes a pajama set off the shelf. While we change, she asks, "Have you been to the mansion on Shelter Island? Is there a lot of damage?"

"Yes. It will take a couple of months for all the repairs to be done. I'll have Emilio find candidates for the housekeeper position, then you can choose one or two."

Dressed in her sleepwear, Gabriella looks at me with sadness furrowing her brows. "How did Martha die?"

"She was buried beneath the rubble," I murmur.

She shakes her head, sucking in a quivering breath. "What will you do with Stefano?"

My eyes meet hers, and not sugarcoating the words, I say, "I'm going to electrocute him until he begs for death, then I'll feed him to the rats."

Gabriella nods, and stepping closer to me, she wraps her arms around my waist. "Thank you for finding me in time."

"Always, *amore mia*."

Chapter 42

Damiano

After leaving Gabriella in Mamma and Vito's care, Emilio drives Carlo and me to the warehouse.

Yesterday was a quiet day for us. Once we all got some sleep, Emilio ordered food for everyone. There wasn't much talking being done, because we were all processing the shitstorm we just went through.

But as I'm on my way to the warehouse, my thoughts are focused on what lies ahead.

Vengeance burns in my chest, an incessant inferno that can only be extinguished with blood.

A fuck ton of blood.

Today, everyone who's hurt me and mine will die. Everyone but Stefano. He will suffer a million times more than Gabriella did before he meets his gruesome end.

After the SUV pulls up to the warehouse, I shove the door open and climb out.

Dressed in a suit, I adjust my jacket before I walk to the side entrance while pulling my phone out to call Tommy.

"Yes, boss?" he answers on the second ring.

"Bring them."

"Be there in ten minutes."

When I enter the building, I head to the room where Stefano is being held. The moment I walk inside, one of my men slaps Stefano. "Wake up."

The fucker lifts his head.

"I told you you were stupid," I mutter. "How long have you been planning to overthrow me?"

"Since you took the seat," he grumbles. "I've been saving money for nineteen years to afford an army."

"And look what all that saving bought you," I mock him. "Before I get started with you, Carlo has a gift he'd like to share with you." I check the time. "In give or take five minutes."

I glance at Emilio. "Strip the fucker and put on the belt."

While the men get to work, ridding Stefano of his clothes and wrapping the stun belt around his waist, I watch.

Emilio pushes a control into Stefano's hand, then I say, "Every time you want a drink of water, something to eat, or even a piss break, press the button."

"What happens if I press it?" Stefano asks.

I nod at Emilio, who presses the button, and the next second, Sefano's ass lifts off the chair he's tied to as the electric current shoots through him.

He slumps back against the chair, completely breathless from the shock.

"You'll torture yourself for every basic necessity you need or die of thirst," I mutter.

"I'd rather fucking die," he spits at me.

I shrug, and when I hear footsteps, I turn to face the door. "Here they are now."

"Who?" Stefano asks.

Tommy and his team herd the di Bellas and Cettina into the room, and when my *guests* lay eyes on Stefano, shock ripples over their faces.

"Stefano!" Cettina cries, and when she tries to rush to her son, Carlo grabs hold of her arm. Her eyes fly wildly between me and Carlo as she asks, "Why are you doing this?"

"What's going on here?" Mr. di Bella asks. "We were told we were coming for the wedding."

Ignoring the man, I nod at Carlo.

He drags Cettina closer to Stefano, where he forces her onto her knees.

"Wait? What's going on?" she asks, panic and fear drenched in each word.

"She has nothing to do with this!" Stefano yells. "Get your hands off my mother, you fucking bastard."

Carlo presses the barrel of his gun to her head, and looking Stefano dead in the eyes, he growls, "A mother for a mother."

He pulls the trigger, and her blood sprays over Stefano's legs before she drops dead by his feet.

"You fucker!" Stefano shouts. "You fucking fucker."

Carlo watches with satisfaction as Stefano begins to sob while I turn my attention to the di Bellas.

"On their knees," I mutter the order to Tommy and his team.

"No!" Mr. di Bella yells while his wife makes a panicked sound.

"Wait. Tell us what this is about," the son barks.

Once they're on their knees, I pull my Glock from behind my back. My fingers tighten around the handle as I look at them.

"You abused my wife," I say, my tone low with the promise of death.

"We didn't," Mrs. di Bella cries. "I don't know what lies–" Her sentence cuts off in a scream as I train my gun on her son and pull the trigger.

"No!!! NoNoNo!" she wails when he slumps down dead beside her.

"Please! Stop," Mr. di Bella begs.

I move the barrel of the gun to Gabriella's father, and locking eyes with Mrs. di Bella, I say, "You're not screaming loud enough."

When I pull the trigger, her eyes fill with horror and heartache as she watches her husband die.

I want this woman to suffer the most unbearable pain of losing her husband and son, because she was supposed to protect and love Gabriella, and she didn't.

Once the men are dead, I crouch in front of Mrs. di Bella and ask, "How much pain are you in right now?"

She sobs, her body trembling while she gasps for air, then a wounded cry tears right from her fucking soul, and she lets out a harrowing wail.

"Good," I hiss before I rise to my full height, then I order, "Take her to the other room where she can mourn her loss."

I watch as they drag her away and signal for the other men to remove the bodies.

Turning to look at Stefano, I mutter, "Get comfortable, cousin. I'll visit again tomorrow."

Carlo reaches out and presses the button on the control for the belt, shocking the fuck out of Stefano, before leaving the room with me.

"Feel better?" I ask.

"No. I still have to bury my mother tomorrow."

The funeral.

Tomorrow's going to be hard on everyone.

———————————

After the viewing, we all take our seats in the cathedral and Father Parisi says some final words for Aunt Greta.

Gabriella's sitting on my left with Mamma next to her, and I have Carlo on my right.

"Carlo would like to say something before we proceed to the cemetery," Father Parisi announces.

Tipping my head closer to Carlo, I murmur, "You've got this."

He nods as he climbs to his feet, and I watch as my second-in-charge, my best friend, and my brother walks to the front.

He clears his throat before his eyes scan over the pews that are filled with members of the Cosa Nostra.

"My mother was too good for this world," his voice drifts over us with sorrow tightening it.

Mamma lets out a sob, and Gabriella quickly wraps her arm around her.

My women huddle together as Carlo continues, "Christ, Ma, you were supposed to grow old and give me shit about not giving you grandchildren."

Fuck.

I suck in a deep breath as my heart bleeds for my loved ones, the loss of Aunt Greta finally sinking into my bones.

I never showed her any kind of love, but I did love her. After all, I've known her all my life. She was Mamma's best friend and like a second mother to me.

I shift in my seat, my muscles tightening as I firmly shove the sorrow down so it won't overwhelm me.

Today, I have to be strong for everyone as they mourn their loss.

Today, I have to guard Carlo like he's guarded me for nineteen years.

"Ma, you're the only woman I love with all my heart. No one can ever take your place. I'll miss you teasing us, hearing you reading..." his voice breaks, and he clears his throat again.

Knowing he's a second away from breaking down, I stand up and walk to him.

Placing my hand on his back, I lean into the microphone and say, "It was our greatest honor to be loved by Aunt Greta, and she will be missed." I glance up and kiss my fingers. "Rest in peace, Aunt Greta."

When I pull Carlo back to the pews, he whispers, "Thanks."

"Anytime."

I gesture for Gabriella to come and she helps Mamma to her feet.

"Carlo?" Mamma asks.

"I'm here," he murmurs as he moves to her side.

She hooks her arm through his and pats his hand. "That was beautiful. You still have me, *mio figlio*. We'll get through this together."

Jesus, Mamma. You're going to make me cry in front of all my men.

I grip Gabriella's hand tightly as we walk down the aisle, and when we're seated in the SUV, I let out a sigh.

Emilio and Vito get into our vehicle while Tommy and one of his best men drive with Carlo and Mamma.

"Are you okay?" Gabriella whispers.

I lean my head closer to hers. "Yes. You?"

"I'm okay as can be under the circumstances."

The drive to the cemetery isn't as slow as it would usually be. We don't want to be sitting ducks behind a hearse, and soon, we're driven through the iron gates of the cemetery before we all stop in a row.

Angelo pulls up behind our SUV, and when he, Vittoria, Tiny, and Big Ricky get out of their vehicle, I give him a chin lift.

Aunt Greta was a mafia queen so all the heads follow me to the back of the hearse, where we help Carlo pull the casket out.

I glance at Gabriella, and seeing her with Mamma, where my men surround them as they walk to the gravesite, I focus on carrying Aunt Greta to her final resting place.

We set the casket down, and I take my place between Carlo and Gabriella before Father Parisi says a few words.

When it's time to lower the casket, Carlo steps forward, and resting his hand on the polished wood, he whispers, "You were the best mother a son could ask for. *Ti voglio bene*, Ma. *Addio*."

We watch as the casket is lowered, and halfway through, Carlo turns around and walks away.

"Stay with Emilio and Vito," I order Gabriella before I go after him.

When I catch up to Carlo, I hear him take a shuddering breath.

Placing my hand on his back, I say, "I'm here."

He nods and only stops walking when we reach the SUV.

"Christ, Damiano," he groans.

"I know." I step closer to him, and putting my hand behind his head, I let him rest his forehead on my shoulder. "I know, brother."

I keep an eye over our surroundings and everyone attending the funeral while Carlo takes a moment to catch his breath.

When people start to walk in our direction, I mutter, "Lift your head."

He sucks in a deep breath, and when he raises his chin, I watch as he reins in his sorrow.

"You good?" I ask.

He nods. "Yes."

"Let's go to the warehouse," I order.

We wait for the women, and then I say, "Vito, you and Tommy take the women home." I lock eyes with Tommy. "From now on, you'll guard Gabriella and my mother."

"Yes, boss," he says before helping Mamma to the SUV.

"Emilio, you're with us."

Gabriella holds up her hand to Vito and walks to me. Wrapping her fingers around the back of my neck, she stands on her toes as she tugs me down and presses a kiss to my mouth. "Don't be late, *amore mio*."

I nod, then watch as she faces Carlo. "I got a moment with Aunt Greta before I was taken away." My wife swallows hard as she fights her tears. "She asked me to tell you she loves you. It was her final request."

Carlo nods as his features tense.

"She thought of you in her final moments," Gabriella whispers.

He nods again, then I watch as she walks away and gets into the SUV with Vito.

I take another minute to thank the other heads for coming before I climb into the SUV, and Emilio steers us away from the cemetery.

Time to make Stefano scream.

403

Chapter 43

Damiano

Arriving at the warehouse, I get out of the SUV and head to the side entrance.

"Carlo, go torture Stefano," I say. "Just don't kill him yet."

He nods, and I stop by the room where Mrs. di Bella is being held.

"Are you going in?" Emilio asks.

"Yes. Go keep an eye on Carlo."

When I'm alone, I think about everything Gabriella told me.

As ice flows through my veins, I open the door and step inside. I glance at Bobby, who's been guarding her, and nod to the door.

After he leaves, my gaze settles on Mrs. di Bella, who's tied to a chair.

"Comfortable?" I ask.

Her breaths explode over her lips, her skin pale with sorrow. Fear darkens her eyes as she stares at me.

"Gabriella told me what you did to her," I murmur, my tone dark with anger. "What you allowed to be done to her."

"It's all lies," she cries.

I dart forward, and grabbing hold of her neck, I force her and the chair backward until she slams into the concrete floor.

I pull out my gun from behind my back and press the barrel against her quivering lips.

"Open," I order.

She tries to shake her head.

"Open your fucking mouth," I shout.

Her lips part, and I shove the barrel so deep she gags.

"My wife...my fucking queen doesn't lie. It's one of the things I love about her," I hiss. "I saw how you treated her."

She tries to shake her head again, muttering something unintelligible around the barrel.

I look Mrs. di Bella dead in the eye and let every ounce of power radiate from me as I say, "You fucking hurt her for twenty-three years, but thank you for letting me be the first to say the words 'I love you' to her."

Mrs. di Bella's whole body trembles as she gives me a pleading look.

I hold her terrified gaze and pull the trigger. With my hand around her throat, I feel how her life instantly leaves her body, and I fucking savor the moment.

Letting go of her, I rise to my feet. I walk to the door and yank it open, then head to the restroom so I can wash her blood off my skin.

After I've cleaned the barrel of my gun, I tuck it back into the waistband of my pants.

I suck in a deep breath of air and exhale slowly before I leave the restroom to go see what Carlo's been up to.

As I near the room where Stefano's being held, I hear an agonizing scream. I shove the door open in time to see Carlo pressing a hot poker against Stefano's sole.

"Good choice," I say.

"I thought you'd like it," he mutters as he tears the cooling poker away, taking some skin with it.

"Please," Stefano cries. "Please. Enough."

I shake my head. "I haven't even gotten started."

"No," he sobs. "I beg you. I'm sorry. Please."

Walking closer, I grab his face and lean down until I'm looking him dead in the eye. "Not once did Gabriella beg. You're fucking weak."

I shove him backward, then hold my hand out. "Cattle prod."

"I'm sorry. I see my mistake now," he weeps, his eyes feverish on the cattle prod as I take hold of it.

I press the prongs to his skin and watch with satisfaction as his body convulses from the electric current hitting him.

I don't stop until he passes out, then glance at Emilio. "Pour me a drink."

"Yes, boss."

I set the cattle prod down on a table and look at Carlo. "I've decided, once all of this is taken care of, we're going on vacation."

"Where?" he asks as he crosses his arm over his chest.

"I'll let Gabriella choose the destination."

He nods. "It will do us all good to get away from New York for a week or two."

"Here you go, boss," Emilio says, holding out the tumbler of whiskey.

I take the drink and swallow a sip down.

"It's Christmas day tomorrow," Carlo mutters.

"Christ. I forgot." I glance at him. "I didn't get the women anything."

"We've been busy."

At least I can tell Gabriella I killed her family, and the vacation will be good news as well.

When I look at Emilio, he shakes his head. "Anything but shopping, boss."

I almost let out a chuckle.

"I'll call Savannah and ask her to bring something over," Carlo offers. "Jewelry?"

I shake my head. "A new phone and laptop for Gabriella so it's easier for her to make her tutorials."

"And for your mother?" We think for a moment, then he says, "I have the perfect gift."

"What?"

"Audiobooks."

Christ.

I lift my hand and give Carlo's shoulder a squeeze. "She'll love that. Thanks."

While Carlo steps out of the room to make the call, I toss the rest of the whiskey at Stefano's face. "Wake up!"

Emilio moves closer and gives the fucker a couple of slaps.

Stefano lets out a groan, and when he lifts his head, I ask, "Ready?"

Spittle dribbles from his mouth as he shakes his head. "No."

I pass the empty tumbler to Emilio and say, "Give me a knife."

"No. Please," Stefano starts to beg.

"And you wanted to be the *Capo dei Capi*." I shake my head as I take the knife from Emilio. "Pathetic."

I step closer to my cousin, and as I press the blade to his right side, I growl, "You're fucking weak."

Slowly, I push the blade into his flesh, and I drink in the sound of his cries.

I leave the knife embedded in his side so he doesn't bleed too much and order, "Bring the bucket."

When Emilio leaves the room, Carlo comes back in. "All set."

"Good."

I stare at Stefano, whose breaths are fast and shallow, his skin ghostly pale.

"I don't think he'll last much longer," Carlo mutters.

Unfortunately, I agree. The fucker is much weaker than I thought.

When Emilio returns with a metal bucket, a blow torch, and a cage with rats, Stefano almost shits himself.

"*Dio! No! Misericordia, per favore,*" he begs for mercy.

"Take off the belt and strap the rats to him," I order.

409

Emilio removes the belt, and Bobby has to help transfer the rats into the bucket before they strap it to him.

"No! No!" Stefano screams hysterically. "Nooooooo!"

I grab the blow torch and turn it on, and as I hold the flame to the back of the bucket, I watch as Stefano loses his ever-loving fucking mind.

This is what you get for fucking with me.

When the rats try to escape the heat, they start clawing and biting their way into Stefano's stomach, and I drink in every fucking agonizing scream until his body goes into the shock from the rats tunneling their way into his guts.

When his head slumps forward, Emilio checks for a pulse, and only when he nods do I turn off the blow torch.

"Bobby, get the men to clean up," I order.

"On it, boss."

When I walk out of the room with Carlo beside me and Emilio at my back, the corner of my mouth lifts.

Finally, I can take a fucking vacation.

Chapter 44

Gabriella

Even though I didn't have much of an appetite, I made *Coda alla vaccinara* for Mamma, knowing she loves oxtail.

I hope Stefano suffers a lot.

It's all I've been thinking about since we arrived home after attending the funeral.

I can't believe Aunt Greta's gone.

I glance at Mamma, where she's sitting in an armchair with her eyes closed.

"How are you doing, Mamma?" I murmur.

Slowly, she opens her eyes and lets out a heavy sigh. "I keep listening for Greta. It's so quiet without her."

I know.

"Should I switch on the TV?" I ask.

She shakes her head. "I'm actually tired, *cara*. I think I'll go to bed."

"Let me walk with you to your room."

I get up from the chair and help Mamma to her feet.

As we walk to her bedroom, I wrap my arm around her shoulders and give her a sideways hug, then say, "Please let me know if there is anything I can do to make you feel better."

We stop near her door, and she gently pats my cheek. "You're already helping, *mia figlia*."

Hearing her call me her daughter, I wrap my arms around her and squeeze her tightly. My voice is hoarse as I whisper, "*Ti voglio bene, Mamma*."

"*Ti voglio bene, cara*." A loving smile tugs at the corner of her mouth. "You're such a blessing to me."

I pull back and swallow hard on the tears from the special moment we're sharing. "I hope you sleep well."

Mamma pats my shoulder, then I watch as she walks into her room before I pull the door shut so she'll have privacy.

Tugging my cardigan tighter around my shoulders, I walk toward the stairs so I can head up to my bedroom. When I come around a corner, I slam into a solid wall of muscle.

Damiano's hands fly to my shoulders to keep me from staggering backward, and the next second, I'm squashed to his chest.

"You okay?" he asks.

"Yeah. Sorry, I was deep in thought." I glance up and smile at him. "You're home."

"I'm home," he murmurs.

Taking my hand, he leads me to our room, and after shutting the door behind us, I'm pulled back into his arms. He rests his hand behind my head and practically curls his body around mine.

"I missed you," I sigh against his shirt that smells like blood and sweat. "But you need to shower. You smell like death."

Damiano lets out a chuckle, the sound still foreign to hear because he doesn't do it often.

Pulling away from me, he walks to the bathroom and while my man showers, I carefully strip out of my clothes.

The burns on my back are starting to feel better, but the nurse said it might take a week or two before they fade away.

I'm surprised that the stab wound gives me the least pain. It feels more like a slight discomfort when I move too quickly, but other than that, I forget it's there.

Once I'm naked, I tug the covers back and crawl onto the bed.

I lie down on my left side and snuggle into a pillow while I listen to the water running in the shower.

Things feel a bit up in the air because I have to get used to the Manhattan house. I miss the lake mansion, and Aunt Greta, and Martha, and Gerardo.

A heavy sigh drifts from my chest.

I hear the water turn off, and after Damiano's finished, he comes out and switches the light off.

He's also naked as he climbs beneath the covers. Turning on his side, he stares at me for a moment before I pull him into my arms.

He presses his face into the crook of my neck, and when my fingers start to brush up and down his back, his body shudders.

I kiss his hair and hold my man while he decompresses.

Drinking in the feel of his warm skin and hard muscles beneath my fingertips, I once again think about how grateful I am that he got to me in time.

Lifting his head, his eyes meet mine. "Stefano's dead."

I bring my hand to his jaw, and as he presses a kiss to my palm, I whisper, "Thank you."

"I also had my men bring your family to New York."

I'm totally caught by surprise, and a dark frown forms on my forehead.

"Why? I don't want them here."

He shakes his head, then says, "I killed them."

Oh.

For a moment, I blink at my husband, then his words sink in.

Holy crap.

"They're dead?" I ask to make sure.

"Yes."

Damiano has killed everyone who's ever hurt me.

I lean forward and press my mouth to his. "Thank you," I whisper against his lips.

He kisses me tenderly before pulling a little back. "It's my Christmas gift to you."

I let out a soft chuckle. "Only you would think killing people counts as a Christmas gift." Staring at Damiano with all the love I feel for him, I add, "I love it, though. It makes me feel better they're gone and can never hurt me again."

Damiano turns onto his back and pulls me on top of him. "I liked how we slept in the hospital."

"Yeah?" I straddle him, and feeling how hard his cock is, I reach down between us and position him at my entrance. When I take his cock all the way, I moan, "You want to sleep buried deep inside me, *amore mio?*"

"Yes."

I press my chest to his stomach and rest my cheek over his heart. Feeling his cock stretch me to my limits and

415

knowing we're as close to each other as we'll ever be, I whisper, "I like it too."

Damiano's hand finds my hair, and he pulls his fingers through the strands. "*Ti amo.*"

I press a kiss to his pec. "*Ti amo, marito mio.*"

When I wake up, lying on top of Damiano with his cock still buried inside me, the corner of my mouth lifts.

I love waking up like this so much.

He's still fast asleep, and I can't resist pressing a kiss to his skin.

Pushing myself into a sitting position, his morning hard-on pushes deeper into me, and I let out a moan.

Oh yes.

My eyes drift over every sculptured muscle in his chest and abdomen while my fingers trace the curve of the lines carved into his sides.

Dio. My husband is pure perfection.

My core clenches with need, and as my gaze flits between his face and his body, I slowly begin to move.

Having Damiano asleep beneath me as I start to fuck him is one hell of a turn-on.

There's a tightening sensation in my abdomen, and with my palms and fingers feasting on his chest and abs, I move faster and faster.

Damiano lets out a groan, and his muscles tense so much I'm almost delirious from rubbing my hands all over him.

"*Dio*," I gasp as I fuck him as hard as I can. "Fucking you while you're asleep is the hottest thing ever."

My breaths explode over my lips, and when an overpowering orgasm rips a cry from me, Damiano grabs hold of my buttcheeks and starts to thrust up into me.

"You like that, *amore mia*? You like fucking me while I'm out cold?" He groans as he hammers unbelievably hard into me, making my orgasm so much more intense.

"Yes," I sob from the ecstasy holding my body captive.

"Do you want to restrain me so you can have full control?" he growls.

The image alone is enough to make another orgasm hit, and I can only nod as I whimper through the pleasure.

Damiano keeps pounding ruthlessly hard inside me. "Do you want me powerless beneath you?"

"Y-yes," I gasp, my clit becoming oversensitive from all the friction.

When Damiano jerks and buries his cock to the hilt, I drink in the sight of his orgasm ripping the air from his lungs and rendering him helpless.

A sense of power floods my veins as I stare down at my husband while he orgasms, and I say, "That's right, *amore mio*. Come hard for me. Fill me with your release so I can give you an heir."

His eyes burn on my face as he thrusts twice more into me, his teeth bared and his muscles straining from reaching his climax.

I'm completely captivated by the hot-as-hell sight of Damiano orgasming, and when he starts to relax beneath me, I lean over him and press a kiss to his mouth before praising him, "You fucked me so well."

He lets out a chuckle while his fingers massage my buttcheeks. "You're a dominant little spitfire first thing in the morning. It's fucking sexy."

Snuggling against his chest, I let out a satisfied sigh. "That was amazing."

"One hell of a way to wake up," he groans as he pulls out of me. "Up and off, *amore mia*."

I climb off him, and letting out a burst of laughter, I run for the bathroom so I can get there first.

I quickly relieve my bladder and clean myself, then hurry out so Damiano can use the bathroom.

My little stunt earns me a slap on the backside before he heads inside.

I straighten the covers on the bed and when I hear the water running in the shower, I join Damiano.

Stepping beneath the warm spray, I reach for the body wash.

He presses a kiss to my shoulder, then says, "Merry Christmas, *amore mia*."

Dio! I totally forgot!

My eyes widen as I turn around to face him. "Merry Christmas." We share a tender kiss, then I admit, "I forgot."

He shakes his head while his eyes fill with love for me. "Next year will be better. This was not how I wanted our first Christmas to be, but at least we're together."

I nod as I start to wash his body while smiling up at him. "At least we're together."

He tilts his head, then says, "Where would you like to go for our vacation?"

"You mean our honeymoon?"

He shakes his head. "Everyone will come with. I think we all deserve a couple of weeks away from New York."

My smile widens, and excitement pours into my veins as I say, "Cape Town. I've heard it's really beautiful there, and if we have time, we can visit the national parks and see all the animals."

"Cape Town, it is. I'll have Emilio make all the arrangements."

Pushing my body up on my tiptoes, I press a kiss to his mouth. "Thank you."

"Anything for you, *la mia regina*."

Chapter 45

Damiano

Amelio arranged a Mercedes van and a Porsche Cayenne for the vacation in Cape Town. As we're driven to the hotel, my eyes are on Gabriella, who's grinning as she stares at the landscape.

"It's so green, and the mountain is stunning," she tells Mamma.

She was surprised when I allowed us all to travel in the same vehicle, and I had to explain the risk of an attack isn't as high on vacation as it is in New York.

"The roads aren't as busy as in Manhattan," Gabriella mentions. "It's nice."

I give her hand a squeeze and lean into her. "Are you happy, *amore mia*?"

She smiles at me, excitement making the green flecks in her eyes brighter. "Yes. Thank you for arranging all of this for us."

"Emilio did all the work," I mutter.

"You're welcome, boss," the fucker says from the driver's seat.

"Don't make me throw you out of the car," I grumble.

When we pull up to The One & Only that's situated near the waterfront, I slide the door open and climb out.

My muscles are stiff from all the traveling, and I suppress the urge to stretch while my eyes flick over our surroundings.

"Welcome to The One & Only," an African man greets us with a friendly smile.

"Thank you," Gabriella replies while she keeps her arm wrapped around Mamma's lower back.

"I'll get us checked in," Emilio says.

When Gabriella leads Mamma to a garden at the side of the hotel, Carlo and I follow behind them with Vito and Tommy sticking close to us.

"There are dark gray slate stones and green reeds and plants. It's so pretty here, Mamma," she tells my mother. "Try to picture paradise. That's what it feels like."

Christ, I chose the perfect wife. She's so good with Mamma.

Gabriella points to the right of the hotel. "When I checked the surrounding area on Tripadvisor, it said there's an aquarium. Can we visit it?"

"Sure," I mutter.

"And there's a market that's open on Saturdays," she mentions. "I'd like to get some souvenirs."

"Okay, *amore mia*."

"And there's a scratch patch where a person can get all kinds of crystals and stones. It's only an hour's drive away."

I nod. "Whatever you want."

Gabriella lets go of Mamma and moves closer to me. Vito quickly hooks my mother's arm through his and leads her into the hotel lobby.

My wife wraps her arms around my neck and pulls me down for a kiss. "Don't worry. I'll make sure you get plenty of rest," she assures me before pressing her lips to mine once more.

"We're all set," Emilio says. "I just have to take the cars down to the parking area."

The four extra guards I brought along on the trip go with Emilio so they can bring the luggage to our rooms.

Another African man gestures at a golf cart. "I'll drive you to your rooms."

I let Gabriella and Mamma get on first before I take a seat beside my wife.

Vito sits next to Mamma, and Tommy grabs the seat beside the driver.

As we're driven around the side of the hotel, I have to admit, Emilio has outdone himself. Passing over a wooden bridge, we find ourselves on an island where the rooms are hidden between thick greenery, and seagulls cry overhead.

It really feels like paradise.

The golf cart comes to a stop, and to our right is a restaurant and pool area that has a zen feel to it.

"Your mother will stay on the ground floor, and we've given Mr. and Mrs. Falco the room above her so you're close to each other," the concierge explains.

"Thank you," Gabriella murmurs as she glances at our surroundings. "It's so beautiful and peaceful here."

The concierge unlocks the door to Mamma's suite, and when we walk inside, he explains where everything is.

I glance at Vito, and he quickly steps forward to handle the concierge while I walk out onto a small veranda that has a stunning view of the waterway that encircles the island.

Once the concierge leaves, I watch as Gabriella leads Mamma through the suite, explaining in detail where everything is.

I pull out a chair by a small round table and sit down, not wanting to rush the women.

With my eyes following them, I'm once again struck by how amazing Gabriella is with Mamma.

She was made for me.

She's my better half in every way.

When Emilio and the other guards bring in the luggage, I climb to my feet and walk back into the room.

"Vito, my keycard."

He hands it to me, and I say, "Stay with my mother until she's comfortable."

"Yes, boss."

Taking Gabriella's hand, I pull her out of the room and up the stairs to our suite.

I scan the keycard and shove the door open.

Once we're inside, I bring my hands up and frame her face, my eyes drifting over every beautiful inch of her.

"There are no words to describe how much I love you," I murmur.

Her smile softens. "I love you too."

"It's you and me forever, *amore mia.*"

She pushes herself up on her tiptoes, and against my lips, she breathes, "Forever."

As I kiss her with a hunger only she can create in me, I once again thank all that's holy I took her for myself.

Gabriella

It takes a whole week for Damiano to finally relax, and I'm proud to say I even have him wearing jeans and a T-shirt.

But he still walks around with a murderous expression on his face that scares the hotel staff half to death.

"Stop scowling at everyone," I whisper as we walk down a path that leads to the market.

There are sailboats in a small bay area and the summer sun shines brightly down on us.

"I'm not scowling," he mutters, just as a mom and a toddler walk by us.

The poor kid takes one look at Damiano, then his bottom lip trembles, and he cries at his mom to pick him up.

"You're making children cry," I say as I slap his arm, then I spot a floating deck where seals are sunbathing. "Oh my gosh! Look. Seapuppies."

I hurry to Mamma's side and quickly explain, "There are seals bathing in the sun. They're so fat but cute."

"They stink," Damiano mutters under his breath.

A baby seal clambers onto the deck and makes a barking sound as he climbs all over the others to get to his mom.

"Oh, they're loud," Mamma mentions. "And Damiano's right. They smell quite bad."

I glance at the seals again before pulling Mamma in the direction of the aquarium so we can get out of the sun.

I spend time at every display explaining what the different fish look like before Vito comes to take Mamma from me.

The next room is dark, and there are cylinder tubes with tiny jellyfish moving through the water.

Damiano catches my eye from the other side of the display, and I watch as he slowly walks closer to me, a look of awe on his face.

"What?" I chuckle when he stops to just stare at me.

"Have I told you how fucking breathtakingly beautiful you are?"

"Language," a mother hisses as she shoots Damiano a glare.

His features quickly settle into a ruthless expression as his dark gaze flicks to her, and she quickly grabs her children's hands and hurries to the next room.

I close the distance to Damiano and shake my head at him. "My scary mafioso." I give him a serious look. "Are you happy?"

"Of course." His features soften as he brushes his knuckles over my cheek. "Why do you ask?"

I poke my finger at his chest. "Then smile before they kick us out."

The corners of his mouth lift as he mutters, "The things I do for you."

"It's because you love me," I chuckle.

I take his hand and weave our fingers together before we continue to walk from one room to the next.

When we leave the aquarium, we head to the market, where we saunter from stall to stall until it's time for lunch.

Once we're back at the hotel and seated at a table, I read the menu to Mamma so she can decide what she'd like to eat.

"I'll have salmon sushi," Mamma says. "And a glass of white wine."

I glance over the menu again. "I'll have the wagyu beef tacos and zucchini tempura."

"And to drink?" the waiter asks.

"Just a Coke with lemon and ice, please."

While everyone else places their orders, I glance out the windows at the beautiful view of nature and the waterway around the island where our rooms are.

Damiano takes hold of my hand and sets it down on his thigh while brushing his thumb over my wedding and engagement rings.

When I glance at him, a soft smile curves his lips, and seeing the loving expression on his face, my heart swoons.

He's trying so hard to be less brutal on our vacation.

I lean closer to him and press a kiss to his mouth. "Thank you."

"Anything for you, *amore mia*."

When I pull back, I stare deep into his dark eyes, thinking how lucky I am to be his wife.

Out of everyone, my god of vengeance chose me.

Tilting his head, he asks, "What are you thinking about?"

"That I'm the luckiest woman alive."

The corner of his mouth lifts. "Not half as lucky as I am."

I give him a tender kiss, then whisper, "*Ti amo, il mio re.*"

Epilogue

Damiano

(Twenty-two years later…)

Walking out onto the veranda, I glance at the lake before my eyes drift over my guests.

Everyone's at the mansion for a cookout to celebrate Mamma's eightieth birthday.

She didn't want anything formal, so I only invited the other heads and their families over to spend the day with us.

I head toward where the men are sitting and take a seat.

Dario points to where the kids are standing in groups, and he lets out a chuckle. "Rosie is following Enzo around. He can't shake her."

I watch as Dario's sixteen-year-old daughter sticks to my second-oldest son like glue. When Enzo stops and wraps his arm around her shoulder, the poor girl almost melts into his side.

Fuck.

I better have a talk with Enzo, who's just turned twenty. I don't want him getting any ideas until Rosie's eighteen.

Thankfully, he gives her a brotherly hug before letting go of her.

My gaze follows Enzo as he walks to where his brother, Christiano, is talking to Angelo's sons.

When my firstborn glances at Sienna, one of Franco's daughters, I let out a sigh.

"Your son is staring at my daughter," Franco mutters.

"They're all fucking staring at each other," I grumble.

Dario lets out a chuckle. "Love is in the air."

"The fuck it is," I grunt before climbing to my feet and walking to my sons.

Christiano notices me first and comes to throw his arm over my shoulders. "Having fun?"

"Not with you undressing Sienna with your eyes."

He lets out a bark of laughter then shakes his head. "I'm not." A serious expression tenses his features, "But if I were, would that be a problem?"

"Christ," I sigh. "No, but ask Franco's permission before you decide to date his daughter."

"Of course."

I narrow my eyes on him. "So you are interested in Sienna. She's older than you."

He just shrugs. "Only by three years."

He gives me a playful smirk before walking to where Georgi is talking with Valentina. I watch as he goes to stand between his sister and Renzo's son, being an overprotective big brother.

I taught him well.

Fuck, at least everyone's keeping it in the Cosa Nostra family.

"Why are you scowling?" Gabriella asks as she comes to stand next to me.

"The kids are growing up too fast," I mutter.

"What do you mean too fast? They're already adults," she argues.

"Not Gianna." I look at my fifteen-year-old daughter, who's sitting beside her grandmother. "She'll always be our baby."

I wrap my arm around Gabriella's lower back and tug her to my side. "Everyone looks happy."

She nods. "It was a good idea to keep things casual today."

We walk toward the water's edge, and I glance at the lake before looking at my wife. "Are you happy?"

She nods as she snuggles into my side. "I love having the whole family here, and Mamma's having a lovely day."

I turn to look at my mother, who's laughing at something Gianna says.

Letting out a content sigh, I search over everyone until I find Carlo where he's sitting with Emilio and enjoying a beer. He never married and still follows me like a shadow, but soon Christiano will take over from me, and we'll both retire.

"What are you thinking about?" Gabriella asks.

"It's time for Christiano to step up as the next *Capo dei Capi*."

"When will you make the announcement?" she asks.

"Now is as good a time as any." Walking to the middle of the lawn, I call out, "I have something to say." My eyes find Christiano. "Come here." Then I look at Enzo. "You too."

When I nod at Carlo, he sets his beer down, and getting up, he walks toward me.

Once they all join me, I place my hand on Christiano's shoulder. "You're twenty-two, and it's time for you to take over the position as *Capo dei Capi*."

My eldest looks exactly like me, and I know he'll rule the Cosa Nostra with an iron first. The same way I have.

My gaze flicks to Enzo, and I say, "You'll be your brother's underboss. You'll protect him at all costs."

"Yes, Papa," Enzo replies as he moves to stand beside Christiano. "You'll both do whatever is needed to keep the family safe."

My sons nod, then Carlo pats Enzo on the back. "Finally, I get to sleep in. Good luck, son."

I scowl at Carlo. "What do you mean you get to sleep in? You're still going to protect my ass."

"Can your ass get up at eight instead of the crack of dawn?" he asks.

Shaking my head, I watch as all the men come to shake my sons' hands. It's time for the next generation to take over, the moment bittersweet.

Gabriella wraps her arm around my back and presses a kiss to my cheek. "Does this mean we'll get to travel more?"

"Maybe. I'll keep an eye on the boys for a year or two. Just to make sure they don't fuck up."

She leans her head against my chest. "We raised strong men."

"We did." I press a kiss to her hair.

As I look at the family I've spent most of my life protecting, I know I'll never fully step down.

I'll protect them until I exhale my final breath.

The End

435

PUBLISHED BOOKS
In Reading Order:

MAFIA ROMANCE

THE KINGS OF MAFIA SERIES
Mafia / Organized Crime / Suspense Romance
(Can be read in this order or as standalones)
This series is not connected to any other series I've written,
and there will be no spin-offs.

Tempted By The Devil
Craving Danger
Hunted By A Shadow
Drawn To Darkness
God Of Vengeance

THE ST. MONARCH'S WORLD
(The Saints, Sinners & Corrupted Royals
all take place in the same world)

THE SAINTS SERIES
Mafia / Organized Crime / Suspense Romance
(Can be read in this order or as standalones)

Merciless Saints
Cruel Saints
Ruthless Saints

Tears of Betrayal
Tears of Salvation

THE SINNERS SERIES
Mafia / Organized Crime / Suspense Romance
(Can be read in this order or as standalones)

Taken By A Sinner
Owned By A Sinner
Stolen By A Sinner
Chosen By A Sinner
Captured By A Sinner

CORRUPTED ROYALS
Mafia / Organized Crime / Suspense Romance
(Can be read in this order or as standalones)

Destroy Me
Control Me
Brutalize Me
Restrain Me
Possess Me

CONTEMPORARY ROMANCE

BEAUTIFULLY BROKEN SERIES

Organized Crime / Suspense Romance
(Can be read in this order or as standalones)

Beautifully Broken
Beautifully Hurt
Beautifully Destroyed

ENEMIES TO LOVERS

College Romance / New Adult / Billionaire Romance

Heartless
Reckless
Careless
Ruthless
Shameless

TRINITY ACADEMY

College Romance / New Adult / Billionaire Romance

Falcon
Mason
Lake
Julian

438

The Epilogue

THE HEIRS

College Romance / New Adult / Billionaire Romance

Coldhearted Heir
Arrogant Heir
Defiant Heir
Loyal Heir
Callous Heir
Sinful Heir
Tempted Heir
Forbidden Heir

Stand Alone Spin-off
Not My Hero
Young Adult / High School Romance

THE SOUTHERN HEROES SERIES

Suspense Romance / Contemporary Romance /
Police Officers & Detectives

The Ocean Between Us
The Girl In The Closet
The Lies We Tell Ourselves
All The Wasted Time
We Were Lost

STANDALONES

LIFELINE
(FBI Suspense Romance)

UNFORGETTABLE
Co-written with Tayla Louise
(Contemporary/Billionaire Romance)

ACKNOWLEDGMENTS

And so the Kings of Mafia has come to an end. Thank you so very much for the endless support I've received with this series. I appreciate every reader.

Your excitement when I release a book means everything to me, and I'm planning an entire new massive mafia world for you all!

My editor, Sheena, has nerves of steel with all the deadlines wooshing past us. Thank you for putting up with me and always being honest with your feedback. I appreciate you so much!

To my alpha and beta readers – Leeann, Brittney, Sherrie, and Sarah thank you for being the godparents of my paper-baby. Thank you for all your time and feedback.

Candi Kane PR - Thank you for being patient with me and my bad habit of missing deadlines. Thank you for being my friend and always being there to calm me down.

Sarah, from *Okay Creations* – I love, love, love the Kings of Mafia covers! Thank you for doing such an amazing job with them.

My street team, thank you for promoting my books. It means the world to me!

A special thank you to every blogger and reader who took the time to participate in the cover reveal and release day.

Love,
Michelle.